A BEASTLY INCONVENIENCE

"Dead? That boy?" Eve gaped foolishly, scarlet lips parted. "Did he have an accident?"

"I don't know. Russell sent for the police."

"Police! Oh, how inconvenient!"

"Very," Meredith said drily. "Especially for Lorrimer."

Eve clapped her hand over her mouth like a guilty child. "Oh, I'm sorry, Merry, I didn't mean it to come out the way it sounded. And you must be terribly shaken. Would you like a brandy? Let me pour you one. What a perfectly horrible, beastly thing to happen . . . But, you know, just before the wedding like this—you have to admit it's like a bad omen."

A bad omen. Meredith refused the brandy and went upstairs . . .

SAY IT WITH POISON

ANN GRANGER

AVON BOOKS NEW YORK

AVON BOOKS
A division of
The Hearst Corporation
1350 Avenue of the Americas
New York, New York 10019

First Avon Books Printing: April 1993

AVON TRADEMARK REG. U.S. PAT. OFF. AND IN OTHER COUNTRIES, MARCA REGISTRADA, HECHO EN U.S.A.

Printed in the U.S.A.

RA 10 9 8 7 6 5 4 3 2 1

To John

One

The lift was out of order again. Weary from a busy day, crushed from the homeward journey in a crowded tram and dusty from walking along the sun-drenched street Meredith Mitchell glared at it resentfully. Not that it was unheard-of for it to be out of action, nor surprising. The lift was a museum-piece, composed of ornate cast-iron bars like a monkey-house in some Victorian collector's private zoo. The bars burst at the top into metal acanthus leaves and the winding-gear, proudly displayed in full visibility, resembled something from a *Boy's Own* annual. Affixed to one metal acanthus stalk and stamped with German words, a metal disc indicated that the lift had been installed at the height of the Austro-Hungarian empire. Some wit had obtained, probably on a trip across the border to Vienna, a picture postcard reproduction of a portrait of Franz Josef and sticky-taped it up inside. There it remained, treated by the elderly Croat janitor with the kind of reverence normally reserved for holy pictures. Meredith grimaced at the old emperor with his blue military-style coat, brass buttons and walrus moustaches. Today Franz Josef had the lift all to his imperial self.

She picked up her briefcase and set off to climb the gentle curve of the stone steps, hugging the stair-well wearily. Despite chipped paint, cobwebs in the arches and an air of slowly sinking into dust, the apartment block still had a *fin-de-siècle* elegance about it: the staircase up which Meredith now toiled to the third floor was wide enough to accommodate crinolines. But the heating seldom

1

worked well, the plumbing was erratic, there were rats in the cellars and sometimes one took a wrong turning and arrived on the higher floors. Meredith had once walked out of the flat late at night and found a rat washing his whiskers on her doorstep. Nevertheless she liked this building and did not envy other members of the consular staff their more modern flats in soulless concrete blocks out in the wilderness of the new suburbs. It put things in perspective; it tipped the visitor a wink both conspiratorial and slightly malicious, like that of a faded old *boulevardier* who had not lost all his dash. Time, after all, takes care of all our aspirations, one way or another.

She arrived before her own front door, panting slightly and beginning to perspire on the airless landing. Marija, the cleaner, had been today and polished up the brass letterbox which still read *"Briefe"* in worn Gothic script. Not that any modern postman troubled himself to haul his bag of letters up here. All post was left in numbered metal boxes affixed to the wall downstairs in the entry. Other people's post, that was. Meredith's personal post, when she received any, arrived courtesy of the Outward Bag Room in London, in a canvas sack with the diplomatic mail delivered by the regular courier. But the truth was she rarely received any personal letters.

People at home don't forget you after you've worked abroad for a number of years but keeping in touch becomes more and more of an effort. At least that was what Meredith told herself. Lives diverged and with less and less in common you drifted apart. Both Meredith's parents were dead. She had no brothers or sisters. She kept up an intermittent correspondence with a couple of old schoolfriends—one of them hadn't written last Christmas, only sent a card and next Christmas probably even the card wouldn't make an appearance—but they were both married with growing families and rightly realized that Meredith wouldn't be interested in the minutiae of their family lives. Her one close relative, a cousin, was the only one who did not come into this category. Eve Owens led an eventful life in which domestic events tended to be overshadowed by happenings in what she called "the business." The two of them did manage to keep in touch, just. Whether that was a good thing was another matter.

A letter had arrived today, filling Meredith with pleasure and unease. Reading Eve's news was always unsettling. It stirred old, half-buried memories better left undisturbed. Toby Smythe the vice-consul, who always got to the personal mail first, had brought it in to Meredith with a meaningful, "Here you are!" which was explained by the fact that Eve had thoughtlessly written her name and address on the back and Toby had read it. Unasked questions had radiated from him but the steely look in Meredith's eye stopped him putting them to her—for the time being. She had taken it with a crisp thank you and had not opened it, even after he had reluctantly taken himself off. She put it on her desk and sat looking at it before stuffing it hurriedly in her pocket, still unopened. It reminded her of its presence now, as she rummaged for her key, rubbing stiffly against her fingers and crackling.

"You wait a bit!" said Meredith silently to the letter. She let herself into the flat. Marija had left but an odour of wax polish lingered. Meredith dropped her bag, hung up her coat and went into the kitchen to put the kettle on. As was typical in flats of this age, the living rooms were enormous and the kitchen a tiny marble-floored galley where the cook had sweated, hardly able to turn round, while the family had sat and shouted at one another from either end of their vast drawing room. Meredith fiddled about, taking her time, concocting a peanut butter sandwich she didn't want. She finally carried letter, tea and sandwich through to the spacious lounge and put the tray down on the obtrusively modern wooden furniture which officialdom decreed should be supplied for her. The moment she had been putting off had arrived. She sat down in the last of the evening sun and, after a mistrustful stare at the smooth ivory surface of the envelope, opened it.

No wonder it was so stiff. It contained a letter and a card. The card, it was soon apparent, was a tastefully engraved wedding invitation. For a moment, Meredith

thought Eve proposed taking the plunge for the fourth time
but quick scrutiny revealed that the bride-to-be was Sara,
Eve's daughter and Meredith's godchild.

A fresh wave of remorse enveloped her with a distant
memory of a chilly church and a wailing baby. There, in
memory's eye, stood Eve looking young, pretty and
charmingly maternal. Beside her stood Mike, the proud
father—he had been so proud of his baby daughter. Another couple had also been godparents besides Meredith
but she had quite forgotten their names. She had been a
very young godmother and the occasion had weighed on
her shoulders. She had felt a dreadful responsibility. She
had also been a prey to guilt, a guilt which made her want
to hate Eve, whom she really loved. She had been locked
in that particular kind of adolescent purgatory with senti-
ments which frightened her, which she did not understand,
which exhilarated and made her miserable at the same
time.

They had made a charming, outwardly united trio, the
pretty wife and mother, a beautiful baby, and the proud
young father and husband. Standing directly opposite to
them, Meredith, pressed against a pillar, skulking behind the
high carved stone font, had wanted to die, sink through the
uneven slabs which floored the ancient church, sink
straight down to the crypt beneath and join the dead who
were beyond all fleshly torment. She had believed then she
must be the wickedest person in the world. The vicar intoned the question to the godparents, "Dost thou, in the
name of this child, renounce the devil and all his works,
the vain pomp and glory of this world, with all covetous
desires of the same, and the carnal desires of the flesh, so
that thou wilt not follow, nor be led by them?" Despite her
every effort to prevent it, her gaze had been dragged up
and she had met Mike's eye across the font and felt that
everything in her heart must be branded on her forehead
for them all to read.

"Response!" the vicar had prompted testily.

Meekly she had mumbled, "I renounce them all ..."
and to this day did not understand why an immediate bolt
of lightning had not struck her dead, right there on the

worn stone slabs. Even now, sitting here with Eve's letter
and the card in her hand, she seemed to smell the candle
grease, the earthy dampness which lurks around old
stones, the dust in the hassocks. She could hear in her
mind the splash of water, the rustle of the priest's wide-
sleeved surplice, a surprised little squeak from the infant
in the crook of his arm.

Sometimes, Meredith reflected later, you grow out of
adolescent confusion and sometimes it just matures into
confusion on an adult scale, and then there is no other way
to deal with it than to run away. No other way out. In due
course, Meredith had set out on a wandering existence.
Posting to posting, country to country. She was British
consul here, thirty-five years old, good at her job.
Meredith, said everyone, is a career woman. She was also
a fugitive.

Fate, however, has a nasty way of hanging on to your
coat-tails. Here was that squawling infant, grown to
womanhood and about to marry. Malicious fate must
have been waiting for this day, sneering at Meredith and
doing a ghostly triumphant little dance in the corner of
the lounge as it watched her read. And it was, undeni-
ably, a nasty shock to think how quickly the years had
flown by.

"Cripes," Meredith muttered. "How old is she?" She did
some rapid sums on her fingers. Nineteen. "Blast, I never
sent her an eighteenth birthday present. When do they cel-
ebrate coming-of-age now? Eighteen or twenty-one? I'll
have to give a splendid wedding present. Who on earth is
she marrying?"

Inspection of the card announced this to be one Jonathan Lazenby. As for wedding present, Eve would have to
be consulted. The last thing Meredith remembered sending
her god-daughter was a *Beano* annual. She began to read
the letter.

"You will try and come, won't you, Merry?" Eve's
sprawling handwriting swooped back and forth across the
page, occasionally falling off the edge altogether, leaving
words curiously truncated. "We're such a small family. No
proper relatives at all and the Lazenbys will probably turn

up in force. It's just a little family wedding, you see, and it will embarrass Sara if our side of the church is empty. She's being married in our little local church which is more or less disused and has to be opened up specially. I do hope it doesn't smell of damp hassocks. It's got nice stained glass and should look good in the wedding photos. I've lost touch with all Mike's family. I should have kept in with them, I suppose, for Sara's sake but I didn't after the way things turned out. PLEASE DO COME!"

"The way things turned out," Meredith repeated. She sat for a few minutes, the letter in her hand, in a world grown still. A blue-bottle colliding with the window-pane recalled her to the present. The fly lay on its back, buzzing uselessly. She got up, shovelled it up on Eve's letter and dropped it out of the window. A burst of warm, late afternoon air gusted in, bearing on it the sound of trams clanking a block away. She suddenly found herself filled with an overwhelming nostalgia for England and a home which was not something she carried on her back like a snail: a dim, beckoning impression of a world of double-decker buses, chintz covers, summer rain pattering against window-panes and toasted tea-cakes.

Why not accept? She had more than enough leave due to her and did need a rest. It would be nice to see Mike's daughter married. Mike would have liked it, too. How would it be possible to stand in church and not remember that other service, the questions and the responses? How not to think of Mike? Because she still did, more often than was good for her and certainly more often than was any use. She pushed the invitation back into the envelope. A decision could wait. Not for long because the wedding was not that far away, but it could still wait for a week until her reply went into the next UK-bound sack. It had been a long day, she felt sticky and dusty and her indecision clung to her with a multitude of other, unresolved feelings. She went into the bathroom and turned on the taps to wash the whole lot away.

* * *

"I don't like weddings," said Alan Markby firmly. He peered up at a hanging basket. "The heat's affecting this thing. I'd better move it."

"Bit late," said Paul, his brother-in-law, turning the steaks on the barbecue. "I'm afraid the lobelia's pretty well smoked by now. Keep away, you kids!"

Laura, Markby's sister, uncoiled from a deckchair and organized her brood into a corner where they sat with cans of Coke and, Markby noticed resignedly, hideous red ice lollies on sticks which dripped faster than small mouths could eat them and were peppering the flagstones of his patio with violent scarlet patches. He wondered why he had asked them over to ruin his Sunday afternoon. Bad conscience, he thought.

Laura, veiled behind outsize sunglasses, turned up her face to the sun. Fair-complexioned, her blonde hair was turning to a Scandinavian whiteness as the English summer progressed, and she was nicely tanned. She was displaying long, shapely legs and Markby thought with some humour that he had never seen anyone who looked less like a successful solicitor in a reputable and old-established county firm.

"Here we go!" announced Paul. "Steaks for us, hamburgers for kids, sausages for those who want them."

As they ate, conversation turned again to the wedding invitation pinned up on the larder door in Markby's kitchen.

"It's flattering to be asked to give the bride away," said Laura coaxingly. "Especially when her mother's the famous Eve Owens."

"It's only flattering if you're an old family friend. I knew Robert Freeman slightly. I played golf with him and had a few drinks with him. But he wasn't Sara's father, only stepfather number two, and he's been dead eighteen months. I've met Sara two or possibly three times. She dresses like a visitant from outer space, bounces about like an untrained puppy and saves whales. Eve Owens I've met about the same number of times, and I'm hardly a fan of those films of hers. The last time I saw her, on screen or off, was at poor old Bob Freeman's funeral when she

looked stunning in black and was surrounded by photographers. I don't say she wasn't decently grieving
but when she let fall a single rose into the open grave,
flashlights went off in all directions. The whole thing
was grotesque and this wedding is going to be on a par
with it. Paparazzi pushing each other out of the way
trying to snap the bride's glamorous mother and yours
truly in a top hat trying to look as if he knew what he
was doing there." Markby raised a haunted face from his
steak. "God, they'll call me 'Eve Owens' latest escort!' "

"You should be so lucky."

"Got a bit of newspaper I can stick down under those
kids? They are making a bit of a mess of your patio,
Alan," observed Paul amiably.

"For chrissake, it looks as if they've slaughtered a pig.
Whatnot's dropped his hamburger—the grease will leave a
mark."

"His name is Matthew! Alan—you ought to know your
own nephew's name!"

A diversion followed whilst the children were cocooned
in newspaper, too late to save the damage.

"You can't refuse to give the bride away, Alan. It would
be churlish."

"I don't like weddings. I've never liked weddings. I
didn't like my own much and that was a portent if ever
there was one."

"You ought to get married again. You're forty-two. You
ought to have a family."

"No thanks," said Markby, staring morosely at grease
sinking into his flagstones. "As for marriage, once was
enough. Matthew, stop popping the fuchsia heads, if you
don't mind."

"It makes them open up."

"They'll open up by themselves, thanks. Can't I turn
down this wedding thing? Why has she asked me? She
rang me up and said Robert would have liked it. Pure rubbish. He wouldn't even have thought of it!"

"If he was alive, he wouldn't have to. He'd give his
stepdaughter away himself."

Markby surrendered. "All right, I'll do it. But it's a mistake, I feel it in my bones!"

"Mum, Vicky's picked all those red and purple flowers . . ."

TWO

Meredith had never thought of her cousin as any kind of country mouse. To bury herself away from all her friends and professional colleagues was simply not Eve's way. As Meredith drew up before The Old Rectory, Eve's present home, and switched off the engine, she wondered whether it had been the idea of Robert Freeman, Eve's last husband, to buy this attractive if slightly crumbling yellow brick pile in the rural setting of the Oxfordshire-Northamptonshire border.

The village was called Westerfield, or so a sagging sign half obliterated by long grass informed approaching travellers. It lay some six miles from the market town of Bamford and to find it on the ordnance survey map had required squinting at tiny print before discovering the name, printed hard by a symbol and the laconic indication "earthworks." Exactly what comprised the earthworks goodness only knew; there were no tangible signs anywhere that she had yet seen showing where these historical curiosities might be found. They were probably just a series of bumps in some farmer's field betraying bronze age fortifications. Man had long tilled the soil at Westerfield.

Primitive man had probably had his shaman or druid priest but eighteenth-century Westerfield had had a rector to watch over its souls, collect its tithes and represent authority. And he had lived here. Eve's house stood at the end of a tree-shadowed gravel track. Opposite stood the church with which it had once been associated, half-hidden behind the trees in an untidy churchyard. Meredith could only see that the church was late Gothic and appeared to be locked and deserted. The rectory, or what

could be seen of it from behind a high brick wall and
closed wrought-iron gates, was Georgian with some late
Victorian additions. Unsightly pipes swarming up the exte-
rior bore witness to likely Edwardian attempts to modern-
ize the place. A television aerial atop the roof indicated the
priorities of a later generation.

Meredith got out of the car and shivered in the dank
coolness, rubbing at her bare forearms as she peered up at
the first-floor windows. Behind her the wind soughed
mournfully in the church-yard trees and without warning
something large flew out of nearby branches and flapped
away, making her start. But it was only a wood-pigeon
which landed on the television aerial and cooed at her.
Meredith grimaced and shook the bars of the gates. They
were locked and now she could see that there was a per-
forated metal disc on one gatepost and a button.

There was something else, too. Tied to a bar of a gate
was a brown paper bag. It was secured by a length of pink
satin ribbon tied in a bow and pinned to it was a small
card of the kind florists affix to bouquets delivered on order. The curious and rather unpleasant thing was that this
card had a black border and was the type which usually
accompanied wreaths or floral tributes intended for the
graveside.

Meredith stepped closer and peered at the card. In
printed lettering it read "Welcome Home, Sara." No signature. She frowned. No doubt the anonymous well-wisher
had good intentions but it was a silly mistake to make, to
pick out a black-trimmed card. It was then she noticed that
the bottom of the paper bag was wet. Whatever it is, it's
leaking, she thought and put out her hand to touch the sod-
den paper.

Her fingers came away sticky and stained scarlet. She
gave a gasp and tore at the pink bow, destroying it. The
paper bag fell down on to the ground and burst open. Inside was a grisly bloody mess. Meredith dropped on to her
heels and gingerly pulled the paper away. It was an ox
heart.

"What a perfectly filthy practical joke!" she muttered
and was glad she had found this nauseating offering before
anyone else. Meredith picked up bag, heart, ribbon and

card and carried them at arm's length across the track to the far side where a ditch full of nettles bordered the track. She dropped the whole lot into the middle of the nettle-bed and saw it disappear from sight. A dog or some night-prowling predator would find the meat and dispose of it by morning. Meredith wiped her fingers carefully and gave herself a mental shake to dismiss the unpleasant image. Just then, she heard the faintest crunch of the gravel surface of the track behind her and whirled round.

Behind, some twelve feet away, a man stood watching her. He was as unlikely a figure as any she could have imagined in the quiet of the country lane. He was of middle height, slender and pale and could have been almost any age between thirty and fifty. He wore a dark suit and looked almost obsessively clean and tidy so that for a wild moment she took him for an undertaker inspecting the church-yard with a view to some future professional visit. But then he spoke.

"Kind of unpleasant," he said. The voice was American but the accent careful, the words clearly enunciated in a slightly old-fashioned, prim manner. He did not sound shocked, only disapproving.

Meredith said hotly, "Yes—did you know it was there?"

The corners of his mouth turned up but his pale grey eyes remained watchful. "I just saw it as I was coming down the track. You got to it first." He moved forward and held out his hand. "You'll be the lady consul. My name is Elliott—Albie Elliott. I'm a friend of Evie's. I'm staying here, too." He jerked his head towards the rectory as he spoke the last words.

A little unwillingly, Meredith took the soft white fingers in her palm. She spoke her own name automatically, although obviously he already knew it. "Wasn't it there when you went out?"

Elliott blinked. "I'd have noticed it, wouldn't I? But I went out early this morning. I've been into the little town near here—Bamford they call it. One horse place. I took a ride in on the bus. It was interesting but I don't say I'd do it again. There was nothing on the gate when I left, but, like I say, that was at nine this morning."

Several questions sprang into Meredith's head, but the

only one she asked, was, "Have you come for the wedding?"

"Oh, yes—the wedding." Elliott rubbed his smooth palms together. "Evie wants me to stay on for that. Not too many people on your side of the family, I understand. But I don't know that I can spend much more time here. I have business back home." On his finger was a large, singularly unattractive dark red stone in a clumsy setting. "Mine's a business visit," he said.

"Film or television?" she asked promptly. It was presumably one or the other, unless Eve had decided to write her memoirs. But it was difficult to know what to make of Mr. Elliott, other than that at least in one way he operated under false colours. Behind the "preppy" accent, the carefully clipped hair and dark "Ivy League" suit, to say nothing of the monster fraternity ring—all of it so consciously WASP—lay pure Bronx. Meredith was sure of it.

Elliott's mouth turned up again. "I both produce and direct *The Inheritance.*" He paused and, seeing that she looked quite blank, added with a little note of annoyance which made his voice more nasal, "It's an on-going saga of three generations of New Jersey bankers."

"Oh, a soap opera!" said Meredith, enlightened.

"That's right. Surprised you haven't heard of it. But let's see, you've been in . . .?" He paused.

"In Yugoslavia. *The,* um, *Inheritance* hasn't reached them yet, I'm afraid."

"It will."

"I shouldn't think they would know what to make of it." That sounded rather rude and she regretted it, but Elliott did not appear to take offence.

"It has something for everyone. It's my baby. My idea. I set it up. I make sure we stick to the original formula. But right now, it needs a little something . . ." His eyes drifted towards the rectory again.

"You want Eve to take a role in it?" she asked, surprised.

"Yes, ma'am. We have action, drama, pathos, passion and we're not afraid to be controversial without actually upsetting anyone, you understand." Elliott paused and frowned as if not entirely pleased with this wide-ranging scenario. "But we need a touch of class," he said, reluctantly, adding with returning optimism, "Evie can fix that." He turned bland eyes on her. "Shall we go on up to the house?"

"No, wait, just a minute!" Meredith put out a hand to prevent him. He paused and fixed his pale expressionless gaze on her. "What are we going to do about—about that?" She pointed towards the nettle-bed and the grisly mess it concealed.

"Do we have to do anything?"

Taken aback, Meredith gaped at him. "Yes!" she said at last, finding her voice.

He looked disapproving again. "What are you planning, lady? You want to pick it out of there and go on into the house, waving it in front of you?"

"Don't be silly!" she returned angrily. "Of course not!"

"Fine. So leave it there. Let me take care of it, right?"

There was an edge to his voice which had not been there before. Meredith found herself taking a second look at him. The pale grey eyes didn't seem nearly so fish-like and blank. There was a hard glint in them. But as she watched the look, it faded. Elliott smiled placatingly. "You don't need to worry about it right now. You just arrived. Why not go in and say hallo first? Evie's waiting on you. Why spoil the reunion? Evie's talked about nothing else since yesterday but that you're coming. I tell you, I've been real curious to see you."

Meredith repressed a desire to snap, "So, what do you think, now you have?" Instead she said in a starchy voice, "All right. But we will talk about it later."

"Sure," said Elliott smoothly, giving her the unwelcome impression that he had dealt with her as capably as he might have done with a temperamental actress on one of his sets. He crossed to the gates with a brisk step and pressed the button. A disembodied, crackling voice dimly identifiable as Eve's asked who it was.

"It's Albie, Eve honey," said Elliott. "And I got your cousin right here with me."

A sudden jarring electronic buzz made her jump out of her skin and resulted in the opening of the gates. Ahead of her now Meredith could see on the wall of the house the conspicuous blue-coloured box of a burglar alarm. Between security gate, high wall and burglar alarm, Eve seemed pretty well fortified. Presumably in the country these days one could not take chances. Certainly not if one had nasty-minded practical jokers about.

As if in echo of her thoughts, Elliott murmured a reminder, "We don't mention that little package back there, right? No point in upsetting Evie."

Meredith nodded in reluctant agreement. In the countryside of her childhood people had habitually left their doors open all day, even when they left the house to go to the village shop. Country trust and village shop had both disappeared. Property prices had gone up a bit, too. What did a house like this cost nowadays? she wondered as she climbed the steps to the front door. Plenty of "period character," no doubt five or six good bedrooms and a couple of maid's rooms in the attic, two bathrooms probably and perhaps a separate loo in the downstairs cloakroom, several good receptions and an enormous kitchen (stone-flagged she imagined and now doubtless housing a dishwasher and other mod cons), a sprawl of out-buildings and a large walled garden . . . By the time I come to retire, she thought wryly, I shall be lucky if I can afford to rent a bed-sit! As this thought ran through her head, the front door was thrown open.

"Darling!" cried Eve flinging out her hands in a gesture of greeting. "How lovely! Here you are at last!" Meredith was enveloped in a warm embrace and a faint aroma of some very expensive perfume. "Come right in!"

"My car's still outside."

"Oh, bring it in later. No one uses that road. It's very quiet here! Oh, I know, give Albie your keys. He'll drive it in."

Elliott grimaced and held out his hand. A little embarrassed, Meredith handed him the keys. "That's kind of you."

"Why not?" he said enigmatically.

Meredith was propelled through the hall and into a drawing room. Her shoulders were grasped. "Now then!" declared her cousin happily. "Let's have a good look at you!"

They were standing in an elegantly furnished drawing room. There were few signs of its original clerical use. Now the walls were peach-coloured, the windows draped with the looped net curtains once associated with Viennese cafés, the one painting an indifferently executed portrait of Eve herself, and there wasn't a book to be seen. Instead, glossy magazines were strewn across the coffee table. Even the rector's affronted ghost had fled.

"I am so happy to see you, Merry . . ." Eve said. Her voice, which had been raised in enthusiasm, suddenly sank to become almost inaudible. "Damn it, I think I'm going to cry!"

"Don't!" Meredith exclaimed. "Don't be daft, Eve. I'm not about to present you with an Oscar."

"I just need you!" Eve said fervently. "I'm run off my feet. This wedding . . . and everything else. You're always such a tower of strength, Merry!"

"Less of the 'tower', please! I can't help being a bean stalk."

There was the sound of a car being parked outside the front door. The gates clanged shut distantly. Elliott reappeared, holding out Meredith's keys.

"I put your valise in the hall. Anything else you want me to do, Evie?"

"Bless you, darling, only to come and join us and meet my cousin properly." Eve turned back to Meredith. "You look so well!" she said emphatically. "Doesn't she, Albie?"

Elliott, standing a little to one side with his hands folded, allowed himself a spontaneous answer. "How the hell should I know, honey? I never met her before till ten minutes back. Sure, she looks great."

"You look fantastic, Eve," Meredith said sincerely.

Eve radiated well-groomed charm from every pore. Her beautiful face seemed little changed since Meredith had last seen her cousin, some six years earlier. Elliott was nodding. He was watching Eve in a slightly proprietorial way, like a proud parent.

"You must be gasping for a cup of tea," said Eve, suddenly practical. "That long drive. Lucia—she still cooks for me—has gone to the dentist. I do hope she's going to be all right for this evening. Jonathan is bringing Sara down from London and I've arranged a little dinner party. Sara is longing to see you and I want her to stay a few days and discuss all the last minute wedding details. There's so much to do—you've simply no idea. I'll fetch the tea—just sit down there and relax!"

"Don't bring me tea!" said Elliott hurriedly. "I've got work to do. Besides, you girls want to talk. I'll see you both later." He walked out with his brisk light step.

"Who is he?" Meredith asked in a hoarse whisper. "He says you're going to lend a touch of class to his appalling soap epic!"

"I'll tell you about it later—" Eve glanced furtively at the door. "Albie is a sweetie. I've known him for years. I'd love to work with him again. No, don't come and help. I can manage!" She departed to fetch the tea, her heels clicking on the parquet floor.

Alone, Meredith wandered across to the other side of the room and gazed at the portrait. A date, just beneath the signature in one corner and above a slight chip in the frame, showed that it coincided with Eve's last marriage. A wedding present to or from the bride? The artist's name was unfamiliar and difficult to make out, his brushwork clumsy and style slap-dash, but he had an eye for colour and had caught something of Eve. Looking at it, Meredith realized that Eve had changed, only a little, but it was there. The dark tawny-blonde hair still looked much as it did in this painting. The fine violet eyes stared out as confidently but in real life the skin beneath them was just starting to sag a little. The jaw line in this picture was firmer. Either the artist had flattered or, again, the slight loss of tension of skin and muscle had come over the last year or so. What the artist had done was blatantly to ignore the fine mesh of faint lines which had marked Eve's skin since she turned thirty, the legacy of hot bright lights, dusty, windswept, sun-drenched locations, heavy stage make-up and the famous wide, beautiful smile which had slowly led to crow's feet in the corners of the eyes and little vertical lines either side of the mouth.

In the portrait Eve wore a dress the colour of her eyes. Eve's appearance had always been the subject of meticu-

lous care. Today she was wearing black pants, a loose
white silk tunic and a wide black belt. In it her body had
appeared slim, supple and full of a youthful elasticity. Eve
was nine years older than she was but Meredith accepted
without rancour that, presented with the two of them, any
man would only have eyes for Eve. She thought of Elliott
and that almost paternal look he had given Eve and a
slight frown momentarily creased her forehead. Then she
sat down in one corner of a very comfortable sofa uphol-
stered with some exotic design of birds and foliage and
waited for Eve to come back.

Her cousin tottered in shortly, bearing a large tray laden
with miscellaneous china. Eve and domesticity had always
gone ill together. Meredith repressed a smile and took the
burden from her to set it down on the coffee table, pushing
aside the glossy magazines.

"What have I forgotten?" Eve peered at the assortment
on the tray. "Those are some of Lucia's biscuits. We don't
need forks for biscuits, do we? I haven't brought any. The
lemon is for me, unless you like it too."

She subsided onto the sofa beside Meredith and
splashed tea haphazardly into the cups from a rather nice
Victorian teapot. They chatted together for some time, exchanging general gossip and then Meredith brought the
conversation back to Elliott's soap opera, prompted by real
curiosity.

"Are you going to do it, Eve? It's a bit different from
films."

"Oh, I haven't made a cinema movie for ages. Let's
face it," Eve said with sudden candour. "None of my films
was ever a box-office record-breaker."

"I liked that one you made years ago, when you wore
that fur bikini and were chased round by radio-active dino-
saurs."

Eve's mascaraed eyelashes flickered. "Oh, that one. Did
you really? It wasn't one of the best." She brightened and
wagged a slender, well-manicured forefinger. "But the special effects in that film were quite advanced for its day. Of
course, now the movie-goers all cut their teeth on *Star
Wars* and *Indiana Jones* and our poor old creaky monsters

make audiences laugh . . . except for the kids, who still love them."

"I still love 'em," Meredith said grinning. *"King Kong* was one of the best films ever made. I think so, anyway."

"I hope you're not suggesting I starred in that!" Eve said severely. "It was well before both your time and mine. As a matter of fact, Albie and I go way back to my movie-making days. But he's been in television for some time. He's doing well. He's had several successes but *The Inheritance* is the biggest and the chance to star in it, well . . ."

Meredith made a mental resolve to see an episode. In the meantime there was little more she could say about it. Instead, she said, "I'm looking forward to seeing Sara again. Give me a clue about a wedding present and tell me about the boyfriend, sorry, fiancé. Where did she meet him?"

A shadow crossed Eve's face and a new line was added to the fine mesh beneath the make-up. She put down her cup abruptly. "You know I had a lot of trouble with Sara, don't you?"

"You did hint at it in one of your Christmas letters."

"It was much worse," Eve said. "Much worse than I wrote to you." She made a gesture of despair which though no doubt genuine still managed to look slightly theatrical. Meredith felt a sudden pang of pity for her. "I messed it up," said Eve bleakly. "I messed up being a mother, Merry."

"Oh, come on. You're devoted to Sara, I know it!"

"Yes, I am!" Eve's fists clenched in frustration. "But I still made a rotten hash of bringing her up. Mike wouldn't have approved."

Another, more painful twinge shrivelled Meredith's heart. "No, I suppose not."

"Mike was so practical. He was good for me, Merry!" Eve sighed. "If we hadn't split up when Sara was eight, if he'd been around, it would have been different. We were going to get back together again, you know, when that damn kid—"

Meredith put out a hand and touched her cousin's arm. "Don't get worked up about it now, Eve. It's over and done with." Her words sounded hollow in her own ears. She knew it wasn't. Aloud she said, "You did your best for Sara, Evie."

"No, I didn't! I did sod all! I never had any time, you see. And my second marriage to Hughie—well, I'm not going into all that again. You know the sordid details. But it took my attention off poor Sara even more. Then suddenly, she wasn't a little girl any more but a teenager and running wild with the most undesirable crowd you could imagine." Eve paused and pushed the tea-tray away. "Who wants tea? It's gone five. How about a proper drink?"

"Not for me, thanks. Later."

"Don't mind if I have a gin?"

"Of course not. It's your house."

"Old fashioned drink this, nowadays," Eve said when she returned after a few minutes with her gin and tonic. "They all drink weird preparations these days with exotic names. I'm getting outdated, Merry. I'm forty-four and finding it harder and harder to relate to anything my daughter says or does."

"So do most parents, I imagine. It's nothing to do with age. It's a mother/daughter thing."

"Sara will be twenty next month." Eve seemed not to have heard the interruption. "It was poor dear Robert who drew my attention to the mess Sara was in. Naturally I refused to believe it at first. We were living in London at the time. Everything was going especially well for me and I just didn't want to know about anything nasty in the woodwork. Then one night Sara came home from a party at about three or four in the morning. She made a bit of a row and I half woke as one does and thought, drat that kid! But I didn't get up. Good mothers get up. I was always a rotten one, so I just put the pillow over my head and tried to go back to sleep. She carried on crashing about for a bit and then went quiet. By then it had seeped through even to me that something was wrong and I did get up and go and see what she was doing.

"She was awfully drunk and had thrown up everywhere. You never saw such a mess. Then she'd gone to her room and collapsed in a chair with all the lights on and still in her party frock. There was vomit everywhere. I stood looking down at her and thought, dear God, she's just seventeen. What on earth have I let happen?"

"Look, Eve," Meredith said firmly. "You can't blame yourself. Lots of kids go through that sort of phase."

"That wasn't the worst of it!" Eve retorted fiercely, her fingers gripping the gin glass. "She wasn't asleep or passed out drunk, she was sitting there mumbling to herself. I tried to get her together with some idea of getting her to bed. I shook her by the shoulders and shouted at her. Eventually she seemed to take in that I was there and who I was. She started trying to tell me something but I was so angry and so—so bewildered, not knowing what to do, that I really didn't pay much attention. I remember saying, 'Tomorrow, tell me tomorrow'—I just wanted to get her to bed, you see. But all the time I was helping her undress she kept repeating the same thing until I was forced to take it in. 'We couldn't wake her up,' she kept saying. It became—" Eve paused and shivered. "It became so sinister. I was frightened, yet I still didn't want to know. In the end I asked, 'Who?' She gave me a name but it meant nothing to me."

Eve fell silent and Meredith waited. "The next day the police came round." Eve's voice had become bleak. "Some poor kid had died—a mixture of drink and drugs, I'm not sure what sort. That's what Sara had been trying to tell me. They couldn't wake her up and they were all too frightened and too drunk to call a doctor or telephone anyone's parents. If they had, the kid might have been saved. As it was, they all panicked. They had some pathetic belief—they were only children after all—that if they left well alone it would all come right—the girl would just wake up again with nothing worse then a splitting head. As it was she never came round. It was a dreadful thing. We went to the inquest. The dead girl's parents—I'll never forget the mother, her face . . ."

"It wasn't Sara's fault," Meredith said.

"No. But it had to be someone's, didn't it?" The violet eyes in their mascara frames flashed aggressively.

"The drug-pusher's."

"Easy to say that."

"True, also. Look, they home in on kids like Sara and others with money."

"And with parents too busy to notice? Why not say it?"

"It was a sad case. But it wasn't your fault or Sara's, Eve." Poor Eve was suffering from guilt, too. Meredith knew all about that. *Forasmuch as this child hath promised by you her sureties to renounce the devil and all his works . . . ye shall provide . . . that this child shall be virtuously brought up . . .* She'd given the baby a set of silver feeding tools and called it a day. Impulsively she asked, "What happened to the other godparents? Besides me, there was a couple. Will they be coming?"

"No," Eve said absently, staring into her empty glass. "You mean Rex and Lydia. They divorced. Lydia married an oil sheikh. Rex is based in Florida and manages sports stars. That's where the money is nowadays. The youngsters don't want to be movie stars any more. They want to play tennis." Eve threw back her head and turned haunted violet eyes towards Meredith. "When that girl died, it was a foul business but it saved Sara. It frightened her so much she was prepared to listen to us at last. Even so, it took myself and Robert a long time to get her even part way back on an even keel. Robert never lived long enough to see her come good because he had his last heart attack in the middle of it all. It was a dreadful time and I never want to go through another like it ever again! She was scared and she wanted out of it but at the same time she was loyal to her friends. She refused to believe badly of any of them. We never found out who supplied the drugs at that party, all the youngsters closed ranks. No one knew anything. Anyway, we sold the London house and moved down here. Sara hated it at first and missed her so-called friends. She scooted off to London at every opportunity but eventually she started to see them for what they were. Robert was right. He said distance would lend perspective to her view. She started to get herself sorted out. That was when Robert died, so suddenly. Sara was very upset. She had respect for Robert and talked to him much more freely than ever she did to me. I thought she might just go to pieces again but luckily she met Jonathan Lazenby, oddly enough at Robert's funeral." She paused. "He's a financial adviser—"

Eve must have caught a hint of disapproval on her cousin's face because she added emphatically, "No—not like Hughie."

"I should hope not! If he were, Sara would be better off with an out-of-work young actor filling in time as a barman! What does it mean, Eve? Financial adviser could be anything from a bookie to manager of the Bank of England."

"Well, investments, pension schemes and things . . . I don't know! He works in the city and he's doing very well. Sara thinks the world of him and he isn't like her former friends, thank God!" Eve tossed down her gin and tonic in a defiant manner.

"I see. What about wedding presents?"

"Oh, there's a list going the rounds somewhere. People have crossed things off and I don't know what's left. Ask Sara tonight. I hope she went for that dress fitting . . ." Eve's expression grew preoccupied.

This wedding, thought Meredith, is going to take up every minute of time any one of us has.

Later, when she had unpacked, Meredith went out for a walk round the village, letting herself out of the gates. Lucia the cook had returned from the dentist and was busy in the kitchen. Eve was resting. Meredith glanced uneasily at the nettle-bed as she passed by it, but drew back from disturbing it to see if the package was still where she had thrown it. Eve was right. We shut out unpleasantness. We know about it all right, but just don't choose to face it. Anyhow, Elliott had declared he would deal with it. Perhaps he already had done so. He was smoothly efficient, Mr. Elliott, and unlikely, Meredith felt, to be squeamish. He wasn't around. It was a toss-up whether he was working in his room or burying the evidence. What are the odds, Meredith mused, that he did that while Eve and I drank tea and reminisced? Yes, that would be the best time to do it. She turned back determinedly, picked up a stick and poked aside some of the nettles. There was a patch of broken stems and a dark smear on the underlying grass. Nothing else. Mr. Elliott had dealt with it. Meredith threw away the stick and walked on.

The evening was pleasant, the village, she thought, not. It clearly wasn't the kind which won competitions for being picturesque and Meredith did not think that the memory of her gruesome find influenced her view of it. Westerfield was not large but it was sprawling and lacked any kind of distinct centre. The outskirts were marked by a long single row of dilapidated town-style post-war council houses, set down amid the surrounding farmland without any regard for suitability and gazing out over open fields. After that came a mixed bag of bungalows and cottages, until one reached a rounded bend in the road like that of a hockey stick. The bend marked on two sides a triangle of overgrown grass and weeds around a rusting bus stop pole, scattered over with a confetti of cigarette ends and sweet wrappers. Beyond the triangle of green stood a public house which must be one of the oldest buildings. It was called the Dun Cow. Next to it stood a pair of early nineteenth-century farmworkers' cottages and running alongside them, away from the triangle of grass, the track which led to the church and the Old Rectory. There was none of that feeling of community which she would have felt in a Yugoslav village. There were not even any people about.

Meredith walked towards the Dun Cow. But the pub had a closed and deserted look too. Its sign, depicting an amiable, unlikely proportioned beast, swung and creaked in the breeze above its half-timbering. Small, dusty windows were dark blank eyes and its stout plank door refused to yield to her hand. On the door was a small plaque which informed her that the licensee was one Harry Linnet. She glanced at her watch. It was well after six but if Mr Linnet was in there somewhere, polishing up the glasses, there was no sign of him. Perhaps he just opened up when he felt like it. Meredith fastidiously wrinkled her nose. The smell of stale beer, ash-trays and Jeyes fluid seeped from the building. Meredith suspected that inside it would prove similar to a pub outside Dover into which she had been lured by an outward appearance of old-world charm after disembarking from an uncomfortable cross-Channel trip on the car ferry. The inside had proved to be cramped, grubby and dominated by one-armed bandits, space invader machines and cigarette dispensers and had pumped unwanted reggae music into her ear.

She turned her back on the Dun Cow, tossed back her straight mop of brown hair, shoved her hands disconsolately into the pockets of her jeans and observed her surroundings with deep mistrust.

She was reluctantly forced to admit she was more a stranger here in her own country than anywhere. Every home leave, every gap between overseas postings emphasized that she had become as much a foreigner as all those other bona fide foreigners amongst whom she normally lived. She had paid the penalty of spending too much time globe-trotting and living in alien climes, necessitated by her consular job. She, who in her own small way represented England abroad, had slowly and inexorably turned into another foreigner whenever she came home.

At that moment a strange, inarticulate cry pierced the air and made her jump. An extraordinary figure, a human spider in a cloth cap, appeared round the side of the right hand half of the pair of farmworkers' cottages—the one with the tidy garden—and scurried, screeching hoarsely, towards the front gate.

"Git out of it, you foreign blighter!" it howled and Meredith wondered, startled, if she was meant, so clearly did the epithet echo her earlier musing. As she watched, the figure began to pelt an unseen object with the small stones with which its pockets seemed to be filled.

"You bin in my carrits, dang you—git out of it!" The apparition danced in an ungainly fashion by the gate and raised clenched fists into the air. "I'll have your skin, you furry foreign varmint, if you don't keep off my spring cabbidges!"

A siamese cat leapt up on to the wall between the cottages and, pursued by a hail of abuse and pebbles, jumped down into the other cottage front garden, which by contrast was a riot of neglect. The other cottage door opened and a youth in a worn red sweatshirt and jeans emerged.

"For God's sake, Bert!" he called, "stop making all that fuss!" The voice was educated and the manner, despite the words, patient and pleasant. Meredith found herself thinking ridiculously that he looked like a very nice boy.

"One of them foreign moggies of yours has been digging in me carrits again!" yelled the ancient old man. "And burying his business in me lettusses! I seen him—with his evil black face and crookedy tail. I tole you to keep them brutes out of my veg!"

The boy stooped and scooped up the siamese cat which sat up in his arms directing supercilious looks at his assailant who now became so enraged that Meredith began to fear he would have a fit.

"Wait a minute," said the youth reasonably. "It's because you keep weeding and raking the soil. Of course the cats go there. I can't help it and neither can they. Why don't you put some chicken wire over the cabbages?"

"And why don't you," howled Bert, brandishing his fist, "keep them foreign creatures off my gardin? Evil-looking brutes they is! Look like devils not cats! Dogs is kept under control and so should them devilish cats be!"

"I've explained before, you silly old bugger!" said the youth wearily. "A cat is a feral beast. That means it roams by nature and its owner can't be expected to control where it goes."

"I'll have the law on you!" sputtered the other.

"For goodness sake! That is the law! I've just explained it! A cat is a feral beast and a dog isn't. Dog owners are obliged to keep their animals from straying. Cat owners aren't—can't be."

Bert scurried bandy-legged and arms flailing across to the dividing wall and peered malevolently from beneath the brim of his cap. "Clever, you think yourself, don't you? Well, I got a right to protect my property! That's the law, that is! And I'm telling you, I'm going to put poison down! That'll take care of them foreign brutes! I got the poison and I tole you before I'll put it down if you don't keep them animals off my gardin!"

The boy's face reddened. "Listen, Bert!" he said sharply. "If you do, I'm the one who will have the law on

you! Tom and Jerry are valuable animals and if you go deliberately poisoning either of them, you'll be the one in
trouble. Got that?"

They glared at one another and the old man growled and
turned and stomped away. When he had gone, the boy
looked across to the watching Meredith and called,
"Hallo! Are you lost? Can I help?"

A little sheepishly, because it did look as though she
had been eavesdropping on the quarrel, she walked across
to his gate. "No. I'm visiting in the village and was just
looking round. I didn't mean to listen in on your conversation with the old man."

"Conversation?" he returned good-naturedly. "No one
has had a reasonable conversation with old Bert Yewell for
years. He's potty. What they call a local character. Unfor-
tunately, Tom and Jerry do dig holes in his garden. He's
inordinately proud of it. He's won prizes at shows with onions and things. I told him to put down wire or even twigs
to keep the cats off until the plants get big enough to with-
stand a bit of scratching around. But the old fool is so obstinate. He's standing on what he reckons are his rights."

He had walked down his overgrown front path as he
spoke and now he and Meredith stood together with the
unpainted gate between them. Viewed nearer to hand,
he was older than she had supposed him at a distance, not
a "boy" at all, but a young man of twenty-five or so and
she felt embarrassed at her mistake. He was still holding
the cat and rubbing at one of its smoky ears. She noticed
that his fingers were streaked with pale lines of what
looked like dry clay.

"Will he really do it, put down poison?" she asked worriedly. She stretched out her hand and Tom sniffed at it
disdainfully and permitted her to stroke his head.

The young man frowned and glanced towards Bert's
cottage. "He might. He's been threatening to do it for
ages. I'm sure he's speaking the truth when he says he's
got some. That garden shed of his must be full of God
knows what. Warfarin, Paraquat, the lot. He doesn't keep
it locked and I stuck my head in there one day looking for
Jerry when he went missing. Jerry is Tom here's brother."

He indicated the cat in his arms. "I never saw such a clutter. I mean, I'm not tidy . . ." He waved a hand nonchalantly at his overgrown garden. "But Bert's shed must be the most dangerous place in the village. Some of the stuff he's got in there is so old it must have destabilized and if the bottles were opened the fumes alone would knock you rigid. It wouldn't surprise me if the whole lot didn't go up one night with an almighty bang, taking old Bert with it with any luck!" He grinned.

Meredith smiled back. "I'm staying at the Old Rectory."

For a brief moment the grin on his face seemed to freeze. Then he said easily, "That's the Owens' house."

"Yes. I'm Eve Owens' cousin."

"Are you?" He stared at her thoughtfully and to her anger she felt herself flush. She knew what he was thinking. How ever did this plain Jane manage to be related to a beauty like Eve Owens?

"Yes!" she heard her own voice reply too sharply and cursed inwardly.

He apologized gracefully. "Sorry if I was staring. But I know the Owens a little. Well, the beautiful and celebrated Eve doesn't deign to notice me much, but Sara and I used to be good friends once."

"Oh?" Meredith was interested. "I'm looking forward to seeing Sara. I haven't set eyes on her for several years."

"You'll find quite a change in her, then," he said casually. "My name is Philip Lorrimer. I'm a potter." The clay stains were explained. "My studio's round the back. It's a poor but honest living." He smiled at her sardonically.

"I'd like to take a look at your studio some time, if I may."

"Sure, any time." He allowed the cat to jump down from his arms. It walked away, twitching its tail and sat down on the doorstep. Another cat, almost identical, joined it and the two sat side by side. Lorrimer said, "Sara used to come over and help me out at the studio sometimes, before she got engaged and disappeared off to London."

"Was she good at throwing clay—isn't that the expression?"

"Christ no, she was awful. Everything she did looked like the sort of thing mental patients turn out. She was okay painting designs on the pots. She got under my feet, really." He shrugged.

"Will you be coming to the wedding?"

He pulled a face. "Shouldn't think so. I'd lower the tone."

"The church isn't much used, I understand. Is there no present incumbent of the living?"

"Not as such. We're part of a team ministry here. That means that we get whoever draws the short straw and has to drive out from town to hold a service for the sake of our souls. They can't think our souls are all that important because the bloke only comes once a fortnight. I suppose on whatever list of priorities they draw up, we come after the beleaguered inhabitants of vandalized tower blocks in the inner cities."

Meredith said slowly, "This village . . . I know I've only just arrived in it—but it doesn't seem to have any heart to it. It looks sort of disembowelled. Has it got a school? I didn't see any sign."

He shook his head. "No. Kids are all bussed to town. The old school house was sold off and turned into a retirement bunker for the Lockes." He paused. "It's all right, the village, when you get used to it. Even old Bert is all right when you get used to him." He jerked his head towards the Dun Cow. "Even the beer Harry dishes out is all right when you get used to it. But I don't suppose we'll see you in the Dun Cow, not if you're staying with Eve. You'll be with the sherry brigade."

He said this with a pleasant grin, but she still didn't like it and disliked particularly the feeling that she had been put right. But after all, she, a confessed stranger, had quite gratuitously criticized his village.

"I'd better get back," she said. "Nice to have met you."

"See you about, I dare say," he returned. "If you're staying."

She walked off up the track towards the rectory but turned at a bend in it to glance back. Lorrimer was standing on his doorstep watching her. He gave her a cheerful wave. She forgave him the crack about the sherry. She had invited it. He was obviously such a nice boy—man! she corrected herself crossly. Lord, it's a grim sign if a hulking chap like that looks like a boy to me! What do they say? When the policemen start looking younger . . .

Three

The last time Meredith had seen her god-daughter Sara had been spectacularly garbed entirely in black, an outfit comprising a very short skirt, tights and laced ankle boots of the kind worn by children at the turn of the century. Her long hair had been bleached to a tinselly gold, her round, pretty, childish face with its snub nose had been unattractively plastered with lurid make-up and the whole lot had been crowned by a fur cap of the sort worn by Soviet army infantry, complete with red star.

"Merry!" cried Sara enthusiastically now, throwing her arms around Meredith's neck. "Oh, it's lovely to see you again!"

No one could fail to respond to the spontaneous warmth of this greeting. "Hallo, yourself," said Meredith, returning the hug. "I hardly recognized you."

Nor had she. All the changes had been for the better. The hair was no longer tinsel-gilt but had gone back to its natural light brown. The make-up was nowhere near so thick and the lurid purple eye shadow absent altogether. Best of all, although still slightly eccentrically dressed, Sara had discovered that there were other colours than black.

"You look great," Meredith said. "The last time I saw you, you looked like the witch of Endor."

She did not know whether the word "witch" had come up out of her subconscious, but it served to jolt her into remembering her grisly find on the gate. Yet how impossible it seemed that anyone could wish this happy, spontaneous girl any harm. But someone did. Or perhaps that someone was just stupid with a misplaced sense of humor. Such people existed.

Jonathan Lazenby, whom Meredith had been curious to meet, turned out to be a spruce young man of about twenty-five, possessed of brash good looks. There was a city pallor about him and beneath careful grooming and expensive tailoring, Meredith detected a certain street-wise wariness. Not, perhaps, out of the top drawer, but heading for the top with unerring aim. He talked loudly and with a relentless cheeriness behind which he watched them all shrewdly.

When introduced to her by Sara, he stepped forward in a confident manner and gripped Meredith's hand in an aggressively firm handshake. Meredith retrieved her mangled fingers and managed a smile.

Sara, bobbing around them like a happy puppy, declared, "I used to want so much to be like Merry. Travel about, see all sorts of exciting places and meet people. She's been everywhere!"

"Not quite everywhere," Meredith protested. "Quite a few places. I don't know that I want to be anyone's role model, Sara—if it's all the same to you."

"She did say, 'used to want'," Lazenby interpolated quickly, "Sara has grown up a little since then." In time, but only just, he added, "I mean, of course, she no longer suffers from schoolgirl crushes."

"Doesn't she?" asked Meredith mildly.

But Lazenby's attention had been taken by someone else, someone he evidently recognized, a large, untidy, loose-jointed man who had approached their group and stood blinking his eyes in a manner which suggested to Meredith that he probably wore spectacles in working hours but was fighting off the admission that he needed them all the time. Lazenby bounded forward again, sticking out his hand in the same assured manner and exuding his clubman bonhomie. "Ah, Russell!"

Do they, wondered Meredith, teach the high fliers this way of impressing themselves on newcomers in some kind of business school? Russell himself looked unenthusiastic as he returned Lazenby's greeting. After acknowledging it briefly he turned to his hostess and said, "Good evening,

Eve!" and presented her with a bunch of chrysanthemums in cellophane tied up with a mauve bow.

"Why, Peter!" exclaimed Eve, convincingly acting the role of a woman who had never received a bouquet in her life. She had appeared in the midst of them, bandbox fresh and bright as always in what at first glance looked like a long pink chiffon dress but was revealed when she walked, to be flared pants. Meredith wished she had the nerve to wear such an outfit and then thanked her lucky stars she didn't, because she had neither Eve's build nor style and would only have succeeded in looking like a badly made Christmas cracker.

"How perfectly sweet!" said Eve fondly, "I'll tell Lucia to put them in water straight away! Merry dear, this is Peter Russell. . . . My cousin and dearest relative, Meredith Mitchell. Peter is our local doctor."

"In a manner of speaking," Russell said gently. "I live in the village. My practice is part of a group one, based in Bamford. It's nice to meet you, Miss Mitchell."

Team ministry, group practice, Meredith thought. Had this village nothing left of its very own?

Eve had clicked away across the parquet floor to give the flowers to Lucia. Russell, having shaken hands with Meredith, turned to Sara and said casually, "I thought you'd be here, Sal, and didn't want to leave a lady out. Here you are—" He handed over a small box of mint chocolates.

"Oh, thanks, Peter!" said Sara, grabbing them in an unlady-like fashion. "My weakness! You remembered. I ate myself sick on them last time I was here, Merry."

Lazenby said sourly, "You'll get fat!"

An expression of doubt crossed Sara's face and she glanced at him almost guiltily.

Peter Russell said crisply, "At her age, she'll burn it off. If she were inclined to put on weight, she'd be fat now. Let her start worrying when she's forty."

Lazenby said nothing and across his face passed the sulky look of the precocious child who suddenly doesn't get the plaudit it expected.

"But I have, actually, left a lady out," Russell said apologetically turning back to Meredith again. "I didn't know you would be here, Miss Mitchell."

"I shouldn't expect you to bring me either flowers or chocolates if you did," she said, surprised. "But thank you for the thought."

"Neat . . ." murmured Elliott, sitting in a corner nursing a glass of tawny liquid. Meredith had already noticed the bottle of Southern Comfort amongst the bottles on a nearby trolley. In the background, a telephone was ringing.

Russell smiled. "I'm glad to meet another member of the family. Sara has told me that you are the intrepid lady who sets out for obscure destinations with the purpose of keeping the flag flying."

"We do our best," she said, liking him.

"I hope you don't provide hand-outs to yobbos who go abroad and disgrace their country by their behavior before ending up destitute!" Lazenby said aggressively.

Eve reappeared. "My dears, that was Alan Markby on the phone. He's going to be late and says start without him. I think we'll have to, if he's very late, because Lucia is just a bit cross already—the teeth, you know—and asking her to keep the food waiting might not be a good idea."

"This is the fellow who's giving Sara away?" Lazenby asked pugnaciously.

Russell murmured, "Markby's a busy chap. He'll try and get here on time if he can."

"He was a friend of Robert's!" said Eve firmly.

There was an awkward silence. Sara began to fiddle with her engagement ring. It struck Meredith that there was something haunted about Sara's endearing little pug-dog face. Her usual spontaneous exuberance was a little forced tonight.

They had almost given up on the latecomer and were about to go into the dining room, when voices were heard in the hall. A very tall and rather thin man with a narrow, intelligent face, long straight nose and bright blue eyes strode into the room pushing back untidy fair hair and declared breathlessly, "Sorry!"

"Just in time!" Eve said swooping down on him. "Now, you don't know my cousin Meredith—and Jonathan,

Sara's fiancé, and Albie, where are you hiding, darling? Alan Markby, everyone, who was a friend of dear Robert and has so kindly agreed to give Sara away!"

They all murmured their various greetings except for Lazenby who said loudly, "Great!"

Eve tucked her arm through Markby's and he looked slightly alarmed at the proprietorial gesture. "Come along, everyone!" she ordered and set off, taking Markby with her. He had rallied, Meredith noticed with some amusement, and was managing to say all the right things. Eve was beginning to sparkle in the way which signalled the arrival of a new male in her circle.

Elliott, who had said very little all evening, materialized at Meredith's elbow. "Watch that guy . . ." he said. "He's a natural." He disappeared again before she could reply coherently.

The dining table was a large circular one. Meredith found herself with Peter Russell on her left and Alan Markby on her right. Eve sat to Markby's right, Lazenby to hers, Elliott to his, Sara between Elliott and Russell. A large floral arrangement in the middle partly screened Meredith from Lazenby opposite her and allowed her to observe him covertly without having to talk directly to him. She supposed that if she could not admire him, she ought at least to respect him. He was certainly full of energy, more than capable, shrewd and clever. She wished she could also have found him likeable. But ambition always made her feel nervous and Lazenby struck her as very ambitious.

She became aware that Peter Russell, on her left, was also watching Lazenby. But suddenly he turned aside and began to talk to Sara. Alan Markby and Meredith were left eyeing each other with mutual caution.

He asked determinedly, "How did you cope with a long drive single-handed across Europe?" I did it once, years ago—with my then wife. We drove down to Greece."

"A fascinating trip."

"Not half," he said morosely. "Being shut up in a car with someone brings out all the weaknesses in a relationship. It delivered the *coup de grâce* to my marriage. That's not to say I shouldn't like to do it again spending less time arguing over the maps and more time exploring."

"You can drive back with me as far as northern Yugoslavia, if you like, and make your way on your own from there," Meredith offered.

"What?" He stared at her in the startled way he had done when Eve took his arm. Then he laughed, "You don't even know me!"

"Cripes," she said crossly. "I'm only offering you a lift across Western Europe." She flushed, struck by a thought. "I'm not trying to seduce you!"

"I wasn't flattering myself you were. What I meant was, you don't know I'm not some kind of maniac."

"You're going to give away my god-daughter. You were a friend of Robert's, so Eve tells me. I know you're not Jack the Ripper."

"Well, no . . ." he said slowly and with some—she felt—private amusement. "Thanks for the offer, I'll maybe take you up on it one day."

"I might not make it again." In fact, she thought, I won't. What possessed me to make it in the first place?

"Listen," he said, suddenly earnest and leaning towards her. "I wasn't that much of a close friend of Bob Freeman. It knocked me sideways when Eve asked me to give the bride away. An honour and all that—but I wouldn't want you to get the wrong idea . . ."

"Wrong idea about what?" she asked coldly, still feeling ruffled.

Before he could answer, Sara's clear young voice pierced through the buzz of conversation. "Well, I think it's rotten that cottages cost so much now that the real village people can't buy them! It's unfair!"

"No, it isn't, Sara!" said Lazenby vigorously. "One can't expect rural property value to be exempt from market forces."

"But there aren't any children in this village," Sara insisted, leaning across the table. "Have you notice, Merry? That's because all the young couples have left."

Russell said evenly, "Young families leave because there is no school. I confess that in buying Rose Cottage

I helped deplete the local housing stock in the way Sara criticizes. Sorry, Sal, I just fancied living in the country."

"I didn't mean you, Peter. You understand village life and you're the doctor for a lot of villagers so they're pleased to have you live amongst them—even if they've got to go into Bamford to the medical centre if they want to consult you, which seems barmy to me . . . I'm talking about other people. Townies. Well, like Mummy and me, I suppose. Or commuters. Or like the Lockes, who criticize everything. As for there being no school, it's because there aren't any children!" Sara concluded triumphantly. "It goes round in circles. It's like the chicken and the egg."

"You can't expect the Education Authority to keep a village school going for half a dozen kids!" Lazenby snapped. "It wouldn't be cost-effective."

"They do it in France!" Meredith heard herself say argumentatively. "The French have a definite programme aimed at keeping their villages alive."

"It's part and parcel of French agricultural policy!" Lazenby said, giving her a dirty look. He knew when he had opposition. "That's quite a different question."

"The French know how to live . . ." said Eve dreamily and quite meaninglessly—but nonetheless with the desired effect. The sting went out of the conversation.

Without warning Alan Markby said in a fierce undertone, "I sometimes wonder why people move out into the country. They end up destroying what they say they want. If they want it. Generally, the first thing they try to do is change everything. Have you met the couple Sara mentioned, the Lockes?" When she shook her head, he said, "Well, you will. They bought the old schoolhouse. They got a chap in to landscape the old playground into gardens and then discovered there was a right of way over it. There was a hell of a fuss before Major Locke got permission to re-site the path round the property. Local people objected vigorously—they didn't see why they shouldn't walk through the Lockes' garden, just as they had walked through the school grounds. It was a real battle, with battle-lines. Locke badgered everyone but didn't like being badgered back in return. He even came to me and complained about being harassed. Silly idiot."

Meredith opened her mouth to ask why Markby had been approached by the aggrieved Locke. She supposed it must be connected with whatever Markby did for a living, but she did not know what this was and before she could inquire, he chuckled and went on:

"He got a sort of come-uppance with the septic tank affair. Poor Locke, he just had permission to re-site the footpath and got his gardens all beautifully laid out and something went wrong with his loo. Out came the sewage tanker to pump out his septic tank—and drove straight over his new flower-beds. They couldn't reach the tank any other way."

"You seem to feel very strongly about it," she observed. "But you don't live in the village, do you?"

Surprising her considerably, he said, "No, but I know this village very well. I used to come here a lot as a boy; in fact I stayed in this house. My uncle was the last incumbent here."

"I see . . ." said Meredith thoughtfully. "I hadn't realized yours was a local family. I apologize."

"What for? Yes, my family had a long association with the area. It owned quite a bit of land at one time, though it's all been sold off now. My uncle Henry, who was my father's eldest brother and the last rector here, was a funny old boy, a bachelor who lived among his books. An Edwardian type, you might say. A gloomy place it always seemed to me, full of dark furniture and oil paintings of dead birds and a musty smell that was probably dry rot. When Bob Freeman bought the place he had to spend a lot of money on it. It was in a pretty dreadful state. The architect from the Diocesan Office had been out and more or less condemned it which was why the Church was anxious to sell it off. I don't know what Bob paid for it in the end but he was probably in a position to strike an advantageous deal, especially given that property prices around here have gone through the roof since. Lazenby over there probably sees that as a chance to make money. But Sara's right, local young couples can't afford to buy. Nearly all the young people have left the village. Only the old 'uns who won't budge and mean to die here, remain."

He fell silently suddenly as if embarrassed by his own loquacity. Meredith thought, you might not know why Eve picked on you to give the bride away, but I know. You look right, you sound right and you're a scion of an old county family. She's cast you, just as Elliott wants to cast her in his soap opera and for the same reason—you'll give the occasion a touch of class.

Aloud she said, "I've met one local inhabitant, the potter, Philip Lorrimer."

As she spoke the name one of those silences fell which sometimes occur in a buzz of conversation and the words dropped into a pool of stillness. The atmosphere changed immediately. Sara shuffled about, Lazenby looked wary and Russell said abruptly, "Oh, him!"

"Don't know him," said Markby, frowning. "Potter, you say? Has he been here long?"

"Oh, yes . . . such a funny boy . . ." said Eve. "I believe he came to live here about a year before Robert bought the rectory. He's an indigent artist, if you can call him an artist. He makes clay pots, ash-trays and cream jugs and so on with 'a souvenir from Devon' or whatever on them. He sells them round the country and makes just enough to live on. But it's not as though he were a painter or a sculptor."

"Or an actor, Evie?" asked Elliott a little waspishly.

Eve was unruffled. "Exactly, or an actor. I mean, clay pots, I ask you! Anyway," Eve dismissed pottery with a graceful wave, "I believe they get odd-sized legs."

"What?" Meredith burst into laughter. "The clay pots?"

"No, darling, the potters. From pedalling away with one leg at that wheel thing. Shall we go into the drawing room for coffee?"

In the drawing room, they rearranged themselves and Meredith found herself sitting on the exotic sofa next to Lazenby. Lucia, lips clamped together, was making the rounds with a tray of coffee cups. Lazenby leaned towards Meredith cautiously as if he approached an uncertain-tempered family pet. "I understand you haven't seen Eve for some time, but I suppose you're able to keep track of her through her films." He took a cup of black coffee.

"I've seen all the films, certainly," Meredith agreed, taking her own coffee from the tray, "although Eve hasn't made one for quite a while. I believe she does quite a bit of TV work now and that, I'm afraid, I've missed."

"Oh, yes, television . . ." Lazenby muttered, scowling. "She's told you about this soap opera project?" He glanced to where Eve sat between Peter Russell and Albie Elliott. Elliott had come to life and was waxing eloquent which almost certainly meant he was extolling his "baby." Lazenby gave him a look of some dislike.

"A little. I've never seen the programme. Eve tells me it's very popular and seen by millions."

"Elliott was saying that, I suppose?" Lazenby demanded aggressively. "That's sales talk. It was very popular—but the ratings have been dropping in the States. The episodes reach us several months after they've been screened there. The British ratings are still healthy but will go down if they follow the American trend." He set down his cup untasted and leaned forward again. "That's why the fellow is desperate to bring in a new character and a new story-line. He's got a lot of money tied up in the series. He's had problems with other things and *The Inheritance* is his big money-spinner. But he's a pretty smooth operator. He's gambling on bringing in a known star. That's why he's sitting there now, buttering up Eve."

"I see," Meredith said thoughtfully, sipping at her coffee. It was very strong in the Italian fashion. Eve and Elliott were both talking animatedly. Lazenby appeared to make a decision to take advantage of their preoccupation to confide in Meredith further.

"The problem, as I understand it, has been how to introduce a new character into the story. It's been running for years and almost every permutation of family intrigue had been used. The viewers are starting to recognize the scripts. As Sara's explained it, Eve's character is to be introduced as a woman from the central male character's past, who has some kind of hold over him—I mean she knows of some hanky-panky or other—which forces him to make her his business partner. It's a role for a villainess. Rather sexy, I understand." Lazenby's full upper lip curled in disdain. "It will involve, I'm told, several bedroom scenes."

"All pretty low-key, I'm sure!" Meredith said calmly. "Elliott is after what he calls 'class'."

"Yes, yes!" he said hastily. "But all the same, sex sells. But Eve—I mean, at her age . . ."

Meredith glanced at him speculatively as he fell momentarily silent. He flushed under her scrutiny, suddenly looking younger and less assured, picked up his coffee and drank it. When he had finished, he went on, "Don't misunderstand me! Eve has the looks for it. But she should be thinking about the future and about her image. Does she really want that kind of role at this stage of her career?"

"I'm sure all this has been discussed." Meredith was beginning to suspect that it was not Eve's image and whether it would suffer that obsessed him.

"There's Sara," he said with a return to his aggressive way. "She ought to think about Sara."

The party broke up relatively early. Lazenby, it transpired, had to drive back to London that night because he had an early meeting on the morrow. Russell pleaded early surgery. Markby left with them.

An air of lassitude fell over the company. Elliott said, "I'm bushed." It seemed to be the general feeling. Meredith made her good nights and went up to bed.

It was a pretty room. She did not know whether Eve had taken the trouble to decorate this house or had just employed some fashionable interior decorator to set it all up for her. She suspected the latter. If so, he had not done a bad job on the whole, although Meredith herself preferred to leave old things looking old. But Alan Markby's description of the rectory as it had been indicated what an unwelcoming place it must also have appeared. It was understandable that the new owners had wanted it cheered up. She wondered what he did for a living. She never had found out.

She was about to get into bed when there was a tap on the door.

"Merry? you aren't asleep yet, are you?"

"No, of course not, come in!" Meredith re-tied the belt

of the dressing gown she was about to take off and went to open the door.

Sara was standing rather forlornly on the sill. She asked, "Can I come in and yammer?"

"Okay," said Meredith resignedly.

Sara moved uncertainly into the room and stood for a moment as if making up her mind about something. She was clad in a cotton nightshirt emblazoned with a large picture of Snoopy and pink nylon fur bedroom slippers and with her scrubbed, shiny face she did not look a day over fourteen. She seemed suddenly to make up her mind, hopped up into the basketwork chair by the dressing table, kicking off the slippers and tucking her feet under her.

"Right," said Meredith, taking up an uncomfortable perch on the dressing table stool. "Spill the beans."

Sara did not return her grin. Instead she chewed nervously at her lower lip and fixed Meredith with large, thoughtful blue eyes. "What do you think of Peter Russell, Merry?"

Meredith, who had been bracing herself to answer a similar question by on the subject of Jonathan Lazenby, blinked. "Nice man, I suppose. Rather old-fashioned sort of family doctor."

"He's keen on Mummy."

"Oh, is he?" Meredith tried not to sound cross. "Well, then, I should leave that to run its own course, Sara, and not try and help things along if that's what you have in mind. Lots of · harm in this world is done by well-intentioned people."

"It would be nice for Mummy," Sara insisted, clasping her hands. "Mummy's been unlucky with men."

Has she? Not that I've ever noticed it! thought Meredith uncharitably. She was feeling sleepy and could do without all this.

"Both the men Mummy was happy with died. Robert was awfully nice. He didn't even mind when people called him 'Mr. Owens'. No one ever called Mummy Mrs. Freeman. I suppose that's because she's so well known by her own name. But some men wouldn't have liked being called by their wives' names, as if they were some sort of hanger-on. Robert didn't mind. He thought it was funny."

"He was fairly successful in his own field," Meredith pointed out. "He didn't have to worry about it. If he had been a less secure person in himself, it might have worried him more."

Sara thought this over. "Then there was Daddy. I wish I remembered him better. I was eight when they split up. When I try to remember his face, it's sort of fuzzy. Mummy's got some old photos but I can't say they make him real to me. I mean, in them I'm a little fat kid in a velvet dress and an Alice band and I can't believe that's me, either. Everyone looks like a stranger."

Meredith got up and walked across to the window, her back to her god-daughter. The curtains were not quite drawn and she could see the stars and the moon. As she watched, the moon disappeared behind scudding clouds, reappeared briefly and disappeared again. Her problem was not trying to remember Mike, it was trying to forget him. Perhaps it was all a mistake, coming here. Mike's daughter was burbling away behind her and the words washed about Meredith's ears. She was almost afraid to turn round and look at the girl.

"But they were going to get back together again." Sara's clear tones pierced her thoughts. "Mummy told me about it. They had talked it all over and were going to try again."

"Yes," Meredith said blankly.

"But they didn't because Daddy was murdered. That was horrible. And for nothing."

"I remember it," Meredith said.

As if she would ever forget. Eve had Hollywood ambitions in those days and moved to California with Mike, who had found work as a script-writer. Eve was not the first person to let Hollywood go to her head. She plunged happily into the parties and intrigues, the casual comings-together and partings. Inevitably the marriage fell apart. Whether the fact that Mike had actually walked away had struck Eve like a bucket of freezing water or she had just been piqued was unclear, but she had set about getting him back. She and Mike had been working together in their separate capacities on the same film set. Meredith remembered Eve's letter. "Mike and I see so much of each other that, really, getting divorced seems so silly especially as

Mike dotes on Sara. So we're going to have dinner and really talk it through and see if we can't get together again. I'm sure it will work this time."

That reconciliation had never taken place. Violence, unforeseen and unnecessary, had intervened. Mike had returned to his own apartment one evening to find a teenage drug addict ransacking it for money or saleable valuables. The kid had been armed and shot Mike dead. Just like that. Later the youngster had tried to sell the gun to pay for a fix and that had led to his arrest and conviction, despite his denials and claim to have found the gun in a rubbish bin. He had previous convictions for breaking into homes, locked cars, anywhere where either money or something he could sell could be found and it was known he had visited the building to see his uncle, the janitor, in a vain attempt to borrow money.

"It's a pattern," the worldly wise and world weary Los Angeles homicide department lieutenant who dealt with the case was reported as saying. "Eventually they wind up killing someone. It happens all the time."

Only that time it had happened to Mike. Meredith stared thoughtfully at Mike's daughter.

As if reading her mind, Sara asked, "I don't look much like Mummy, do I? Do I look like my father?"

"Yes, a little. More like him than your mother, certainly."

"Hughie was horrible," said Sara with sudden vigour. "I don't know why Mummy married him, unless it was on the rebound after Daddy."

"Probably."

Eve had been grief-stricken, mostly with shock, Meredith suspected, at Mike's sudden and violent death. But a year later she had married a smart-talking, smart-looking financial dealer whose grandiose projects were too late discovered to exist mainly on paper and in his head. Nor had he been easy to get rid of.

"I always hated him," said Sara bitterly. "He terrorized her. She was really scared of him. He was horrid over the divorce, too. He got a lot of money from Mummy, you know. She had hardly anything left."

"Lucky she met Robert Freeman, then," Meredith said and wished she hadn't.

But Sara took the words at face value. "Yes, it was. And the thing is, Robert left Mummy pretty well off, so she can marry Peter even though Peter hasn't got any money, do you see?" She leaned forward eagerly. "It would be nice for Peter, too, because his wife died. She was ill for years and he was devoted to her and looked after her . . . and then she died very suddenly and he was very cut up. So he's had a rotten time, too, and ought to have another chance."

"Got it all worked out, haven't you? But I stick by what I said, Sara. Don't interfere. If your mother and Russell get together, that's well and good. But it's their business."

"I'm not going to interfere. I just want Mummy to be happy, because I've behaved very badly and given her a lot of worry. I expect she's told you."

"Some of it. Don't brood about it. Put it behind you." Meredith hesitated. "Sara, are you really in love with that young man?"

"Jon? I don't know. I don't know if I can love anyone. I sometimes think it isn't in me. But I'm as much in love with him as I can be with anyone." Sara's hands were clenched together so tightly that the knuckles started through the stretched skin. "And I need Jonathan, Merry! He keeps me on the straight and narrow. If I didn't have him, I think I'd go wrong, just as I did before! Oh, Merry! I couldn't bear it if anything went wrong!"

This last came out as such a wretched cry from the heart that Meredith experienced a stab of alarm. "Why should it go wrong, Sara?"

"Oh, I don't know . . . it might. Nice things do. Nothing good lasts."

Poor kid, thought Meredith. She's searching desperately for a father-figure. She thought she'd found one in Robert and he was snatched away. Now she's fixed on Lazenby. He's not much older than she is but he exudes certainty. Well, if he's what she wants and feels she needs, well and good. I just hope he appreciates her!

"Merry—" Sara said suddenly. "In your job, you give advice to people, don't you?"

"Sometimes," Meredith said cautiously. "It depends. It's pretty limited advice and generally laid down by the rules so I can't claim to be any kind of agony aunt."

"No, but you've got experience of the world."

"Good grief! Well, some. Go on."

"Supposing, supposing someone told you they were being threatened."

"By whom? How? With what?"

"By someone they knew, who knew something about them, something bad they didn't want made public, and that person was going to make that thing public."

"Sara," Meredith said carefully. "Are we talking about blackmail? Because if we are, that's a serious criminal offence and a police matter!"

"Supposing one couldn't go to the police? I mean, it would get out that way, wouldn't it?"

"No. The police have procedures for dealing with blackmail. They do all they can to protect the victim."

"Yes, but this isn't blackmail. I mean, blackmail is leaving bundles of used fivers in a hollow tree or exchanging identical briefcases on Victoria Station."

"Not necessarily. People might use blackmail to get anything they wanted—a job, for example."

"But it's not like that!" Sara said passionately. "It's all legal!"

"Suppose you tell me," Meredith said calmly, "what all this is about?"

Sara's mouth set tightly. "I can't. It—it concerns a friend."

"Well, you tell your friend to think it over and ask her or him if she or he would mind you telling me all about it."

"Okay." Sara slid off the chair and wriggled her toes into the pink fur slippers. "Thanks for listening, Merry. I really have a nerve, pouring all my troubles into your ears and rabbiting on like this when you must be tired. There's no reason why you should be bothered with my problems or my friend's."

Meredith surveyed Sara thoughtfully. Friend be blowed. Sara was in trouble and probably couldn't confide in her mother after all the rumpus of three years ago. In addition, she was scared of Lazenby's disapproval. Meredith would have liked to talk more to Sara about Lazenby but she quashed the impulse, knowing she would be coming perilously close to interfering in the way she had warned Sara not to do in regard to her mother and Peter Russell. Basically there was nothing wrong with Lazenby other than that he was young and full of himself and filled her with an urge to slap him down. Perhaps her irritation with him had only stemmed from the aftermath of a long tiring drive. Even worse, perhaps it stemmed from a subconscious urge to act as Mike's advocate.

"Run along to bed," she said aloud. "Get your beauty sleep and let me get mine." Sara still looked so stricken that Meredith added vehemently, "Cheer up! Nothing is going to go wrong!" and knew that she really must be dog-tired to snap like this.

Alone again, Meredith got into bed and lay staring up at the ceiling in the bedside lamplight. She was unwilling to turn it off because in the darkness faces sometimes danced up out of the past. Besides which, the tiredness had reached the stage when she couldn't be bothered to switch the light off. There were magazines by the bed but they were not the sort which interested her.

When she summoned energy to switch out the light at last, she thought, just as she drifted off into slumber, "that's twice blackmail was mentioned tonight . . ."

Four

Meredith awoke early to the sound of an engine ticking over quietly outside in what, surely, must still be night. She slipped out of bed and padded to the window. It looked out straight down the drive to the wrought-iron gate which was bathed in the headlights of a vehicle. A figure moved across the glare and the distant and very British sound of chinking milk bottles was audible on the still air. She wondered how the milkman would cope with the locked gate. He did so simply by passing the bottles one at a time between the bars and leaving them in a forlorn cluster on the gravel drive. Someone, presumably Lucia, would later be obliged to trek down to the gate and fetch them in. The milkman got back into his vehicle—not one of those slow-moving electric milk floats but a proper open-sided van—and rattled off down the track. Opening the window and leaning out she saw the beam of the headlights become stationary again. He was delivering milk to the doorsteps of Philip Lorrimer and old Bert. The beam moved on again and was lost.

The sky was just beginning to lighten in the east. A few birds were twittering in the trees around the churchyard opposite. Meredith peered at her wristwatch. A quarter past five. She went back to bed but not to sleep. Odd sounds attracted her attention and she lay trying to identify them with mixed success. Various creaks and groans belonged to the old timbers of the house. Alan Markby— mysterious Mr. Markby—said there had been dry rot but it had been seen to. Some of the original timber must have been replaced but not all. The floorboards of this bedroom, for example, had an uneven tilt to them that indicated they

were original. A hollow ghostly gurgle was identified as
the plumbing and almost made her feel she was back in
her flat. A sudden crack from outside was a piece of wood
falling from a churchyard tree. Finally, she rolled over and
drifted into restless slumber.

When she awoke again it was with a suddenness that
sent her heart leaping into her throat. The cause had been
a distant buzz and a metallic clang. The main gate had
been opened. By and for whom? She sat up. It was a little
before eight. The milk bottles chinked again. Whoever
the newcomer was, they obligingly carried them up to the
house. Meredith jumped out of bed, trotted along to the
bathroom, showered and came back without meeting a living soul on either journey. As she descended the stairs,
however, she heard the sound of women's voices, neither
of them familiar. Following that she heard a bumping
noise as if someone wrestled to move an unwieldy object.

When she reached the main hall downstairs Meredith
saw an open door under the stairs. Protruding from it was
an ample female rear encased in an orange nylon overall.
The rear wiggled and began to emerge, revealing the body
of which it formed part. A stout, middle-aged person stood
upright, huffing and puffing and red-faced from her exer-
tions. She was triumphantly grasping the handle of an upright vacuum cleaner she had just hauled out of its lair.

"Mornin'!" she greeted Meredith cheerfully. "You'll be
the lady what's staying. I'm Mrs. Yewell what comes in
daily." She slammed the cupboard door and withdrew a
yellow duster from her overall pocket. "Hopes you slept
well?"

"Fairly well," Meredith replied cautiously. "The milkman woke me up."

"That's our Gary," said Mrs. Yewell. "He's got to start
early 'cos this is the beginning of his round, see? He
comes straight here from the dairy, then goes to Lower
Clanby, round by the big council estate and down to the
air force base at Cherton and then back by them posh new
houses—executors' homes, they call 'em—and then back
to the dairy with the empties. Takes 'im all morning." She
lugged the vacuum cleaner noisily down the hall. "This is

a big house to keep clean, this is. Too much for just the cook to do. 'Specially when people is staying."

Meredith took this as a hint not to get under Mrs. Yewell's feet. She left her revving up the vacuum cleaner and warbling a ditty from *South Pacific* and followed a comforting smell of freshly made coffee to the kitchen.

"How are the teeth?" she asked the cook.

"He take out wisdom tooth—here!" Lucia opened her mouth wide and pointed into the dark cavity. "It is very sore."

"Perhaps you should rinse round with aspirin." Meredith avoided peering into the afflicted mouth. "Or I've got some antiseptic mouth-wash."

Lucia chuckled. "I no need chemist shop mouth-wash. I make it myself, mouth-wash—with this!" She dived into a cupboard and reappeared holding a bunch of sage leaves.

"Is that good for the mouth?" Meredith asked curiously.

"You bet, this is the best!" The sage was waved under Meredith's nose. "And you get very nice, white teeth. I know all medicines. I don't need no chemist shop. In my village in Campania, we have a very clever old woman. She make all medicines, cure everything. She use everything what grow in the country." Lucia put the sage down. "I make eggs?" She made a beating motion.

"No thanks. Just a cup of that coffee would do fine."

When Meredith ventured back to the drawing room it had already been immaculately tidied by Mrs. Yewell who could be located by "Some Enchanted Evening" issuing from the downstairs cloakroom. From the window Meredith could see wedged between the metal bars of the gate what looked like a newspaper. She opened the front door and went to retrieve it.

There were in fact two papers, *The Times* and, discreetly hidden inside it, the *Sun*. It was as she tugged them through the bars that she noticed something else lying on the ground outside the gate. It looked at first glance like a piece of dirty rag, but a second closer look revealed it to have a distinct shape.

Meredith tucked the papers under her arm, stooped and stretching an arm through, picked it up. The object was a rag doll. Its general grimy, tattered appearance suggested it

was very old and might well have been retrieved from a
rubbish pile. But its chief disfigurement was not the result
of wear and tear but deliberately inflicted. Someone had
slashed the face with either a sharp knife or scissors and
crudely daubed it with red paint to resemble bloodstains.
The whole doll was damp right through, which suggested
it had been dropped outside the gate after dark the previous evening and lain there all night. The paper-boy must
have seen it but probably had not taken any particular notice. The milkman delivering his pints at first light might
not even have seen it in the gloom. Mrs. Yewell, probably
intent on pushing along an ancient bike, had not taken any
notice. There was no reason why she should be a particularly observant woman or perhaps she had taken it for a
piece of rag. The doll had been intended to be found by
the first member of the family to go through the gate.

Meredith regarded the doll with deep disgust and rising
anger. The human shape of the thing made it particularly
sinister. It made her think of witchcraft again. The heart
might have been a singularly unpleasant joke, but considered together with the mutilated doll, this was beginning to
take on the appearance of a vindictive campaign. She
wrapped the doll inside the newspapers and turned to go
back indoors.

Elliott, startlingly clad in a spotless turquoise track-suit,
was standing on the top step with his arms folded and
watching her. His pale undertaker's face had an infuriat-
ingly knowing expression on it and automatically she
gripped the paper package more tightly, pressing it against
her. At the same time she felt angry and resentful at the
way the man seemed to appear unexpectedly.

"Found another, eh?" As before he did not sound surprised, only deeply disapproving.

"You know a lot more about this than you're admit-
ting!" Meredith said angrily.

She tried to look past him into the hallway. Interpreting
her glance he said, "It's okay—neither of them is around
yet. You want to show me what you have there?"

Silently she opened out the newspapers and let him see
the doll.

He pursed his lips and muttered, "Tsk, tsk."

"Perhaps," Meredith said crisply, "you'd like to tell me what you know about all this!"

He nodded. "Sure—but it's not much. What do you say, we go inside?"

Indoors he bent over the doll as it lay on a table but seemed singularly loath to touch it. "I've found this kind of stuff before around here. I got rid of it fast."

"As you did the ox heart?" He did not deign to answer and Meredith asked more quietly, "Does Eve know anything about these horrible things?"

"I haven't told her, if that's what you mean. And I wouldn't suggest that you do." He turned away from her. For some reason, he had a large number nine printed on the back of his track-suit. He moved to the nearest easy chair and slipped into it with a cat-like ease, folding his pale soft hands together and resting them on his turquoise knees. "Let me put my cards on the table. I don't want Evie upset. I don't want the kid upset. I want the kid married off and Evie on her way back to the States with me. I don't know what the hell it's all about—but if I can put Evie on that plane, it doesn't matter a damn."

"How can you say that?" she demanded furiously. "I want to know what it means!"

"I can tell you what it means, honey. It means we have a nut around some place. But so long as we keep finding those things before Evie does—or the kid—it doesn't matter. Believe me. I've dealt with kooks before. Movie and TV stars, personalities of any kind, they attract them. These psychos are inadequate people with dull lives who would like to be glamorous and talked about, but can't be. Sometimes they eat their hearts out in silence. Sometimes they flip. If this was the States, I'd worry. I'd hire a bodyguard. But I don't think it's necessary here. Why scare Eve or the girl?"

"I think we should tell the police!" Meredith said firmly.

"Oh, sweetheart," said Elliott reproachfully, opening his fish-like grey eyes wide. "We already have a cop on the scene. One is enough."

"A policeman?" Meredith stared at him. "Who?"

"Markby. Didn't anyone tell you?"

Meredith sat down with a bump on the corner of the sofa, the doll gripped in her hands. "A policeman?" No wonder he had not volunteered his occupation. Policemen, like lawyers and doctors, were coy of giving their profession. People either got nervous or took the opportunity to dump some private problem or grievance on them. But she felt obscurely annoyed that Markby had not told her, forewarned her. It was unfair not to. Goodness knows what sort of unwise confidences people might be led to make if they were blissfully unaware that someone they had met socially under a mutual friend's roof was actually a police officer.

Meredith made an effort to set aside her growing prejudice against the man and be objective. "He might be a good person to consult, even so," she pointed out. "He's giving Sara away. If we tell him, he'll be discreet and not alarm either Eve or Sara."

"If we tell the man," Elliott said patiently, "he'll want to talk to Eve and the kid. He'll want to know if either of them has received letters or other little packages. Policemen ask questions. They can't help it. They frighten people. They can't help that, either. If you tell Markby about that"—Elliott indicated the doll—"you'll regret it, believe me."

"You realize it is possible that one or other of them has received, say, a threatening letter." Meredith frowned, recalling her conversation with Sara. But it didn't hang together. Blackmail was one thing, a hole in the corner affair, surreptitious, fearful of the light of day; practical jokes out in the open were another. They might be anonymous but there was an element of recklessness about them.

"Think I haven't thought of that? I sounded Evie out. All she thinks about is the wedding. Believe me, if Evie has other troubles she would have brought them to me. She always does."

Meredith, irritated by his calm assumption, snapped, "Maybe all this happened before you arrived here from the States. And just maybe you're not her only confidant!"

Elliott's pale face stiffened into waxy lines. "Nobody has Evie's interests more at heart than I do, sister! Nobody, not even you! Okay, you're a relative. But where have you been these last fifteen, twenty years?" He saw the look on her face and permitted himself a malicious little smirk. "Leading your own life, right? Didn't give a damn about Evie or Sara, right? So, why should you? But I do care— because Evie's important to me."

"Oh, yes, the soap opera," Meredith snarled.

"We all have to earn a living, lady."

There was a silence. They glared at one another, at an impasse. "Now what I say is," Elliott recommenced smoothly, "that you leave it alone. That you leave it to me."

"Just as I left getting rid of the ox heart to you? I shouldn't have let you do that. I should have reported that to the police, straight away."

"No!" Elliott's voice was sharp. "And especially not to that guy Markby. He'll turn the place upside-down. Listen," a note of reasonable entreaty entered his voice. "Do you think I haven't thought all this through? That I haven't considered bringing in the cops? That I didn't decide against it for good reasons?"

Meredith said suddenly, "There's no police station in this village. Where does Markby work out of, Bamford?"

"I guess so." Elliott eyed her shrewdly.

"And when I first met you in the lane, you had just come from a visit to Bamford by bus. Did you go in with an idea of talking to the police?"

He rubbed his pale hands together with a sound like fine sandpaper which set Meredith's teeth on edge. "I'll admit I did walk round town to see where the police station was. No harm in knowing. I found it. It looks like all those places do. Full of guys with no imagination, filling in time until they draw retirement."

"I take it you mean you spoke to a desk sergeant."

"Not about the things I found. I told him I was thinking of hiring a car and asked if I could drive here on my US licence. He said, 'Yus, sir, for a limited period.' " Elliott proved a surprisingly good mimic. " 'You'll bear in mind, sir, that we drive on the left-hand side of the road.' " Elliott shook his head. "That's not the place to take this little problem, Meredith." He leaned forward. "We don't need Markby or any of his side-kicks asking questions, making waves. It's three weeks to go to this wedding. Three goddam weeks! That's how long we have to keep the lid on this! Three miserable weeks! We don't need cops. We just keep our eyes open, you and I. Come on now, think about it. We tell Markby or anyone else and there's no way Eve and the kid don't get to know of it. Evie's had a bad time this last couple of years, the kid running wild and all. To say nothing of Bob Freeman dropping dead with a cardiac arrest like he did. Now there's the wedding to worry over. Surely even you can see that the last thing she needs is to be frightened with this?"

Meredith disliked the "even you", but she had to admit he had a point. He saw irresolution and weakening resolve in her face.

"Trust me—we can handle it ourselves."

Once more she allowed herself to be persuaded. She was reluctant to leave things to Elliott but on second thoughts she was also reluctant to take the problem to Markby, after all. "All right, but if either of us finds just one more thing like this"—she shook the rag doll—"we go to the police! And don't hold out on me, Albie. If you find anything, tell me!"

"Trust me!" he repeated. "I have a lot riding on this. There's no way I want anything to happen to either of them."

Meredith, feeling anything but convinced, went upstairs and locked the doll in her suitcase. She did not trust Elliott but she would be keeping an extra sharp eye open herself and next time Albie might not be around to put his persuasive point of view. If there was a next time. She shivered. Her imaginary idyll of home, full of chintzy comforts, had taken a knock or two. She wondered what kind of policeman Alan Markby was. "He should have told me!" she muttered resentfully.

The bright sunlight beamed into her bedroom, making her feel once again that this must be some sort of hideous mistake or mindless practical joke. But it couldn't be denied that out there under the same sun, lurked someone possessed of a singularly unpleasant mind.

Meredith felt a need to get out of doors and blow away

the unclean feeling with which the episode had left her. In the cloakroom (Mrs. Yewell could now be heard washing that man out of her hair in the dining room) hung a motley collection of garments. Two pairs of wellington boots stood on the tiles. She borrowed the larger pair, reflecting ruefully they had probably been Robert's, and the crumpled green anorak which hung above them, most likely Sara's, and set off.

Feeling slightly awkward in her borrowed clothes, she clumped unglamorously down the track towards the lynchgate of the churchyard. Without warning, a rustle from the ditch signalled that she was not alone. She stopped and gasped as a man's form emerged from the undergrowth.

"Good morning!" said Philip Lorrimer, scrambling breathlessly up on to the track.

Already jumpy, Meredith gave way to a spurt of anger. "Good grief," she demanded accusingly, "you made me jump out of my skin! What on earth are you doing?"

"Sorry if I scared you," he said apologetically. "I'm looking for Jerry, one of my cats. You haven't seen him, I suppose? He looks the same as Tom, only slightly smaller, and his left ear is torn."

She shook her head and the hopeful look on his face faded. She noticed he looked pale and drawn, quite grey about the mouth.

"I'll keep an eye open for him," she offered, wanting to make amends for her crossness.

"He does wander," Lorrimer said worriedly. His voice sounded hoarse. "I'm afraid he might have met a fox and got the worst of the encounter. I think that's how he got his torn ear in the first place. Either that or someone has pinched him. People do pinch siamese cats. He's not afraid of anything or anyone and if a car stopped and someone, even a complete stranger, called to him, he'd go straight over to investigate." He pulled out a handkerchief and wiped his mouth.

"Are you all right?" Meredith asked, peering at him more closely. Scrutinized, he looked ghastly.

"Feeling a bit iffy, actually. I threw up my breakfast about half an hour ago and I've had belly-ache ever since."

"Perhaps you ought to see a doctor."

"I haven't got much time for quacks! Not that one who lives locally down at Rose Cottage, anyway!" he said shortly. "I've had these upsets before. I call them the Dun Cow's Revenge! Harry's always forgetting to wash out the pumps." He essayed a wan smile and thrust the handkerchief into his jeans pocket. The jeans were plentifully smeared with pale streaks of dried clay and splodges of paint. Then, without warning, the smile turned to a grimace of distress. He made a gasping sound as if he found it difficult to get breath and collapsed on to the track with his head on his knees, panting and making hideous retching noises.

"Let me give you a hand!" Meredith exclaimed. Thanking her lucky stars she was sturdily built, she grasped his shoulder, hauled him upright and turned him towards his own cottage. He tried to speak but she ordered, "Not now, later!"

Together they stumbled down his garden path and through the open front door. Here Lorrimer shrugged off her supporting arm and staggered unaided into the kitchen at the back and was sick in the sink. Meredith waited. She heard the tap running and then he came back white as a sheet and with flecks of perspiration on his forehead. But he seemed steadier on his feet.

"Sorry about that . . ." he mumbled.

"Not your fault. Look, let me give Russell a call."

"No!" Lorrimer stumbled towards a kind of divan over which was thrown a brightly coloured folkweave rug, although Meredith was too worried about him to take much notice of the general furnishings.

Standing over him, she said, "I'll get you a glass of water," and went out into the kitchen. It was extremely untidy and in the sink she couldn't help notice traces of blood and bile which had not been properly washed away. It did not look like the aftermath of any kind of hangover she had ever come across. She rinsed round the sink again, found tumblers stacked against tins of cat food, washed one out and took it back full to Lorrimer.

"Cheers . . ." he said weakly, taking it and sipping it.

Meredith sat down on a rickety stool opposite him and

rested her clasped hands on her knees. "What have you got against Peter Russell? I really feel you should get advice. He could call in when he gets back from his town surgery."

"I can't stand the bloke and it's mutual." Lorrimer had regained his breath and his colour and was marginally better. "And I don't have much confidence in his doctoring. Around here they say he hurried his wife into the next world."

"What!" she exclaimed loudly.

A dull flush marked his grey cheekbones. "Well, just a local rumour. She was ill for years and if he did it, I dare say he meant it for the best. Euthanasia. Put the poor bitch out of her suffering. She must have been a blight on his life, though—"

"Listen to me!" Meredith said crisply. "That's a very unwise thing to say! It's a serious accusation and actionable."

"Yes, all right . . . you're right. I shouldn't have said it. Who cares what they say round here, anyway? They're all inbred in this village, if you ask me. God knows how their minds work." Lorrimer leaned back against the wall, the tumbler held loosely in his hands. Suddenly he said vehemently, "That bloody old man!"

"Bert?" Meredith guessed.

"He's what I mean about this village. He might have put some muck out to kill the cats and got poor Jerry. I wouldn't put it past him. He's been saying he'll do it and there has been poison put down in the past somewhere around here."

Meredith asked in shocked surprise, "How do you know?"

"Foxes come into the gardens at night, even up as far as the dustbins, foraging. Mrs. Locke found the body of one by her garage when she went to get the car out one morning and made the usual Locke song and dance about it. It had probably been poisoned."

"That could be a farmer or any poultry keeper. It needn't be Bert. Try not to worry."

"I've found a dead hedgehog, too. Now I can't find Jerry . . . I wish I could. Of course I'm worried."

"Cats are finicky eaters," Meredith reassured him. "They don't just gobble up anything like a scavenging fox. And they wouldn't bother to play with anything already dead, say a mouse. They'd rather chase after a live one. But I'll keep an eye open, and if I see him, I'll come and tell you."

It did sound as if someone had put down rat poison. Hadn't Lorrimer said he'd seen Warfarin in Bert's shed? It was difficult to know just how much action an old man like that really would take. Bert shouted and threatened but might not do more than lob the occasional stone at the cats if he saw them scraping holes diligently in his vegetable patch. Jerry had probably just taken himself for a walk.

"If you don't want to see Russell, he's part of a group practice and you could see someone else."

"I don't need a doctor!" he repeated obstinately.

Meredith stared at him in frustration. Then she stopped herself. Just a moment, my girl, she thought, these aren't foreign climes. You're not the consul here and this isn't some distressed British subject on your hands. You don't have to see he gets treatment. If the lad wants to drink bad beer and make himself ill, it's up to him. It's not your pigeon. "Try drinking the beer out of cans!" she advised. "I'll look out for the cat."

She left him in the cottage and retraced her steps to the lych-gate. In its cool shadow Meredith paused to study the church. It was a small solid building of ancient weathered stone. The graves to either side of the path were old, the headstones mossy and illegible, but some attempt had been made at keeping the intervening grass verges cut and tidy. Even so, the place was eerie and there was a dank, mouldering smell in the air. The rounded Norman arch of the doorway was carved with geometric shapes and fantastic grinning heads. They were unpleasant. Tracing the stonework with her finger, Meredith distinguished a serpent coiling his way round and at the very top, with curling foliage about his ears, leered a mocking, ugly face. Christianity and pre-Christianity mingled here. Surely that face leering down at her was the Green Man of ancient belief? She tugged at the round iron handle, but the door was

locked. A notice pinned to it behind a plastic shield announced that the next service would be in a fortnight's
time and the key could be had meantime from either of the
churchwardens, a Mrs. Honey of Home Farm or Major
Locke, whose address was given as "The Old Schoolhouse." The bunker, as Lorrimer had called it. Meredith
smiled, but she did not like it here. Something about the
place discouraged lingering. She turned away and froze.

She was being watched from a short distance away
amongst the gravestones. An elderly figure, stooped and
gnarled and carrying a huge old-fashioned scythe, peered
at her over a headstone. Meredith remained rooted to the
spot. Realizing she had observed him, the figure began to
scuttle away in a fashion which suddenly rang a bell.
Meredith, fully regaining powers of speech and movement,
called loudly, "Bert! Wait a moment" and started after
him.

Bert stopped and stood waiting for her, grasping his
primitive agricultural implement defensively as if he
thought she might prove dangerous.

"Good morning!" she said briskly. "My name is Miss
Mitchell and I'm staying at the Old Rectory."

"Ah . . ." he growled. "I seen you yesterday."

"That's right. I wanted to visit your church but it's shut
up, so I thought you might be able to tell me something
about it."

"Major Locke, he got the key," said Bert sullenly. "I
don't know nothing."

"But you've lived here all your life," Meredith coaxed.
"And you obviously work very hard to keep the churchyard tidy. You must have seen a lot of changes here."

Bert seemed mollified by this approach. "Ah, an' all for
the worse an' all! They pays me a fiver a month for trimming long grass in churchyard." He shuffled forward and
hissed, "I takes it home for me compost!"

"I beg your pardon?"

"Compost!" repeated Bert crossly. "Lovely rich grass
grows here in the churchyard. I takes it home for me compost heap. Marvelous compost it makes. I puts it in me
beans trench. I get beautiful beans out of that churchyard
grass. Beautiful tomatoes and all. Won prizes with 'em and

all due to churchyard grass!" He grinned up at her like a triumphant goblin. He bore a striking resemblance to one of the grotesque heads on the church doorway.

Meredith gazed at him appalled, not knowing whether he realized the significance of what he said or not. Or perhaps he simply did not care that he owed his prize vegetables to the richness yielded up by the mouldering dead of his native parish. Either way, Meredith hoped none of Bert's vegetables found their way into the kitchens of the Old Rectory.

"Foreigners!" exclaimed Bert with sudden ferocity. He stamped the handle of the scythe on the ground. "Village ain't nothing like what it was. It ain't right. I mind when Mr. Markby, the old rector, was living in the rectory and it was a proper parsonage. Mr. Markby, he wouldn't stand no nonsense. He see a choirboy mucking about at the back of the stalls and he'd stop short, right in the middle of what he was saying, walk over there and clip the blighter's ear!"

"A Mr. Markby dined at the rectory yesterday evening," Meredith fished unashamedly.

"I know that 'un. He's a p'liceman!" said Bert sourly. "I don't have nothing to do with the p'lice. Tricky beggars. Snoops. In the old days, Markbys were proper gentlemen. There's none left like it nowadays. Instead we get them living among us as has got the money and nothing else!" Bert snorted and glanced meaningfully towards the distant roof of the Old Rectory. "Fast women. Painted jades! Living in the parsonage as well! Old rector would be spinning in his grave if he knew!"

Eve would appreciate this observation, thought Meredith, amused.

"They lost their money after the last war!" said Bert. "Owned all the land hereabouts, did Markbys, but it was all sold off a bit at a time. Them death duties, that's what did it."

"I see."

"My wife," continued Bert, suddenly loquacious. "That's her, over there!" He pointed to a spot behind Meredith.

She turned, fully expecting that a female version of Bert

had approached unheard and stood behind her, but beheld
instead a tombstone, more recent than most and engraved:

ADA
Beloved Wife of
Herbert Yewell
Died 21 January 1978
Till We Meet Again

Yewell. At one time the village probably contained no
more than five or six surnames and one half of the inhabitants were related to the other half. She wondered how
Mrs. Yewell the daily help stood in connection to Bert and
how much of what went on at the Old Rectory was relayed
to Bert and the rest of the village from this source.

"Yes, that's her!" urged Bert, pointing at the stone.
"That's my wife. She were parlourmaid to old Mr.
Markby, the rector, when she were a girl and I were court-
ing her. Not housemaid, mind you! Parlourmaid!" He
glared at Meredith.

She nodded to show she appreciated the niceness of this
long-gone social distinction below stairs.

Bert gave a gleeful chuckle. "She weren't allowed no
admirers. Old rector wouldn't stand for it. So she used to
come down to the back gate and I'd meet her there of an
evening. I used to wait in Love Lane." Bert glowered
about him. " 'Tis all gone. No decency left. Nothing but
wickedness and vice. Sodom and Gomorrah old Mr.
Markby called such goings-on as you see round here now!
That young fellow as lives next door to me—makes them
little pots. I ask you, 'tisn't no job for a man! Idle bugger,
he is, if you asks me. Seems like he got money in his
pocket, even so. He's propping up the bar of the Dun Cow
every evening. I never 'ad no money at his age. I worked
for my father and got five shillings a week—and Mother
took four of 'em back off me for keep!" Bert contemplated
this ancient injustice with a sort of gloomy satisfaction.
Suddenly his malicious gaze flickered towards Meredith
again. "He has women there!" he said hoarsely. "Fast
women! I hears them quarrelling. Women as ought to
know better!"

Without warning he turned away and began to sweep the scythe through a bank of nettles.

"What else has changed in the village, Bert?" Meredith asked but she knew she asked in vain.

Bert had decided he had spent enough time on her. "Got me work!" he growled sulkily. "They pays me a fiver to do this." He turned his back on her and began to move away, swinging the scythe rhythmically and she couldn't persuade him to utter another word.

Meredith walked away amongst the graves, stopping whenever she saw an interesting headstone. As she suspected, a few surnames occurred over and over again. There were several Yewells. A small newish square of dark marble inlaid flat into the turf indicated the burial of ashes. It read simply "Esther Russell" with a date. Meredith realized it must commemorate Peter Russell's late wife, laid to rest but still the subject of hurtful rumour.

But burials here had once been more elaborate, at least for some. In the far corner of the churchyard an area had been closed off with iron railings. The railings, once highly ornamental, were rusted and broken and the gate which had once completed them was missing. Inside, as if penned in a corral, stood a row of marble tombs. They were all ornate and must have been costly but few were without chips or blemishes and the side panels of one or two leaned outwards at a perilous angle. Someone had stuffed a crisp packet in one of the cracks.

A glance at the inscriptions revealed that this was the open-air mausoleum of the Markby family. They were a history of English social life amongst the squirearchy. Here was Amelia, daughter of Edmond Markby and wife of Robert Lacey, gentleman, who died in 1784 and was buried with her infant daughter. A case of the childbed fever, probably. Here was a false tomb, erected as a monument to brothers whose bones "lay far from their native land." They were named as Francis Markby who perished in "the most frightful storm" in the Bay of Biscay in 1802 and Charles, who died of loss of blood following the amputation of an arm on the field of Waterloo. Meredith found their empty monument curiously moving. In 1851 Samuel Markby died in a "dreadful accident upon the railway, a martyr to the unstoppable progress of the modern age." Had he stood on the track and expected the express to go round him? At least they had found enough of him to bury. But few of the Markbys seemed to have died peacefully in their beds or of mere old age. However, the late rector had gone against family tradition and passed away at the remarkable age of ninety-four after being fifty-seven years a shepherd of his flock. And its last shepherd, as it turned out. He was also the last Markby to be buried in the family plot.

Meredith walked round the tomb of the Reverend Henry and stopped. There are few sights more pitiful than that of a dead cat. What is in life grace, agility, playfulness and bright inquiring intelligence, becomes a meagre scrap of tattered fur. But this one had not the rag-like limpness of a cat struck by a car and hurled on to a verge. This one was stiff in death, its back arched, its forepaws extended, its head thrown back and its jaw yawning wide, fixed open in rigor. It could not have been dead very long. It was a siamese and its left ear was torn.

Meredith fought down a surge of nausea. It was replaced by blind fury. She ran back through the gap in the railings and across the grassy mounds, looking about her wildly, seeking Bert's gnarled figure. That horrible old man! He had done as he had threatened! She came to a halt. Bert was nowhere to be seen. Some kind of sanity returned to Meredith's over-heated brain.

She didn't know for a fact that Bert was responsible. He would deny it. The real question was, should she go and tell Lorrimer? There was nothing to be gained by it. As had she, he would suspect Bert. There would be bitter words and recriminations. A rift between neighbours would be deepened and nothing could be done about it. As for Lorrimer—already under the weather—his distress at seeing his pet like this could only serve to make him a sicker man than he was this morning.

Meredith slowly retraced her steps to the Markby tombs. On the way she saw a small branch which had fallen from one of the overhanging trees. She carried it back and dropped it over the body of the cat. If Lorrimer found it, that was Fate. But she would not tell him. Better he thought Jerry stolen or fallen victim to a fox. That at least was a clean death. Poison was foul.

She walked quickly away, trusting she did not encounter Bert because she would not be able to hold her tongue. Vicious old brute! she thought and longed to tell him so. Behind her, Jerry lay frozen in his death agony amongst the Markby tombs, the last living creature to be laid to rest there.

Five

When she returned indoors, Elliott was on the telephone making an acrimonious and no doubt very expensive trans-atlantic call. He slammed down the receiver as she came in and glared at her. Then he seemed to recollect himself, gave his upper body a little shake and asked, "Nice stroll?"

"Not particularly, no!" she snapped, the query was so inappropriate. She knew she must look dishevelled and up-set and tried to assume an air of calm.

His pale gaze had sharpened. "Find any more keep-sakes?"

"No." She made another effort to sound civil. "No, it was something else. Something else upset me. Sorry to snap at you."

"Always some goddam thing," he said morosely. "One darn thing after another. Scriptwriters. Lazy, overpaid jerks. Four of them working together can't come up with a half dozen decent ideas."

"Four?" Meredith asked startled. "Isn't that rather a lot? Don't they cramp one another's style? You know, too many cooks."

"None of the bastards has any style," said Elliott suc-cinctly. "Only one in a hundred is any good. Mike was good. You ever meet Mike?"

"Of course I did!" she retorted crossly, beginning to be irritated by him again. "Eve's my cousin. I was bridesmaid at their wedding."

And Eve had thrown her the bouquet as she drove off on honeymoon. In her mind's eye, Meredith could see the scene. Eve had worn an Edwardian gown with lots of ruf-

fles and Meredith a sea-green sixties effort in taffeta with
a stiff full skirt. It had not suited her one bit but it had
been Eve's choice. And Mike ... Mike in a hired topper
and morning suit, grinning. ... She could recall every line
of his face, every eyelash. Oh God, when would it ever
stop hurting?

"He was good," repeated Elliott, watching her. "He was
a loss, that boy."

She was spared having to reply by the sound of upraised
voices drifting down the stairs to them.

"Darling, we discussed it all ... they knew exactly what
we wanted."

"They knew what you wanted, Mummy! Not what I
wanted! I didn't like the design. I said so. You all ignored
me."

"Nonsense, Sara! If you'd said so, I'd have told them to
change it."

"Well, now I've told them to change it."

"For goodness' sake!" Eve sounded exasperated. "Alter-
ations at this stage will cost a fortune! Really, Sara, you
might have consulted me first. I am paying for the
wretched dress. And what have you told them to do?"

"Strip off all the frills. Honestly, Mummy, I looked like
a reject from the harem in it. It just wasn't me! So I told
them to strip it all down and just leave the basic dress."

"Really, child!" Eve shouted. "I suppose by frills you
mean very expensive hand-sewn pearl embroidery! How
can they just take it all off? I'll still have to pay for it and
all the work—plus all the work undoing it. If they can
undo it! The material will be marked!"

A door slammed, the voices became muted. Elliott exchanged glances with Meredith. "Kids," he said.

"Are you married, Albie?"

He looked shocked. "No way."

Upstairs a door flew open again. Feet pattered along the
landing and down the stairs. Eve appeared, looking flushed
and unusually out of countenance. "That girl!" she splut-
tered.

"Take it easy, Evie," advised Elliott. "Let the kid have
what she wants."

Eve threw him a look which sparkled with fury but it

bounced off him. Icily she said, "I'm going into Bamford. Do you want to come, Merry? How about you, Albie?"

"No thanks. I have to wait on a call from the States."

"I'll come," said Meredith quickly.

"Then I'll just go and tell Lucia only two for lunch." Eve marched briskly away towards the kitchen.

"Have a nice day," said Elliott and drifted towards the drawing room, looking in retreat, in his jogging suit and clumsy running shoes, like a turquoise exclamation mark.

Eve drove them into Bamford in record time while Meredith prayed they did not meet much oncoming traffic. They parked near the new shopping precinct. Speed seemed to have had a calming effect on Eve but as she fastened the door Meredith heard her cousin mutter, "Drat the locks!" with a return of her former exasperation. She thought for a second the remark applied to what she was doing, but then looked up to see Eve staring across the car park and realized that what Eve had actually said was, "Drat! The Lockes!"

A hair-raising drive had not improved Meredith's peace of mind. A persistent throb niggled at the back of her brain and she was not in the mood for word puzzles. Nor did she want to meet any new acquaintances. She could not push away the mental image of the dead cat. She kept thinking about the churchyard and its grim little secret which had become her secret, too, and wondering whether she ought to have told Lorrimer after all.

An elderly couple approached at a brisk pace. They were so alike that one could have supposed them brother and sister rather than husband and wife. Both were of middle height and spare and trim in build. They wore identical quilted car-coats and grey slacks and wore spectacles. Major Locke carried a large plastic bag embellished with the logo of a chain of food stores.

"Good afternoon, ladies!" he hailed them and lifted his checked cap. Mrs. Locke, who wore a sort of deerstalker of similar check material, smiled graciously.

"Hallo, Major," said Eve distantly. She hesitated and then introduced Meredith.

"You're just the person I want to see, Miss Owens!"

said Major Locke, when both he and his wife had expressed their delight at meeting Meredith. "You'll want a rehearsal for the wedding, won't you? I can open up the church any time, if you just arrange with Father Holland when. Then there's Mrs. Honey . . . she is organist, you know. She wants to talk to you about music. She thought, the two wedding marches as per usual . . . the Mendelssohn coming in and the Wagner going out . . . But hymns, will you want hymns?"

"No!" said Eve crossly.

"It *is* usual. Father Holland will expect hymns."

"Father Holland isn't getting married, my daughter is. All he has to do is officiate. And I hope he isn't going to come out from Bamford on his motorbike!" Eve began to wax wroth again. "I mean, a priest arriving dressed up as a biker with his vestments in a rucksack is not what my daughter's wedding needs!"

"He finds it an economical way to travel," said Major Locke. "I'm inclined to agree with you, however."

"He doesn't have to be economical. I'll send a limousine for him. You can tell him so, when you see him. No, I'll call him myself and tell him so. And Major—I don't want the church smelling damp! Can't you open it up and air it a bit more over the next week or two?"

"It's a question of someone being there, Miss Owens. And the birds fly in if the door is left open."

"Well, I wish you'd do something," Eve said firmly. "You are churchwarden!"

"It really isn't damp," said Mrs. Locke, interpolating. "Not since the last lot of repairs."

"I'll have a word with the padre and with Mrs. Honey," said Major Locke unhappily. "Hope you enjoy your holiday, Miss Mitchell."

They marched away in step and Meredith could see them stowing their plastic bag in the back of an elderly Ford Escort.

"You were not awfully nice to them, Eve," she said mildly. "He was trying to be helpful. If I'd been him, I would have told you to take a running jump."

"They drive me mad!" said Eve with feeling. "They keep angling for an invitation to the rectory but I refuse to

have them over the threshold. They want to know everyone's business, a quite intolerable pair. There's a little
wine place near here. I want to get half a case of a decent
red. The man there is awfully sweet and always carries it
out to the car for me."

"That's because you bat your eyelids at him. If it was
me, he'd tell me to lug it out myself."

"Serve you right for being so independent," Eve retorted.

In the event, Meredith had to admit Eve had no need to
flutter her eyelashes. The man in question was clearly
overwhelmed at having someone in his shop whom he had
seen on the telly and hovered about in an assiduous manner which Meredith found downright embarrassing and
with which Eve coped easily.

"Good job you didn't buy a whole case," said Meredith
as they locked the wine in the boot. "Or he'd have rolled
out the red carpet."

They set off on foot through the town. "You haven't
said a word about Jon Lazenby," Eve observed suddenly.
"Is that a bad sign? Do be frank."

"There's not a lot I can say, Evie. Sorry. He's the sort
of young man who makes me feel nervous. He seems very
bright. I'm sure he'll do well selling pensions or whatever
it is."

"Don't be awkward, Merry. He doesn't 'sell pensions'
. . . he's an investment adviser. Sara's very fond of him."

"No!" Meredith stopped in the middle of the pavement.
"She's not in love, if that's what you mean. She's just got
a bee in her bonnet. And if you took the trouble to listen
to the kid, you'd realize it. She's marrying him for all the
wrong reasons." Eve was looking mildly surprised so she
heaved a sigh and added, "Let's go and have lunch, Evie."

They walked on in silence. Then Meredith said, "You
will be going back to the States with Elliott, won't you?"

"I certainly don't want to stay in the rectory all on my
own once Sara is married. Why on earth should I?" Eve
hesitated. "I know that after all I told you about my worries over Sara, it might sound contradictory to talk now of
going so far away. Believe me, three years ago I wouldn't

have dreamt of it! But this time I shall be leaving her with Jonathan. And she is mad about him, Merry. You're wrong. Oh, I know he suffers from an overdose of ego!" Eve waved a hand, nearly knocking the topmost newspapers from a pile on a street stand. "But he is reliable! Lucia hankers to retire to the States, too. She's cooked for me for years and only came to the rectory out of loyalty. She has a relative who keeps a pizza parlour in Pasadena and wants her to mind the till." Eve pointed. "Look, we can go and get our lunch over there."

"If you really want to know what I think," said Meredith, knowing that she ought to keep silent but unable to. She was following Eve into the restaurant so the words had to be addressed to the back of her cousin's head. "I think Lazenby likes to tell people he's marrying a star's daughter. He's entirely self-orientated. She'll have to conform to his wishes in every way. You do realize that, don't you?"

"Oh, you're exaggerating," said Eve, sitting down and picking up the menu. She avoided looking at Meredith. "He's a sweet boy and making a lot of money."

"That's it, is it?" Meredith asked grimly. "You say you appreciate my being frank, so I shall be. I believe you when you say you've gone through agonies over Sara. But now you've had enough of the role of devoted mum. You want to pass it on to someone else. Lazenby fits the bill and will take Sara off your hands. You can go off and be glamorous in this soap thing."

"That's not true!" Eve's fingers tightened on the menu card and she looked full in Meredith's face now, her violet eyes blazing. People sitting nearby glanced their way curiously. "Of course he loves her! He does! She's my daughter! He must, he must!"

It was no place for an argument. But sometimes Meredith felt she could grab her cousin and shake those lovely shoulders until Eve's head rattled.

When Meredith awoke the following morning it was dull and overcast. "Rain for sure before lunchtime," Mrs. Yewell predicted. "If you means to go out for your walk, Miss, you wants to go now."

Meredith duly collected boots and anorak from the cloakroom. As Meredith pulled on the anorak she noticed a long pale streak on the sleeve that she hadn't seen the day before. She touched it and a small piece flaked off. It looked like dried clay. Meredith zipped up the anorak uneasily and made her way out of doors.

The last place she wanted to go was back to the churchyard, nor did she fancy wandering round the village. She remembered that as yet she had not explored the rectory's extensive grounds, and what was more, something old Bert had said had lodged in her brain.

The garden was kept tidy by Mrs. Yewell's husband Walter who came in on Saturday mornings. So much Meredith had learned. Trimming the grass and hoeing through the main flower-beds between gate and front door seemed to constitute Walter's brief. He was a methodical and unoriginal gardener. These main beds were laid to regimented rows of red salvia which reminded Meredith of the sort of flower-beds which graced public squares in East European countries. But once away from the main body of the house, the garden ran pleasantly wild. A large greenhouse was empty and dusty with cracked and broken panes. Fruit trees were unpruned and unproductive. All kinds of plants grew in wild profusion, jostling with one another for space. Some had been put there long ago in more meticulous gardening days and some were self-set. Meredith was no horticulturist. She distinguished the plants she knew and puzzled over the rest.

Now that, she thought, looks like a crocus. But it's the wrong time of year, surely, much too late? Don't crocuses come out in early spring? It's now early autumn. This mauve-pink flower must be something else. She stooped and peered at it. It was an attractive little plant but it wasn't a crocus, after all. Nor did it appear to have any leaves. The pink flower swayed gently in a gust of breeze and on this dull day provided a welcome splash of colour. Meredith moved on.

The herb garden showed signs of recent cultivation. Here Lucia grew parsley, marjoram and thyme and also sage, bereft now of purple flowers, and yellowish-green shrubby fever-few which still had a few daisy-like flower heads. Mouth-wash, indeed. But it might be worth a try. Sometimes these old folk remedies worked. It wasn't hard to see how someone of peasant ancestry like Lucia could believe in them implicitly. The old woman she'd talked of in rural Campania, had her equivalents here nowadays, with alternative medicine so fashionable. Looking down at these homely plants, Meredith understood why. At least, if you took a medicine based on these familiar friends, you felt you knew what you were taking.

But now Meredith had come across what she was really looking for. In the high brick wall bordering this limit of the rectory grounds was a stout wooden door. Bert's Ada had not been allowed admirers, so she had crept out of an evening "to the back gate" there to meet the lovelorn Bert. It made the imagination boggle a bit. But this must be the gate, sure enough, and beyond it lay Love Lane. From where she stood, Meredith could see an iron bolt at the top of the door. Probably it was rusted fast after all these years. When she came up to it, however, she found this was not so. The bolt was black and shiny and recently oiled. Meredith reached up and drew it back. It slid easily and stained her fingertips with oily deposit. She wiped her hand on her handkerchief and opened the door.

It creaked very faintly but the hinges had also recently been oiled and the creak came from the aged wood of the door itself. Meredith stepped through it, feeling like a character from a Victorian children's tale, and found herself beyond the rectory grounds and standing on a narrow footpath. It ran down the side of the rectory wall towards a distant clump of trees. Love Lane. But now there were few young people left in the village to make use of it. The surprise, however, came when she looked to see what bordered the other side of the lane. She found herself staring over a hedge into the gardens behind the pair of cottages belonging to Bert and Phil Lorrimer.

Meredith's forehead puckered into a frown as she plotted a map of the locality in her head. Yes, of course. The rectory, although well down the track from the cottages, lay parallel to them and its extensive grounds reached right down to meet their gardens with only Love Lane to divide them. The nearer cottage was Philip's. She could see the back door standing open. Further down the garden, opposite to where she stood, was a square, unlovely breezeblock building with a corrugated roof which must be the studio. She wondered if he had had planning permission for it. Probably not.

Without warning, a peculiar and unearthly yowl split the air. Meredith jumped. The yowl came again and she identified it as one of the curious cries made by a siamese cat. There was a gap in the hedge. Meredith squeezed through it into Philip Lorrimer's garden.

The cat was standing a few feet away by the open door of the studio. Its startling blue eyes looked huge in its dark brown, wedge-shaped head and the short mushroom-coloured fur on its body bristled. "Tom!" called Meredith, but he ran away.

She glanced towards the open kitchen door. There was no sign of life. Meredith approached the studio hesitantly and called, "Philip? It's Meredith Mitchell from the rectory. Are you all right? Phil?"

The door creaked in the breeze. From somewhere in the bushes Tom's unearthly plaint rose on the air. Something and not just the eerie sound of the cat's call made the hair on the nape of Meredith's neck stand on end. She walked up to the studio door and put her hand on the latch. Her heart was throbbing furiously and her throat felt dry. She made an effort to pull herself together, jerked open the door and stepped into the studio.

Philip lay sprawled on the floor, his body twisted into an unnatural attitude, the knees drawn up in a foetal cramp, the head thrown back. One arm was trapped beneath the torso and the other flung out reaching for the door towards which he had tried to crawl in his agony. His fingers had scrabbled in the dust of the floor, tearing the nails and rasping the skin from the bloodied tips. Most dreadful of all was the expression on his face, turned sideways and staring up at her. No trace was left of youth or comeliness. The open eyes bulged unseeingly, almost starting out of the sockets. Lips were drawn back in an animal snarl. Vomit stained the dust and, mixed with saliva, had caked on his parted lips.

She dropped on her knees and put out her shaking hand

to touch his temple. Her fingertips could not distinguish any pulse. Meredith scrambled to her feet, pushing down the revulsion which rose in nausea to her throat, her brain beginning to function. A doctor . . . Blast! This damn village had no surgery, she would have to get an ambulance out from Bamford. No, wait—there was Peter Russell. He might not yet have gone to his surgery in the town.

She dashed out of the studio, up the path into the cottage through the open back door and ran from room to room. All were in incredible disorder. Drawers were pulled open and contents tipped on to the floor, books pulled from the bookshelves. But she hardly noticed this as she searched for the telephone. Hell's teeth! He didn't have a telephone! She ran back the way she had come and stumbled panting into the rectory.

"Whatever is it, Miss?" cried Mrs. Yewell, aghast at the expression on her face.

"Dr. Russell's home number . . ." Meredith scrabbled at the directory.

"It'll be on the pad by the phone, Miss—being as he's a friend of Miss Owens. What's wrong, Miss?"

Meredith grabbed the phone, signalling to Mrs. Yewell to wait. "Hallo?" Oh, thank God, he was there. "Peter? It's Meredith Mitchell—"

"What's the matter?" his voice asked sharply.

"I can't explain now . . . I know you've probably got surgery, but this is an emergency. Can you go straight away to Philip Lorrimer's studio, behind his cottage . . . I'll meet you there." She slammed down the phone and turned to a gaping Mrs. Yewell. "Mr. Lorrimer's been taken ill, Mrs. Yewell. Look, don't say anything to either Miss Owens or Sara if either should come downstairs. I must go back."

She arrived back at the studio as Peter Russell's car drew up outside the cottage. Meredith stepped forward to intercept him as he came striding down the path.

"What the hell—?" he began.

"I think he's dead," Meredith said bleakly. She stood aside and pointed into the studio. "He's in there."

He walked past her into the studio without another word. Meredith waited for a few minutes until he came out, his face grey. He said tersely, "Have you called the police?"

She shook her head. "I thought there might just be a chance, if you got here quickly, so I concentrated on getting in touch with you."

He shook his head. "No. Although he's been dead less than an hour, I'd say. Look, I'll ring the police. You stay here. Don't touch anything—anything at all, do you understand?"

Meredith nodded. "You'll have to use the rectory phone. The garden door is open—through there . . ." She pointed towards the gap in the hedge into Love Lane.

"No, it's all right, I've got a phone in my car." He set off and she forced herself to go back into the studio. It was very quiet here now with the dead man. The tragedy of the sprawled, motionless form struck her. A young man in his prime. Now just a lifeless corpse, grotesque, pathetic . . . the hand stretched out in mute appeal, a desperate and useless attempt to reach the door and summon help.

Meredith glanced around and took in her surroundings properly for the first time.

Eve had been unjust in regarding Philip's pottery. It was by no means all cheap souvenir-ware. There were some elegant jugs of unusual but attractive design. Meredith shivered and folded her arms tightly. At that moment a shadow fell over the open doorway. She looked up and saw Old Bert, staring in.

"Stay out there!" she said sharply, moving between him and the corpse.

"What's wrong with him, then?" Bert asked. He peered past her. "I seen the doctor's car outside."

"He's—fainted." Meredith said firmly, realizing he must at least be able to see the pathetic outstretched hand. "Please go away, Bert. Dr. Russell will be back in a minute."

Bert gave her a look of indescribable malice. "Kicked the bucket, has he?"

She drew a deep breath. "Possibly."

"I ain't going to mourn him!" Bert said. "No one ain't going to mourn him, and some'll dance on his grave, likely!"

"You are a perfectly horrible old man and I'd like you to go away." Meredith looked away from him in disgust.

He gave her another malicious leer and sidled away.

Peter Russell came back, breathless. "Police are on their way. I've phoned through to my surgery to say I won't be in until God knows when and someone will have to cover for me. We'll both have to stay until the police get here. Are you all right?" He lowered his head aggressively, jutting out his jaw, and glared at her.

"Yes. A little shaken. Bert was just here."

"Damn!" Russell said vehemently. "It will be all over the village in half an hour. You'd better sit down, but don't move anything."

"I'll go outside."

She went out, pushing her hands into the pockets of the anorak and glowering mistrustfully about her. Bert was nowhere to be seen. She looked for the cat but it had vanished too. Russell came out of the studio and joined her.

"What do you think was the cause?" she asked. "Heart attack?"

He hunched his shoulders. "Not my job to say. There will be a post-mortem." He scowled and she thought he looked thoroughly miserable. "I don't like the look of it."

"What do you mean?" she asked quickly.

"Strictly between us, it looks like some form of poisoning. Bloody hell!" he exclaimed suddenly. "Why did he have to come here? Why did any of them have to come here?"

She stared at him curiously and he turned back to the body and dropped down on his heels beside it, hands clasped and scowling. He was being careful, she noticed, not to touch the corpse again. There was something about his attitude which reminded her sharply and eerily of Elliott bent over the rag doll. An intentness, in Russell's case professional, and a distaste. Doctors get used to macabre sights. Russell's distaste was almost certainly rooted in something other than the sight of an unpleasant cadaver. She said aloud, "I'll go up to the rectory and let them know."

Russell glanced up. "Mind how you tell young Sal. She

knew this boy slightly and he's her own age group. It's nothing to do with her but it's still going to be a shock."

When Meredith got back to the rectory, Eve was in the hall. Her cousin wore no make-up other than lipstick and Meredith was momentarily startled at how lined, almost weather-beaten, Eve's skin looked without its customary mask. Yet in slacks and a cotton shirt and with a silk scarf carelessly knotted round her head Eve still looked attractive, even if she was the nearest Meredith had ever seen to dishevelled. Even now, fetching disarray would be a better description.

"What on earth is going on?" Eve demanded. "I couldn't make head or tail of what Mrs. Yewell said, partly because she shouted it through the bathroom door at me just as I was thinking of stepping into the shower. I thought she meant you were ill at first. Why did you want Peter's number? What's wrong with Lorrimer?"

As briefly as possible, Meredith told her what had happened.

"Dead? That boy?" Eve gaped foolishly, scarlet lips parted. "Did he have an accident?"

"I don't know. Russell sent for the police."

"Police!"

"Don't go overboard, Eve, it's routine where there's a sudden unexplained death."

"Drink!" said Eve suddenly. "He probably drank."

"Shut up, Eve, and don't start speculating. You had better tell Sara and Elliott. Oh, and Mrs. Yewell and Lucia." Meredith paused. "I expect a copper will come round to see us because I found him."

"I do hope it's Alan Markby," said Eve. "Because he's a friend and would make sure we weren't bothered about it. Oh dear, will the press be interested? Perhaps it won't be Alan because he's CID and a chief inspector. He's probably too important. Oh, how inconvenient!" Eve clapped her hands together in frustration.

"Very . . ." said Meredith drily. "Especially for Lorrimer."

Eve clapped a hand over her mouth like a guilty child. "Oh, I'm sorry, Merry, I didn't mean it to come out the

way it sounded. And you must be terribly shaken. Would
you like a brandy? Let me pour you one. What a perfectly
horrible, beastly thing to happen ... I'm very sorry for
Lorrimer, of course, poor young man. But, you know, just
before the wedding like this—you have to admit it's like
a bad omen."

A bad omen. Meredith refused the brandy and went upstairs. She took the rag doll from her case where she had
hidden it. It looked even smaller and grubbier than she remembered. Its head lolled backwards and its wool-strand
hair was sparse and matted. Through a hole in its body
could be seen a lump of kapok stuffing. She saw now, as
she had not noticed before, that someone had drawn faint
biro lines crudely marking the area of the pudenda.

"You," she said softly to it, "you've got something to
do with all this. You've brought some sort of evil here."

Six

Markby thrust his hands into the pockets of the bottle-green walker's weatherproof he wore and cast a jaundiced eye over Lorrimer's untidy, weed-infested garden.

"Been down there, have you, sir?" asked Sergeant Pearce, pointing to the far end of the plot which lay behind an untrimmed hedge of hebe. "The lad turned his hand to a bit of gardening down there."

Markby grunted and walked across to the fence which divided this garden from the next and looked approvingly across into rows of neatly hoed vegetables.

Pearce, divining what was in his chief's mind, said, "Belongs to an old fellow called Bert Yewell. Bit of a local character and a real old grouser. But he's the sort that thrives on disaster. Happy as a pig in the midden now we're here. I had to chase him off. He was getting in the way."

"So do you and I thrive on disaster and unpleasantness," said Markby sourly. "Without them we'd be out of a job. Before you chased the old man off, I take it you interviewed him?"

Pearce nodded. "If you can call it that. I don't think anyone could hold a logical conversation with him. He keeps wandering off the point and talking about the village as it was years ago, and cats. The deceased kept a couple of cats which dug holes in Yewell's garden." Pearce paused. "He was a bit funny about that. Started grumbling about it no end and then suddenly shut up."

"Oh?" said Markby mildly, raising his eyebrows.

"Yes, sir. I was wondering—you know—if he'd put anything down. We'd never get him to admit it."

Markby glanced up at the sky. Patches of dark cloud scudded across it and would bring rain tonight if not by tea-time. Rain might obliterate useful information out of doors. The garden search would have to be stepped up. He turned and walked back to the cottage, Pearce following behind him.

"Have you had a look indoors, sir? It's in a real old mess."

"Yes," said Markby, looking around him. "Someone wanted something badly. I suppose it could have been the boy himself, looking for something. It's a bit rum, though. We'll have to wait for the post-mortem, of course, but keep your eyes peeled. I'm going round to the big house next door, the Old Rectory . . ." He pointed in the appropriate direction. "I want to talk to the person who found him."

"It belongs to the film star," said Pearce self-consciously, "that house does. Eve Owens. Haven't caught sight of her yet. But the lady who found the body is a Miss Mitchell who is staying there and she's a consul. I don't mean a foreign one, I mean one of ours abroad, home on leave."

"I know. I've met her."

Pearce suppressed his surprise. "Oh, there's been a reporter from the *Bamford Gazette* out already. News travels fast. Well, with it happening next door to Eve Owen's home, people are bound to be interested. But I don't think he had any luck getting into the rectory."

Markby allowed himself a smile. "I think Miss Owens and her entourage have seen off more serious press intrusion that the *Bamford Gazette!* Don't give much for his chances."

He had more success, however, and got through the gate and up to the front door of the Old Rectory before finding his way barred by the ample form of Lucia, eyes glittering and arms akimbo.

"You want to see Miss Owens? She is very upset. All these people come, go. This boy die." Lucia signed herself piously. "Is very bad when young man die."

"I really want to see Miss Mitchell," he said patiently.

"She is in the garden." Lucia indicated he should go round the side of the house.

He thanked her and made his way round the corner of the building, past the soldierly rows of salvia and into the wilder reaches of the garden. He came upon Meredith staring moodily at a moss-covered urn and he had time to observe her before she was aware of his approach.

She was, he supposed, in her mid-thirties, pleasantly plain and though not as tall as she had seemed at dinner the other evening in her high heels, still tall for a woman in flat shoes. Her thick, glossy brown hair had been chopped off in a no-nonsense bob. At dinner, she had struck him as a no-nonsense sort of person not without a sense of humour, although the rather curious little dinner party had not given much opportunity for this aspect of her character to emerge. He thought now, as he had then, that she was a woman who had made it in her chosen profession without looks, because she did not need to rely on anything so transitory. She would know her job and do it well. He rather liked the look of her. But that was neither here nor there.

"Hallo, again," he said and when she looked up, added, "You look like one of those Victorian studies. Thoughts on Mortality in an English garden."

"I think I might be excused them," she said coldly. "I did find a dead man this morning."

"Sorry—a bad joke on my part. Misplaced attempt to put the witness at ease. I'd rather like you to tell me about it, if you wouldn't mind."

She did so, concisely and lucidly. She must have been through all this with Pearce already. Sometimes repeating things helped people remember odd facts they had missed the first time round. Sometimes it had the opposite effect and they reduced the tale to a précis. She seemed to be taking care over what she said. She did not interpose her narrative with cries of "It was horrible!" or insist how upset she was, but he had a shrewd suspicion she was very distressed.

"Perhaps we could retrace your footsteps?" he suggested gently.

"All right. I came down here." She led the way towards

a deepening wilderness of overgrown shrubberies and half-vanished flower-beds which affronted his gardener's soul and recalled vanished boyhood days.

"What brought you this way?" he asked, frowning at roses run wild and garden statuary smothered in under-growth.

"Just exploring. I hadn't had a chance to take a proper look round outside the house."

"Are you interested in gardening?" He was startled to hear a note of hope in his voice and covered it by frowning and scraping ivy with his finger from a broken piece of balustrade.

"Not really. I like flowers but don't know how to grow them."

"It's a bit of a hobby of mine," he confided. "Or would be, if I had any time. To say nothing of a decent garden. At the moment I have what estate agents call a patio and I call a back yard, with three or four tubs in it."

"Eve will be glad you're in charge of this," she said suddenly in a low voice. "You're sort of family. This is rather going to hang over the wedding. I don't mean that Lorrimer dying isn't more important—but it's just, well, come at a particularly bad moment. That still sounds trite, sorry. You know what I mean."

"Yes." He paused. "You said at dinner that you'd met Lorrimer."

"Yes. And yesterday morning I met him again."

Markby wrenched his gaze from a collapsed and gnarled lavender bush and gave her a sharp look.

"It was by the lych-gate of the churchyard. He was looking for one of his cats. He wasn't feeling well." Her hazel eyes met his levelly. "He looked ghastly. As a matter of fact, he collapsed on the track and I had to help him back to his cottage. He was sick in his kitchen but he wouldn't let me call a doctor. He said he'd been sick be-fore and blamed the beer at the Dun Cow."

She fell silent and he felt she was debating whether to add something else, but instead she started to walk on, merely saying, "This way."

They had reached the door in the wall. "This is where I went through into Love Lane." She fell silent again.

Inappropriate name, thought Markby and then wondered if after all, it wasn't . . . and whether she was thinking the same thing. He unbolted the door as she watched and stepped through into Love Lane. Coming back, he asked, "Is there another door like this one?"

"In the garden wall? If so, I haven't found it."

"Hmm." He shut the door and bolted it carefully again. Then he took out his handkerchief and wiped his fingertips. From the corner of his eye he saw her fidget. "So this door in effect by-passes the security system at the main gate."

"Yes, but it's kept bolted. No one could open it from Love Lane."

Markby glanced wryly at his grease-stained handkerchief before returning it to his pocket.

She said loudly, "About the cat, the one I heard yowl. It's a siamese and quite valuable. Lorrimer was very fond of cats. What will happen to it?"

"Ring up the RSPCA, I should," he said. "They shouldn't have any trouble finding a home for a pure-bred siamese. Unless we turn up next of kin who want the animal. Lorrimer seems to have been a bit of a loner, however. Pearce—my sergeant—says he wasn't popular in the village. Any idea why?"

She shrugged. "I thought he seemed a nice enough chap. But he wasn't a local and I dare say villagers wouldn't consider pottery a man's work."

"No muck on his boots? Not a weather-beaten son of toil?"

"If you like."

"By that measure, I'd probably fail the test, too," he said affably.

"Yes, you probably would!" was the sharp retort. Then she hunched her shoulders again. "There will be a postmortem, I suppose. When will you get the result?"

"Pretty soon. After you found the body . . . did you come straight to the rectory?"

She shook her curtain of brown hair. "No, I ran up to his cottage, looking for a phone. But he didn't have one."

"Anything else about the cottage strike you?"

For a second the hazel eyes stared blankly at him and then he saw understanding and some consternation dawn in them.

"It was very untidy ... I didn't pay too much attention. It was untidy yesterday morning. But, yes, it was worse. There were books on the floor ... I didn't touch anything. I just looked round for a phone!" She drew a deep breath. "Look, are you treating this as a suspicious death?"

"I'm always suspicious. Healthy young men don't just drop dead."

"He wasn't so healthy. He had stomach trouble yesterday." An obstinate expression crossed her face. "Could it have been suicide?"

"Suicide?" Markby exclaimed startled. "How do you account for the previous bouts of sickness? Trial runs?"

"I don't know!" she said fiercely. "It's just—the alternative is murder, isn't it? I didn't turn that cottage upside-down, but someone did!"

"Yes, I think so. The intruder was in a hurry, may have been disturbed, had to beat a retreat and was probably unsuccessful. Whoever it was may have been ransacking the place while you were making your way through the garden here towards this door. You crossed Love Lane and went into the studio. The intruder saw you through the kitchen window and scarpered." He frowned. "But it's speculation. And it's early days to talk of murder."

They turned away from the gate to walk back through the garden. The renewed sight of the horticultural chaos round them impelled him to exclaim, "I wish I could get my hands on this garden! I remember it when it was kept in order. My uncle had a full-time gardener and woe betide anyone, especially a small boy, who so much as broke off a twig! It would be a real challenge to re-create it! Hallo, that's an interesting inhabitant."

He stooped so suddenly that she nearly fell over him. "What is it?" she demanded. "Oh, that, I thought it was crocus, blooming at the wrong time of year."

"No, it's not crocus, it's colchicum. No relation to the crocus at all, really, despite the superficial resemblance. It is sometimes called autumn crocus or meadow saffron or naked ladies—the last comes from the way it sends up flowers first without leaves and the leaves later." He took a biro out of his pocket and used it to push back gently one of the petals. "See the stamens? Six of them. Crocus has three. Oh, and unlike crocus, it's poisonous."

He straightened up and this time nearly hit her nose with the back of his head where she had been peering over his shoulder. He apologized.

She trod carefully round him and directed a suspicious glare at the plant. "That little flower?"

"All parts of the plant. It's not the only common garden inhabitant which is poisonous. Some ferns are, foxgloves are, larkspur is. So is the peony. A garden is potentially a very dangerous place."

"But you'd have to eat them," she objected. "Who goes about eating peonies and larkspur?"

"Sometimes colchicum is allowed to grow where animals graze and they do eat it and get sick. In the case of dairy animals it's been known to get into the milk and make sick anyone who had drunk it. Children sometimes eat flowers, buttercups for example, and get very ill. Herbalists use these things safely but they are very careful about amounts. Colchicum has been used to treat leukaemia and, I fancy, gout. The Chinese are keen on the peony in herbal medicines. I wouldn't recommend the layman to have a go."

She was frowning and didn't answer. They had reached the house. "Will you want to talk to Eve and Sara?" she asked, stopping by the steps up to the front door. "They are both very upset. I don't suppose they can tell you anything."

"I won't bother them now," Markby said. "But I might be back later for a word." He noticed that she was very pale and added sympathetically, "If I were you I'd go indoors and have a couple of stiff whiskies."

"Don't like whisky," she said wryly and a sudden and surprisingly attractive grin appeared on her face. Then it faded and she said seriously, "While I was waiting for the police to arrive, I had the chance to see some of his pottery. It wasn't that I was being callous, you understand. But it was better than looking at him . . ."

Markby nodded.

"He really was quite good. Some of his work was kitsch, but some of it really had something. If he hadn't been obliged to make ashtrays for souvenir stalls, perhaps he might have developed into a serious artist of some note."

"If and might," said Markby quietly, "are the great imponderables. When you opened the garden door into Love Lane, you are sure you had to draw back the bolt?"

"Yes, sure. It wasn't unlocked."

They parted. As he made his way back to his car, he thought, Perhaps I ought to ask to be taken off this job right now, before I get started. But there was no real reason he could give, only an inner dissatisfaction and perhaps something else. Then he said aloud, "God, no, not at your age!"

Meredith watched Markby leave and went back into the house. As she closed the front door her feeling of despondency was increased by a sense of not having behaved quite as she should. She had dealt with police forces before, but always abroad and in the course of consular duty. Her profession had bred in her a certain caution and secretiveness, an instinctive abhorrence of Telling All. Impart your information on a need-to-know basis. Let that be your guide. And it had guided her now. Like a real old dyed-in-the-wool consular hand, she told herself bitterly, you told him as little as possible!

She had certainly answered Markby's questions, but hardly with a torrent of information. The habit instilled in her of playing her cards carefully one by one and of manoeuvring to protect a British subject in trouble had exerted considerable influence over her part in the conversation, as she now wryly reflected. She should, for instance, have told him about her discovery of Jerry in the churchyard. An obscure instinct not to drag poor old Bert into it—but there again, perhaps he wasn't poor old Bert but nasty old Bert. Meredith sighed. It was not the only thing she hadn't told Alan Markby but she rallied and told herself firmly that, whilst she ought to be helpful, it would not help to muddy the waters. Extraneous matters would only act as red herrings. She had only partly succeeded in convincing herself of this when she heard a thud of footsteps behind her and turning her head, saw Elliott running down the staircase.

He jumped down the last two steps into the hall with a sort of spurious athleticism. He had laid aside his tracksuit in favour of maroon trousers and a colour-teamed sweater of the sort golfers wear with a pattern of diamonds on the front. She reflected, disrespectfully, that what he really should be wearing was a tee-shirt emblazoned with a slogan like "I watch my cholesterol."

"The fellow from homicide gone?" he asked.

"Why do you call him that?" she snapped.

"It's what he is, isn't it?" Elliott pursed his lips. "What did he have to say?"

"It was actually a private conversation—but he wanted to ask about my finding the body, if you must know." She paused and added drily, "What were you afraid he'd say?"

"What was all that with the plants?" Seeing she stared at him in some surprise, he explained, "My room looks out over the garden. I was watching you."

"You had no business to!" she said angrily. But he could hardly be blamed so she added stiffly, "I'm rather unnerved, Albie. I did find the poor young man dead." She walked pointedly away from him.

Undeterred, Elliott followed her into the drawing room. "Don't feel bad about it. Sure, it's a pity. But look at it this way, at least we don't have to keep looking for more nasty little parcels."

"What do you mean?" Meredith felt a tightening of her stomach muscles.

"Who do you think left those grisly little calling cards? The pottery guy, of course."

"You've no right to say that!" she burst out.

"You'll see. Remember, I've been here longer than you. And I've dealt with this sort of thing before. We won't find anything else now he's out of the way."

He sounded so sure that she was shaken. "Why should he do such a thing?"

"He was crazy about the kid, Sara. Come on, it makes sense. Young love—turned sour. Not that I know about these things."

Meredith, eyeing him, said sarcastically, "No, I don't suppose you do."

"Lady," said Elliott, "I know about people. They're my business."

She was tired and suffering from delayed shock and she could not be bothered to argue with him. "There's no way of proving what you say, Albie. I'm sure you know a great deal more than you're telling me. All I can say is, perhaps you ought to talk to Chief Inspector Markby."

"Never volunteer, sweetheart. Did you tell him everything?"

"Yes!" Meredith flushed. "Well, no, not quite."

"Tell him about the ox heart and the doll?" His voice had sharpened.

"No . . ." She pulled herself together. "Until there's a post-mortem, we don't know why Lorrimer died or if it's in any way connected." Her lack of conviction sounded in her voice.

Elliott smiled nastily. "He's dead. Does it matter why? But you did right to keep quiet about the heart and doll. Let's both forget about it, eh?"

"I don't know what your game is, Albie," Meredith said quietly, "but I'm not in the mood to talk about this any more. And Albie—I don't like being spied on!"

"Excuse *me!*" he retorted sarcastically.

Alan Markby went home at the end of a not very rewarding day and wandered out into his back yard—he must remember to call the thing a patio—with a mug of tea in one hand and a bug-killer spray in the other.

The technique for dealing with whitefly is to creep up on them and spray them before they can flitter off the leaves and evaporate in the air to reassemble when you've gone. It required a certain dexterity to spray efficiently and hold the tea out of range of the mist of insecticide. As he

attempted to do both he told himself this was not how it
was done: this was how people poisoned themselves by
accident.

Does anyone ever get poisoned by accident? That was
the question. He put down the spray and sat down on a
rickety bench in the last rays of the evening sun. The
threatening rain clouds had dispersed themselves after all.
The house was an end-of-terrace early Victorian, originally
built to fulfil the aspirations of an emerging middle class
and later fallen on hard times. Now these Victorian properties were fashionable again. The Upwardly Mobiles had
moved into the terrace. Markby, who had acquired his
house before any of them and before the prices of the
properties disappeared into the upper atmosphere, regarded
the newcomers with suspicion. One of them, heaven help
us, had put a satellite dish on his roof. Markby had asked
Laura, his sister, indignantly, "Doesn't the bloke need
planning permission?"

"Ah," said Laura, "there's a grey area there, regarding
satellite dishes. You might get him to take it down. You
might not. Anyway, it would make for bad blood between
neighbours and you might weigh that against the inconvenience of an obvious eyesore. You've got to move with
the times, Alan."

"Why?" he had replied crossly.

Remembering Laura's remarks about bad blood between
neighbours brought his mind back to young Lorrimer, who
had not been much loved by his neighbours although apparently easily able to impress on superficial acquaintance
an intelligent, not to say shrewd, woman like Meredith
Mitchell. It was beginning to look like a definite case of
poisoning according to preliminary examinations. A proper
post-mortem would tell. Deliberate poisoning most likely,
by someone who disliked him more than most. But why?
Quite apart from how.

Meredith Mitchell ... smart girl that one, he thought
moodily, but holding out on something. A nice chap, she
had called Lorrimer. But she hadn't done as Markby had
done which was search through the cottage. Or she said
she hadn't. She could be lying. He did not like to think

she had lied but he was a policeman on a case and he had to consider all eventualities, no matter how repugnant to him personally. By her own admission, she had gone into the place to look for a telephone. She might also have taken the opportunity for a quick search—but for what?

Ample evidence had been there that young Lorrimer was not a very pleasant type at all. He smoked pot. In fact he grew the stuff in a little plot tucked away at the bottom of that overgrown garden behind the hebe hedge. He read the sort of literature which made the soft pornography on sale in the average newsagent look like children's fiction. He subscribed to a particularly nasty magazine which was smuggled into this country and seized by customs' officers if they were able to intercept it. A bit of an oick altogether. But plausible, obviously. That was the trouble with that type. Markby had met them before. Charming, plausible, likeable, accomplished liars. Until you actually had anything to do with them, you just had no clue to their personalities, then you found you were dealing with Jekyll and Hyde. And before magistrates or a jury—if ever it got so far—they were lily-white Dr. Jekylls and got away with murder. Only in this case, just possibly, murder had caught up with Philip Lorrimer.

Wait for the post-mortem, Markby told himself, draining the mug. But it would turn out to be murder, he had a gut feeling about it.

So back to "why?" A number of unpleasant items had been found in the cottage but none of them suggested a motive for murder. Lorrimer's home-grown grass crop was hardly going to trouble the Colombian drug barons enough to warrant a hit-man being dispatched to the village and anyway they didn't poison people, they blew their brains out. The same went for the porn. There was no evidence that Lorrimer was a major link in a chain headed by some Nordic supplier. If he had been, there would have been no goods in his house and he would have lived in a great deal more style. No, it was something else the unknown searcher had hunted for. But had the person who had conducted the hasty search found what he or she looked for? Or had no one, including the police, so far found it?

"If not," he murmured aloud, "the murderer will be back."

Markby began to think about Eve Owens. A truly beautiful woman. The eyes, the bone structure, the figure of a woman half her age . . . the only flaw was the skin, crisscrossed by a myriad tiny lines beneath the make-up. He recalled her at Robert Freeman's funeral, graceful and grieving. And at dinner the other evening, sparkling effortlessly in pink chiffon like a glass of pink champagne. Heigh-ho. Of such stuff are dreams made.

But she was not a dream, she was a real woman and living at the rectory must be a lonely life. Especially since Bob died. Markby thought uneasily about that locked back gate with its oiled hinges and greased bolt. It led into the lane and dead opposite to it was a hole in the hedge giving access to Lorrimer's garden. Who went that way regularly enough to keep the gate maintained so carefully?

She must be in her forties, Eve Owens, and Lorrimer had been twenty-four—which don't mean nuthin'. But these days, people didn't bother to be discreet. If Eve Owens fancied Lorrimer for her toy-boy, she would have moved him into the rectory. Or perhaps she wouldn't . . . because of the daughter? Because she was wary of the gutter press? Or because the affair had already started during the lifetime of the late Robert Freeman?

Or was it the girl who slipped out to meet Lorrimer? he thought. She was engaged to that city whizz-kid. Markby was due to give her away himself and at the reminder a cloud of gloom formed over him. He still was not sure why, even though Laura claimed it was because he was the only respectable acquaintance Eve had. Unkind of Laura, that. Also inaccurate. Altogether a wild statement from a solicitor and one which suggested a certain personal antipathy on the part of his sister for Miss Owens. Eve could have asked Russell. Or one of Bob's business acquaintances. But she had asked him. So, what about Sara? Pretty, lively girl meets handsome, poverty-stricken young artist. . . . That bit sounded promising. But would she risk her wedding on that account?

One ought not to forget Mr. Elliott, of course. Markby had already judged that gentleman more than likely a gay

of the slightly camp variety. Was Philip Lorrimer bisexual?
Did Elliott trip down to the garden gate to meet him like
a latterday Maud?

"Blimey . . ." said Markby into his empty tea mug.

Seven

At the rectory the following day started very badly indeed. As finder of the body Meredith discovered to her displeasure that she had acquired an unwished notoriety. Whenever she set foot outside the gate she was surrounded by villagers who stared at her silently and curiously as if asking whether she was a good witch or bad. This was not the only reason why she and everyone else at the rectory had been reduced to a state of siege. The news of Lorrimer's death on the doorstep of a person about whom the great British public was always avid to read had reached the ears of the national press and now a horde of baggy-eyed and dishevelled persons, who all looked singularly out of place in their rural surroundings, had descended on the village and was getting under everyone's feet. Nor did they share the villagers' reticence.

" 'Ere," said Mrs. Yewell in wonder, "one of them blokes stopped me as I was coming in to work and asks me if Miss Owens was friendly with that there potting fellow. 'You mind your own business!' I told him. Expecting a person to go gossiping with strangers. 'I keeps my own counsel,' I told him."

Meredith reflected that this speech probably gave the gentleman in question more copy than had a simple direct reply. Then, just before lunchtime, Jonathan Lazenby telephoned. He had heard the report on his car radio. What the dickens was going on down there and why had he not been informed?

Meredith, who took this call and was not in the best of moods, replied sharply, "Why the devil should you be?"

"Look here," he said savagely down the line. "The bloody press will be crawling all round the place soon."

"You're too late. They're here already."

"You see? You'll find Eve's picture all over the evening editions even though it's got damn all to do with it. Tell Eve to get her solicitor working, drafting a statement."

"About what, for crying out loud?" exploded Meredith.

"Denying she knows anything about it."

"Oh, marvellous stuff. Just what's needed!" she retorted sarcastically.

"Listen, Meredith!" he returned belligerently, "I'm flying to New York this evening or I'd come down myself! But I'll be back at the weekend and I'll come down there directly. In the meantime, keep Sara there under wraps! Do you consular act. I don't want her pestered by the press, do you hear? And I don't want her going back to her job. They'll track her down there."

Meredith growled and, repressing the urge to hang up on him with difficulty, passed the receiver to Sara.

"What job is this?" she asked Sara later.

"At the Women's Refuge. It's in the East End. It's sort of social work. I help at the crèche." Sara pushed back a stray hank of hair from her pale face. She did not look as though she had slept at all. "I've been doing it for six months. It can be a bit tough sometimes but it means a lot to me. Jonathan doesn't really like me doing it. He thinks I'm going to get beaten up by an outraged husband whose wife we've taken in."

"For once Jonathan could be right. You'd better stay here, Sara. Anyway, Alan Markby might want to talk to you."

"What about?" asked Sara, fear leaping into her blue eyes.

Meredith studied her. "Oh, just trying to find out something about Lorrimer, I suppose. Don't worry about it. Just tell him the truth."

Sara said, "Um . . ." and scuttled away.

Meredith watched her go. She was plainly scared out of her wits but Meredith knew she was going to have to tackle her about what she'd got herself into pretty soon. It would be nice to clear it up before Markby talked to Sara.

I've got to get out of this house for a spell, Meredith thought. But I'm blowed if I'm going to run the gauntlet of those pests hanging round the gate. It was possible, however, that they had not yet discovered the garden door into Love Lane. Meredith gathered up the anorak and boots, collected the tin of cat food she had stowed in Lucia's fridge and let herself out through the gate and into Love Lane. There was no one in the lane itself but there were policemen all over Lorrimer's garden and Tom had probably run miles away. All the same, she scrambled through the hole in the hedge, calling to him and failing to find him, walked up to the cottage and spooned out some cat food into a saucer outside the door.

"Hallo, miss," said the young man she recognized as Pearce, Markby's sergeant. "Not found the moggy yet, then?"

"Not yet. You haven't seen him, I suppose?" Meredith disposed of the empty tin in Philip's dustbin, discovering too late, as it fell to the bottom with a resounding clang, that the bin had been emptied by Sergeant Pearce's indefatigable investigators and the contents removed for analysis. "Sorry!" she apologized.

"That's all right, miss. So long as I know that tin wasn't part of the original contents. If you leave food there on that saucer, I expect a fox or another cat will come up and pinch it overnight. Or even a hedgehog." Pearce was country born.

"It's the best I can do," Meredith said. "The cat might come home eventually. What on earth are all those men doing digging at the bottom of the garden?"

"Best you ask Chief Inspector Markby, miss. He's around in the village somewhere."

Meredith set off down the main road. Outside the Dun Cow she heard her name called and turning saw Markby walking along the verge.

"Good morning!" he hailed her.

"Hallo," she said. "I've just seen your sergeant. They're digging like mad at the bottom of Philip Lorrimer's garden. What are they looking for? Sergeant Pearce was very cagey."

SAY IT WITH POISON

"Not looking for anything. Digging out your friend Lorrimer's private pot patch."

"What?"

"Can't leave it there. Can't burn it off, either. Unless you want this village floating out of its collective skull." He glanced at the Dun Cow. "Can I buy you a drink?"

"Thought coppers didn't buy on duty."

"It's my lunch break," he said.

"Bit early, aren't you? Oh, okay then. I've not been inside that pub yet. But I'm not much of a mid-day drinker."

Inside the Dun Cow was not as bad as she had feared. There was only one fruit machine and nothing worse than a bar billiards table.

"Ah!" said Markby enthusiastically. "I used to be good at that once, when I was a student. Can you play?"

"I have, once or twice. I'm not much good at it."

"Come on, give you a game. Just don't knock any of the pegs down." He handed her a cue and hunted in his pocket for a coin to release the game for them. "I'd like to have a word with Sara about Lorrimer," he said as he leaned over the table. "She knew him, didn't she?"

"Just slightly, I think. Don't you go scaring her!"

"Why should she be scared?"

"Look," Meredith said patiently. "She's young and death is very frightening to the young, especially when it happens to another young person. They don't think they can die."

"None of us ever thinks he's going to die, not really." The ball fell through a hole on the table and rolled back down the shoot to the front. "But you're wrong about youngsters. They sometimes have a better grip on reality than older people. Have you made a will, Meredith?"

"As a matter of fact, yes. What's that to do with it?"

"Surprising number of quite elderly people haven't."

"For the record," she said icily, "I'm not elderly."

He straightened up and handed her a cue. "That was not my meaning. I meant, we don't like to think we will die. Here, your go. Don't poke my eye out with it."

Meredith struck at the ball and the black peg fell over.

"Bad luck," he sympathized. "Just as well you haven't any score to lose."

"I told you, I'm not much good at this ruddy game."
Frustration echoed in her voice. "Aren't you supposed to
be out there finding out how Lorrimer died? Not stuck in
a pub playing bar billiards with me and swigging pints?"

"Then let's go and sit over there." He picked up his pint
and gestured towards the deserted ingle-nook hearth.
When they were seated, he said, "As for how, he was def-
initely poisoned."

"Oh," Meredith said thoughtfully and fell silent, sipping
at her tomato juice, her dark brown hair falling forward
over her face and hiding her expression.

"We took away some utensils from the kitchen. Fortu-
nately Lorrimer wasn't keen on washing up. He let the
crocks accumulate until he ran out. Plenty of dregs and so
on for the laboratory people to play about with. There are
traces in a coffee cup, a cereal bowl and in a milk bottle."

"A milk bottle?" Meredith looked up in surprise, the
curtain of brown hair swinging aside as she turned to face
him. "You don't surely mean that it's one of those cases
where someone has stupidly kept insecticide or weed-killer
in an empty milk bottle?"

Gently he asked, "What makes you think of those two
things?"

She hesitated. "Lorrimer told me that once when one of
the cats went missing he looked in the garden shed belonging to the old fellow next door and there was every kind
of weed-killer, rat poison, you name it, just standing about
in odd receptacles. Bert, that's the old chap, he's the sort
of person who would put Kill-It-All in a milk bottle and
then stick the milk bottle out with the empties. I've read
of people doing such things."

"They do indeed, but I fancy not in this case. The poison, as far as the lab boys can yet tell, is herbal in base.
It's been administered over a period and its effects were
cumulative. Lorrimer told you he had had stomach upsets
before. Each one would have been worse. The day he collapsed in the lane while talking to you, the poison was already well into his system. It only took one more dose."

Meredith grasped at a straw. "Perhaps it was something
he drank himself. A herbal tea . . ."

"No. He would need to drink gallons of such a thing,

huge quantities day in and day out, even to get mildly ill—
and there's no sign he was addicted to such drinks. There
were no empty packets or tea-bags in his rubbish or in his
kitchen cupboards and in any case the brand names ones
commonly sold are safe drunk in reasonable doses. I'm
talking about a deliberately prepared poisonous extract of
some plant."

"You're talking about murder," she said quietly. He had
been talking about murder from the beginning, pussy-
footing round it. Now it was out in the open.

"Yes, I'm afraid so. Lorrimer had a sweet tooth. Lots of
dried sugar crystals in everything. That would have helped
disguise any odd taste."

Meredith thought it over, aware he waited patiently for
her response. She put down the tomato juice and said,
"Look, there's something I didn't mention and I should
have, perhaps. It didn't seem relevant when we spoke before. But I think now it must be."

"Yes?"

"I told you he was looking for a cat when I met him in
the lane. I didn't tell you I found it in the churchyard,
dead. I thought Bert had poisoned it. I heard him threaten
to. The cats dug in his vegetable patch. I didn't tell
Lorrimer." She hunched her shoulders. "I thought he'd be
upset and nothing much could be done about it. He
couldn't have proved the old man did it."

Markby obviously made an heroic effort not to swear
out loud but she would not have blamed him if he had
done. He got to his feet. "Perhaps we had better go down
to the churchyard and you can show me where you found
the animal. I wish you'd said before."

He could not prevent his irritation sounding in his voice
and she felt herself flush. Because she did not like being
ticked off, even if she was in the wrong, she retorted mul-
ishly, "I would have done so, if I had thought it important!"

"Why don't you let me decide what's important,
Meredith!" he said crossly.

"It was just a dead cat!" she snapped. "Do you want to
know the whereabouts of every deceased creature, animal
and human?"

"Yes," Markby growled at her, "in this case, I do. It was probably dead because it drank the same milk! He put some in his coffee and over his cornflakes and some down for the cats ... Come along!"

Following him out of the Dun Cow, she complained bitterly, "If you're so keen to know everything, then I should point out to you, since your men have inexplicably appeared to overlook it, that this village is overrun by pressmen and they are laying siege to the rectory and causing us considerable inconvenience."

"That's your problem, or Eve's, since she is the householder. It's frankly the least of my worries."

They had paused by his car for him to get his wellington boots out of the back. Meredith watched him tug them on and retaliated. "You mean, they are just allowed to make a nuisance of themselves? They're even pestering the staff."

"It's a civil matter not a criminal one. Let me know when one of them assaults a member of the staff on the public highway."

"I thought," Meredith said starchily, "that when one reported things to the police in this country something was done."

Markby straightened up with a suddenness which startled her enough to make her jump back. "Now look here, Meredith! You're not the ruddy consul here. This is a murder inquiry. You've got no authority and what's more you've got no experience of this sort of thing, not here in this country, anyway. You're not in Ruritania or wherever the place is now! And you haven't got diplomatic immunity. You can't go ringing up the Ministry of Foreign Affairs and complaining you are being bothered by undesirables! I'm sure you are more than capable of seeing off a few miserable pressmen. Don't bother me about it!"

She was temporarily reduced to a seething silence and trudged, glowering, hands in pockets, beside him as they set off down the lane. At the entrance to it, a gentleman with designer stubble and a black leather jacket emerged from the hedge.

"Are you making any progress, inspector?"

"Go away," said Markby. "You'll get your information at a press conference, if I hold one."

"He'll follow us," muttered Meredith.

"I'll have him for obstructing the police if he does it too obviously."

"Oh, I see, one rule for you and another for us?"

"Only so far as it's the difference between invasion of Miss Owens's privacy, which I should think she's pretty used to, and investigating a murder. Okay, where was this dead animal?"

"Over here . . ." Meredith led the way to the family tombs. The branch she had put over the corpse was still there but Jerry's remains had disappeared.

Markby sighed resignedly. "Only to be expected, I'm afraid. A fox probably dragged it off in triumph last night. We shouldn't have found it, even if you had told me at once." He stared morosely at the monument to the gentleman who had stood in the path of the express. She saw him frown and turn his eyes towards the next one, that of Reverend Henry Markby. "Bit of a mess," he said. "This plot, I mean. I suppose I ought to get hold of a stone mason and get him to tidy up the damaged monuments."

"They're no worse than the rest of the headstones. There aren't many recent burials here." Meredith was struck by a thought. "Where was Robert Freeman buried?"

"In Oxford. He died in the John Radcliffe. I suppose Eve could have had him buried here . . . but right opposite the house would have been a little macabre. Years ago they didn't mind having their dead buried within sight. I don't suppose Uncle Henry gave a second thought to all those ancestors under the turf across the road. I was always scared stiff of this churchyard when I was a kid visiting him here, just because all these monuments had my name on them. I kept thinking some old josser would pop up out of the ground and tell me off about something." He leaned disrespectfully against the headstone of the railway enthusiast. "Did you never meet Bob Freeman?"

"No, I was overseas when they married. Whenever I came home, they were always away."

"He was a pleasant sort of chap. Very steady, old-fashioned in his ideas. Dependable."

"Then he must have been good for Eve," she said, not meaning to make the remark out loud.

"Ever meet either of her previous husbands?"

"I met Hughie a couple of times. He was a bit of a creep, I thought. Mike I knew quite well." Markby was looking at her thoughtfully and she wondered if by some tremor of the voice or expression in the eyes she had betrayed herself. To distract him, she pointed across the turf. "Peter Russell's wife's ashes are over there."

He glanced away from her, thank God. "Oh yes, that was a sad affair, I remember the inquest. Suicide. She had been ill for years, bedridden. She finally took an overdose. Couldn't face any more."

"So that's what happened," said Meredith softly and Markby gave her a curious glance. "Poor Russell . . ." she said aloud. But to herself she was thinking, That was a pretty vicious lie Lorrimer repeated to me. He must have known it. This reflection left her feeling less for Lorrimer than she had done, and she disliked it, not wanting to think ill of someone so recently dead.

Markby, watching the conflict in her face, observed, "Talking of inquests, you'll be needed at this one, but it should be pretty soon and quite straightforward."

Meredith nodded, absently running her finger over the arch of one of his ancestors' chilly gravestones.

Markby was called back to Bamford at lunchtime. The laboratory had sent over its detailed report. He sat with it before him on his desk, wishing he had stopped to eat a ploughman's at the Dun Cow before he'd left the village.

The report confirmed earlier speculation in some detail. The poisoning had taken place over a period of some months. He sighed. He was going to have to dig into Lorrimer's past and find all the fellow's contacts, unravel his business dealings, pry into his social life . . . It would be time-consuming and most of it fruitless and a waste. But somewhere in there was the reason why somebody hated, no, more than hated, feared Lorrimer enough to want him removed for ever.

Pearce put his head round the door. "Young lady to see you, sir. A Miss Emerson."

Markby uttered a startled exclamation and scrambled to his feet as Sara was ushered in by Pearce who had a simple look on his face. No wonder, thought Markby, the girl was very pretty. Eve Owens's daughter might be expected to be good-looking, but in fact she did not resemble her mother much. Her hair was fair and her eyes blue, and only around the mouth and chin could a likeness to her mother be seen. There was a china doll clarity to her complexion and the youthful plumpness he recalled from a chance encounter some two or three years previously, had given way to a more mature roundness of young womanhood.

Old men chase young girls, thought Markby. And it's not surprising. The sad thing is, they sometimes catch them and then they find out what very old men they are. It's not just the body, it's the mind. The minds of the young are like blotting paper. They soak up information, impressions, experience. Later on it takes a hammer and chisel to engrave it on a brain turned to marble. And the young are a strange mixture, selfish and callous, yet so often easily hurt and frightened.

He wondered, looking at this girl, which of these qualities was uppermost in her at the moment. He knew he was at a disadvantage. He wondered if she knew it. Perhaps she did. Youthful mistakes she would continue to make a-plenty. But beneath all that she was an intelligent young woman. He pulled out a chair for her politely, finding himself adopting an avuncular air which he disliked and she probably despised. "What's brought you along, Sara?" He hoped his stomach wouldn't rumble.

"You told Merry you might want to talk to us." She sat with her shapely round knees pressed together and her hands clasped. She wore a royal blue linen culotte skirt and a white shirt beneath which she was obviously braless. The sunlight shone from the window on to her face at an angle and showed up the pale golden down on her cheeks. Her blue eyes stared directly at him. "So I came here, because I don't want you coming to the house. That sounds rude . . ." She paused and frowned, her smooth forehead puckering. "I know you're giving me away and you were Robert's friend and Mummy likes you and all the rest of it. I don't mean I don't want you to come to the house as a friend. But I don't want you coming as a policeman."

"Generally, people don't," he said wryly.

She flushed. "It's not because we're crooks! We don't have anything to hide! But Mummy's upset. It's the wedding and this—this awful thing which happened to Phil . . ."

"Ah yes, Mr. Lorrimer," said Markby easily, settling back into his chair. "Tell me about him, Sara."

"Why me?" she returned fiercely, glaring at him.

"Because I never met him and I know little about him and so I must talk to people who did know him. I have, you see, to get to know him, to get to know him very well."

She looked impatient, slightly aggressive and scornful. "I can't tell you anything about him. I used to see him quite often when I lived at the rectory but I've a flat in London now and I'm engaged. Philip wasn't a boyfriend. He just lived nearby."

"When you saw him, was it just round and about in the village or at his cottage?"

A flicker in the blue eyes. A fraction less assurance in the bold manner. "Both. I mean, not at the cottage much. At the studio because that's where he was most of the day. It was quite interesting watching him work. Well, it was for a bit. After a while it gets pretty boring."

"Never try your hand at it?"

"Once or twice." She hesitated and then said frankly, "I wasn't any good."

"And what did you talk about, as you watched him work?"

"Nothing—all sorts of things. He explained about pottery. He talked about things which happened in the village."

"Did he ever talk of feeling ill?"

Now the loss of composure was more obvious. She was getting agitated.

"No—only hangovers. He used to go to the pub, the Dun Cow, most evenings. I went there with him once but I didn't like it. It was full of peculiar people."

"Peculiar people?"

"Yes, you know ... funny old men with terrier dogs on bits of string and awful boys with spots and their motorbikes parked outside."

"Did you know Mr. Lorrimer smoked cannabis, Sara?" Markby asked mildly.

"No!"

"Have you ever tried it?"

She hesitated. "Sometimes, at the parties I used to go to. I don't go to them any more."

"What about Mr. Elliott?" he asked suddenly.

"Does he smoke marijuana? How on earth should I know? And even if I did, which I don't, I wouldn't tell you! I'm not a snooper!"

"All right, did you ever meet any of Lorrimer's other friends or did he tell you about them?"

"No. I don't know if he had any. I met someone who did business with him—a man. He came to the studio once while I was there to see about an order. I don't know his name, but I think his shop was here in Bamford. Look, that's all I can tell you." She got up. "I haven't seen Phil for months."

"All right. Thank you for coming in."

She hesitated. "Merry says there will be an inquest."

"Yes, but you won't need to come."

"Will there be a jury?"

"No, it's only a preliminary inquiry. There may be a fuller inquest later, perhaps with a jury. It depends on the coroner." They both stood up. "As you rightly pointed out when you came in here," Markby said gently, "I do wear two hats in this business. As a policeman I'm paid to make a nuisance of myself. As a private individual I consider it an honour to be asked to give you away. I dare say, though, you'd rather someone else was due to take that responsibility."

"It doesn't matter who does it," she said frankly. "I don't mind you doing it. I wish it was all over with."

"Bit of an ordeal, getting married," said Markby with a flash of memory.

"I'd rather have got married in London," she said. "Not in that fusty old church in the village."

"Oh? Whose idea was it, to use the village church?"

"Jon suggested it. He said his family would like it.
They're all a bit dull and stodgy and when he said he was
going to marry an actress's daughter they didn't like it too
much and Jon said being married in the village church
looked sort of nice and cosy and folksy and they'd like it."

"In-laws . . ." murmured Markby, another memory
jogged. "I see."

Sara was shown out by the besotted Pearce, passing by
a flushed young constable on the desk. Markby, watching
through the half-shut door, reflected that if Sara was going
to make a habit of dropping in at the station, he'd have to
arrange for bromide to be put in the canteen tea.

He pulled out the Yellow Pages and listed all the gift
shops in Bamford and the two nearest towns. He gave the
out-of-town lists to Pearce, saying, "This'll wipe that
smirk off your face!" and took the Bamford ones himself.
He was in luck. The second shop he visited stocked pottery made by Philip Lorrimer.

"Yes, I went out there," said the owner, a harassed individual with thinning hair and a testy manner. "I liked his
work. It sold quite well, especially the ash-trays and coffee
mugs. He was unreliable about deliveries though. It didn't
matter so much to me, because I could drive out and pick
up the stuff myself, but I think he lost a few orders elsewhere because of it."

Mr. Furlow, the shop-owner, did not remember seeing a
girl there. He would not have taken any notice if there had
been. He supposed young men like Lorrimer always had
girls around. No, he had never seen Lorrimer ill. He was
sorry Lorrimer was dead. They had been planning a new
line in personalized coffee mugs. They'd have made nice
little gifts, Mr. Furlow explained.

Markby stared round his shop, filled with nice little
gifts. Stuffed toys hideously over-priced. Grotesque porce-
lain figurines. Remarkably vulgar comic items. Printed
tee-shirts. Large pink and blue nylon furry dice. In the
background were a number of unpacked boxes.

"Christmas stuff," said Mr. Furlow.

"It's only September."

"Got to have it on the shelves by the middle of next month," said Mr Furlow severely.

Markby retreated, but at the door paused to ask curiously, "Who buys it?"

"All sorts," and Mr. Furlow confidently. "Youngsters collect the stuffed toys and these here." He picked up a specimen. "Got suction pads on its paws. You stick them on your car window."

"Very dangerous," said Markby sternly, "obscuring your view." He walked away wondering if after all, when the history of the culture of our times came to be written, it would all come down to personalized coffee mugs and stuffed animals clinging by suction pads to car windows.

"Meredith," Sara said at breakfast on the morning of the inquest. "I want to come with you."

"No, you don't, Sara, it will only upset you." Meredith pushed away her cup and glanced at her watch.

Sara leaned forward earnestly. "I won't make a fuss. I'll just sit quiet. But I've got to come. Honestly, Merry, I must!"

"There will be some nasty details discussed," Meredith argued. "What's the point in it?"

"The point is, I want to come and I'm not a child!"

Meredith stared at her god-daughter's flashing eyes and then let her own gaze drop to the ruby cluster on the third finger of Sara's left hand. "Fair enough. You're not. Come along then, I'm going to be late and the coroner will tell me off."

It was an unpleasant hour. Sara kept her promise and sat without moving and for the most part in silence, but when the medical evidence was being given she uttered a whimper like a hurt puppy. Meredith gripped her hand and felt her god-daughter's fingers close on hers. Sara's palm was damp with perspiration.

Outside, in a chilly breeze, they faced one another. "I did warn you," Meredith said.

"Yes, I know." Sara stared at her feet.

Peter Russell, who had given evidence as the first medical man on the scene, came striding up to them at that moment, the wind playing havoc with his thinning hair. He glowered at Meredith and looked solicitously down on Sara.

"What on earth are you doing here, Sal?" He turned aggressively on Meredith. "Why did you bring her?"

"I wanted to come," Sara said, before Meredith could answer. "I asked Merry to bring me. She didn't want to." She drew a deep breath. "Excuse me. No, Merry, don't come!" She turned and bolted towards the door marked "Ladies."

"Poor little thing," Russell muttered.

"She knew Philip. It's upsetting."

"Nasty little creep!" Russell exclaimed. "Lorrimer, I mean!" He saw she looked startled. "He was no loss. See here, I'm a doctor and like priests we hear and learn all sorts of things we can't always repeat. Take it from me, Lorrimer was a wart on the skin of humanity." His gaze drifted towards the door of the ladies."

It opened and Sara came out, composed but even paler. Russell walked to meet her and stopped over her. "If you're still feeling upset about this in a day or two, Sal, call by my surgery and I'll write you a prescription."

"Okay, Peter, thanks," Sara mumbled and he looked suddenly quite miserable.

Oh, lor, Meredith thought. Trust poor little Sara to misread the signs and get it all wrong! It's not Eve that Russell is interested in—it's Sara herself! He might be old enough to be her father, but the poor bloke is head over heels in love! Desperate about it, too, probably. Thinks he hasn't a hope in Hades. Nor has he, probably.

First love is always painful, she reflected ruefully, but last love can be a wretched, painful business, too. The fear of being too late and seeing happiness appear suddenly on the road in front of you and disappear again before you can catch up with it. Poor Russell.

"Come on," said Meredith resignedly. "Let's go home."

The scene had not gone unremarked in other quarters. Alan Markby had come out of the court-room and was waiting his chance to speak to Meredith and more especially to Sara, whose obvious distress he had noted. He saw her bolt into the ladies' room and frowned thoughtfully. He waited patiently and unobserved until she came out and he saw Russell go to speak to her—and the expression on the doctor's face.

"Talk about a dying duck in a thunderstorm," he muttered. "Staring at the kid as if she were the Grail. Where, if anywhere, does all this fit in?"

He stepped forward with the intention of finding out and found his way barred by a sprightly figure in a check cap.

"Locke!" said the figure. "Major Locke, retired. The Old Schoolhouse. You'll remember me perhaps, chief inspector."

"Yes!" said Markby briefly, trying to get round him and catch Meredith and Sara before they drove off.

"I've been trying to have a word with you fellows. Your sergeant said I should see you."

Markby sighed. "Yes, Major Locke?"

"It's about this fellow, Lorrimer. I expect you recall my right of way trouble."

It was as well he had a good memory and was not misled into thinking the major referred to some intimate surgical problem. "Yes, Major Locke. I thought all that was settled. In any case, this is hardly the moment." Markby cast an agonized glance towards his retreating quarry. "I'd really like to—"

"I thought you'd remember," said Major Locke complacently. "Well, when local people were so difficult about it, I got up a petition amongst the new residents in the village. I thought we'd all stand together. After all, there was a principle at stake. Agents sell off these white elephants of buildings as suitable for conversion and all the rest of it and when a fellow tries to do it, he finds some pettifogging mediaeval regulation in his way. But that fellow Lorrimer, he was just damn rude and wouldn't sign. And he'd always been so pleasant until then. Butter wouldn't melt in his mouth, in fact. He was deuced offensive—and to my wife."

"Really, sir?" Meredith was opening the car door. Markby tried in vain to catch her eye.

"We had a real stinker of a row, he and I, and after that

we didn't speak. The thing is, I felt I ought to tell you that
he and I were on bad terms. In case anyone else told you.
What with his being murdered."

"I hadn't got you down as a suspect, major," said
Markby wearily. "But thank you for coming forward."

"He was an impudent young fellow! A wrong 'un, if
you ask me." Locke leaned forward and added mysteri-
ously, "Made a bit of trouble for others, too."

"Look," Markby said hurriedly, "I'm much obliged, but
if you would just excuse me . . ."

"That's why they had the—"

"Good-bye!" Markby exclaimed and broke into a run,
leaving Major Locke standing with his mouth open. He
was too late. The car with Meredith and Sara had pulled
out into the main road and was already receding from
sight in a line of traffic. "Hell!" Markby said with deep
feeling.

They drove along the road until they reached the B road
turn which led to the village. Meredith took it and a little
way along drew into the entry to a field and stopped. She
turned in the seat and surveyed her silent passenger.

"Want to get out for a bit?"

"I'm okay."

They sat in further silence for a while. Meredith wound
down the window. It was a pleasant, peaceful autumn
morning. Red and yellow leaves drifted down from the
trees. "Listen," she said at last. "You know I'm on your
side, don't you?" Sara nodded. The fingers of her right
hand fiddled with the ruby cluster on her left, turning it
round and round. "Have you thought any more about what
you mentioned the first night I was here?"

"Yes, and I shouldn't have mentioned it to you, Merry.
I'm sorry I bothered you with it."

"But you did and I can't just forget it. What did you tell
Markby, Sara, when you went to see him the other day?"

"Nothing. I couldn't tell him anything. I said I used to
know Phil when I lived here for a bit. Then after Robert
died, I got the job in London at the crèche and got a flat.
And I knew Jon by then anyway, so I didn't see Phil any-
more."

"You didn't see him the day before he died?"

Sara's blue eyes fixed her in horror as if Meredith had revealed some supernatural gift. "No, of course not!"

Meredith took a deep breath. "I think you did. I think the afternoon when your mother and I were in Bamford, you walked down to see Lorrimer. If I had to guess, I reckon you went the back way, through the garden door."

"No!" The desperation in Sara's voice was heart-breaking but Meredith steeled herself against it.

"There was a fresh clay smear on the sleeve of your anorak the second time I borrowed it. Sara, I'm on your side! Look, it's not some dreadful criminal offence to go and see someone who was at one time quite a close friend. You did see him, didn't you?"

Sara bit her lip and nodded. "Yes. I was upset about the row with Mummy over the wedding dress. I don't want to cause her any worry, Merry, I've done enough of that. But the dress—if you saw it you'd know what I mean. It's the sort of thing in which someone like Mummy would look stunning, but I'd just look vulgar. Jon's family—they're really ultra-respectable. They turn their noses up a bit at me already. If they saw me coming down the aisle dressed up like someone in an old forties film musical—well, I can imagine their faces. Jon would be embarrassed. I can't wear that dress the way it is, Merry, but Mummy just won't see it!" Sara clapped her hands together in frustration. "She never asks!"

"I know," Meredith said. "When I was her bridesmaid she had me tricked out in taffeta with a puffed-out skirt. I think I must have looked like one of those celluloid dolls people win at shooting booths. Go on."

"I wanted to talk to someone, anyone! You'd gone into Bamford with Mummy and Albie was on the phone to the States. Albie's nice, you know. He is, really. I like talking to Albie. He always listens and says funny things and cheers me up. He's been Mummy's friend for years and years and always stood by her when she's been in trouble . . . like when she was trying to divorce Hughie and of course, when Daddy died."

Why did everyone talk about Mike? It was as if they were all obsessed by him and felt he had to be brought into everything. Eleven years dead and gone. No, just gone. Not dead. Not in me. Sometimes, thought Meredith, I wish he were. I wish I could forget him. I wish he'd go away and not always hover at my shoulder like this.

"So I went to see Phil," Mike's child was saying. "I went the way you said, through the garden. Phil was in his studio."

"What did he say?"

"He said—he said he knew I was visiting but he hadn't expected to see me. He asked me if I wanted any coffee."

"How was he? I mean, cheerful? Working? Did he look ill?"

"He said he wasn't feeling very well. He was working but it was all going badly because he felt rotten. He was in a bad temper. . . . He said he was just going to break off and make himself the coffee."

"And you went with him up to the cottage?"

"Yes . . ." Sara shook back her loose hair and her voice gained more assurance. "We went into the kitchen and Phil made coffee for himself but not for me because I didn't want any. He drank a lot of coffee. He used to put three spoonfuls of sugar in every cup. I don't know how he could . . ."

"Yes. What else did you do?"

"Nothing!"

"Come on! He didn't suggest you smoke a social joint, by any chance? He did have cannabis in that cottage, didn't he? The police found it."

Sara swallowed. "Yes, he did suggest it but I refused. I did—I did at one time . . . a long time ago. But I haven't, not for ages . . . I didn't want to start again."

"So, what then?"

"He grumbled about the old man next door to him. Nothing else. I came away and left him there." She turned large, luminous blue eyes on to Meredith. "I didn't go back and I didn't see him again, honestly, Merry. There's nothing to help Alan Markby and I don't want to tell him. It won't make any difference. The inquest is over." She leaned forward and grabbed at Meredith's arm. "Don't tell him, Merry! He'll come asking me questions again, he'll want to know why I didn't tell him about it! I don't want him asking me questions. Merry, don't make me—please!"

"All right, all right!" Meredith soothed.

"Thanks." Sara fell back in her seat. "You're all right, Merry."

"Soft, more like." Meredith hesitated. "About your mother, Sara, I doubt she's interested in Peter Russell and I'm not convinced he's interested in her. So don't go trying to further any little romance there, will you? You could come an awful cropper. And about the other matter you mentioned, the friend you say you have who has been threatened—"

"Oh, that's all right," Sara said quickly. "Things have changed."

"Oh? Since when?"

"They just have. It's okay, Merry. Just forget about it."

Meredith stared at her in some exasperation. "For crying out loud, you come to me with this story—" She broke off and, trying to keep her voice level, went on, "All right, we'll leave it. But I think you should tell Alan that you saw Phil the day before he died. It will help him fill a kind of diary of Lorrimer's last days."

"No!" Sara glared at her fiercely.

"Why not?"

"He'll come to the rectory and Mummy will find out and start worrying about me. She'll wonder why I went to see Phil—and it doesn't matter that I saw him!" Sara was beating her clenched fists on her knees, then said in a pitiable voice, "Oh Merry, why does everything go wrong?"

"It's called life," Meredith said unsympathetically. "And you'd better start getting used to the idea. And while you're about it, here's another fact to mull over. You're nineteen, not a kid. Don't expect people to treat you the way they did when you were a lisping tot. They won't. They expect you to make responsible decisions. I think you're right about the dress, but you shouldn't have gone behind your mother's back. She is paying for it. Explain to her how you feel politely but firmly. And I want you to think again about talking to Alan Markby—and about talking to me."

Her god-daughter's pretty snub-nosed face was set obstinately in its frame of long fair hair. She reminded Meredith of a stubborn pekinese. She wound up the window and switched on the engine. It had been a long morning and for one day enough was enough.

Eight

"Oh, sorry, Mrs. Yewell!" said Meredith apologetically, coming into the drawing room and finding the daily ferociously beating the sofa cushions. "I didn't know you were still in here—I'm used to hearing you sing."

"Singing!" exclaimed Mrs. Yewell in a muffled voice. "As if a body was ever likely to sing another note, that's what!"

"Is something wrong?" asked Meredith cautiously, peering at her.

Mrs. Yewell raised a flushed, puffed face from her task and stood clasping a cushion to the bosom of her already well-filled orange overall. "What's to sing about? What with the disgrace of it and the shocking things said. And all of it's lies, wicked lies, every word!" She grew visibly more heated as she spoke, her round face glowing crimson and shiny with emotion.

"Who has said what, Mrs. Yewell?" asked Meredith practically.

"Lies!" repeated Mrs. Yewell fiercely. "To think I've lived in this village all my life. Born and bred here, and Walter, he was, too.... You go over to that churchyard and see how many Yewells is buried over there, go on!" ordered the daily as if Meredith had demurred.

"Yes, as a matter of fact, I had noticed," she said hurriedly.

"Ah!" said Mrs. Yewell, sounding marginally more composed. "Us and the Stouts are the oldest village families and there's no Stouts left now except old Fred and Myrtle as is married to Harry Linnet at the Dun Cow. She was a Stout. Last of the Stouts to leave was young Trevor

115

when he married and got the job in the bus garage in Bamford. Couldn't get a council house here and couldn't buy, of course, prices being what they are. That leaves us Yewells and we've always had a good name! Grandad was parish clerk to Reverend Markby. Dad, he was air-raid warden during the last war. Not that we had no air-raids, not proper. But he had to go round on a bike in case folk left a light showing, on account of the air-field at Cherton. All Yanks it was. Used to come in the Dun Cow."

"Mrs. Yewell," said Meredith impatiently. "This is all very interesting but what's actually happened to upset you this morning? Not war-time American pilots in the Dun Cow, I'm sure."

"Upset? I'm upset right enough!" retorted Mrs. Yewell vehemently. "It's what folk are saying about Uncle Bert and all on account of that there murder. Terrible business that is. We never had nothing like that in the village in the old days when it was all village folk! We didn't go murdering one another. Couple of lads might have a bit of a dust-up of a Saturday at closing time outside the Dun Cow and that was it. They didn't go murdering and poisoning! And Uncle Bert, he never had nothing to do with it!"

Meredith recognized the daily's reminiscent rambling now as the desperate search of a frightened and ill-educated mind for a lost security and eyed her thoughtfully. Mrs. Yewell gave her a look of infinite majesty and hurled the cushion on to the sofa like a Juno who had borrowed one of her husband's thunderbolts.

"Who is gossiping, Mrs. Yewell, and what have they said?"

"They all is, behind our backs!" said Mrs. Yewell darkly. "Especially that trollop what lives down in what used to be tied cottages. It was Mary what told me—Mary, what does for Dr. Russell over at the Rose Cottage. Pearl, she says—that's me . . ."

Pearl? thought Meredith. That was a choice of name which tempted fate. Alas for Pearl's parents. Red-faced, brawny Mrs. Yewell tipped the scales at fifteen stone.

"Pearl, she says, you oughta know what folk are saying."

"Very kind of Mary, I'm sure," Meredith observed drily.

The dryness was not lost on Mrs. Yewell who appreciated it at its worth. "Ah, you're right there, miss. Pleased as punch she was to be able to tell me. Couldn't keep the smile off of her silly face. Folk says, she sez, folk says as your Uncle Bert has got his shed full of poisons and that young Mr. Lorrimer, he drunk one of them by mistake."

"I'm sure that's not true, Mrs. Yewell. Tell the people who say so that the police have established that's not so."

"You can't tell 'em anything," said Mrs. Yewell. "They makes up their own silly minds. Now I'm not saying it isn't partly the old fool's own fault. If Walter has told Uncle Bert once about clearing out that shed, I'm sure he's told him twenty times. But it's like talking to a brick wall. He's turned eighty, you know, Uncle Bert, and when they get that age you can't argue with them. And I know he said things he ought not to have done to Mr. Lorrimer about them cats. Well, they kept digging in Uncle Bert's veg. Naturally he got upset. But he wouldn't never really put down poison. He just said it. He says all sorts, Uncle Bert, and don't mean it. He don't know it. He don't know half the time what he does say. And the other half he knows what he's saying but don't mean a word of it. He's past eighty. They gets like children. Says things to be awkward."

"Look here, Mrs. Yewell," said Meredith briskly. "I think you ought to go along to the kitchen and have a cup of tea with Lucia."

" 'Tisn't our elevenses, not yet," said Mrs. Yewell obstinately. "I got the downstairs lav to do yet."

"A change in routine won't hurt for once, not in the circumstances. Go and sit down for a bit. If you like, I'll clean out the downstairs cloakroom."

But that was trespassing on Mrs. Yewell's preserve. "I can do my job, miss, even if I am a bit put out over Uncle Bert!" she said starchily. "I don't need no one to do my job for me!" She bustled out in high dudgeon.

Meredith left the house and walked down the lane to the cottages. The press had departed for the moment, that at least was some consolation. The police had gone, too, for the time being. Numerous tyre tracks churning up the grass verges were mute witnesses of the crowds which had briefly descended on them. Meredith put her hands in her pockets and stared at Philip's front door. After a moment, because there seemed to be no one about, she opened the gate, walked down the path and, shielding her eyes with her hand, peered through the unwashed window of the sitting room. It was in incredible disorder, even worse than when she had been in there seeking the telephone. The police had made their own search and she wondered whether they had had any more luck than the murderer.

The furniture, such as she could see of it, was old, poor and rickety. It was the sort of thing picked up for a pound or two by the sort of firms which specialized in house clearances and sold whatever was got for whatever it fetched, bundles of forks and spoons for fifty pence, chairs a fiver each. Philip had probably bought this lot in Bamford and if the furniture together, upstairs and down, had cost him more than fifty quid she'd be surprised. He had probably lived on breakfast cereals, bacon and sausages, cheese and baked beans. His electricity bill was probably high because of the kiln . . . and there was the cats' food, the two siamese had to be fed properly. But apart from those expenses he had lived cheaply which was not surprising because he could not have made that much from the pottery. Yet he had been, according to Bert, always "propping up the bar in the Dun Cow." How could he afford that? By selling a little of his home-grown cannabis in pubs in Bamford? Not likely, it had only been a plot the size of a pocket handkerchief.

Meredith moved away from the window and walked round to the back of the cottage with the idea of calling—she feared vainly—for Tom. Markby had said they had not yet contacted any next of kin. But there must be family somewhere and if Philip had money to spend in the Dun Cow, quite possibly it had come from relatives who "subbed" him with a ten-pound note in the post from time to time. If so, he hadn't kept the letters or Markby would have found them and traced the family from them. She felt irritably that there was a gap in their knowledge. She, who was a new arrival, could not be expected to know much about Philip. But apparently no one did.

Unless Sara did. Meredith stopped and bit her lip. Sara, when she had first come to live in the village with Eve and Robert Freeman, had spent hours down here at the cottage, talking to Philip, watching him work, trying her hand at throwing clay. If anyone knew about Philip, Sara did.

A movement in the next garden caught her eye. Bert emerged from his shed and scurried down his path carrying a shallow wooden box and leaving the shed door creaking and swaying in the breeze behind him. Meredith went to the fence and called over it, "Good morning, Bert!"

Bert came to a halt, glowered at her from beneath his cap brim and then moved a few feet closer to the fence. "What's good about it, eh?"

"Mrs. Yewell, your niece," she said, "was telling me that there's been gossip in the village about your shed. I know the police don't think it had anything to do with it, but you really ought to clear it out, you know."

"She's me niece by marriage, Pearl is," he said pedantically. "Walter, he's me nephew. And Pearl, she's me niece by marriage. And I don't give a tinker's cuss for what they says in this village. They're all daft buggers, any road."

"Can I come round?" Meredith asked. "I'd like to see your garden. I hear you've won prizes."

Bert brightened. "Ah, you can squeeze through that hole there in the fence where the planks is missing, thin body like you."

"No wonder the cats came through," said Meredith, complying. "Have you seen Mr. Lorrimer's cat, by the way? I'm trying to catch him."

"No, I ain't seen it!" said Bert crossly. "And if I does, I'll chuck a brick at it. If it's gone off, good riddance. Dead, I hopes, like the other one."

"What about the other one?" she asked sharply. Bert leered at her and she went on, "I found the other one dead in the churchyard, but I didn't want to tell Mr. Lorrimer so I covered it over with a branch. Did you move it?"

"No, I never!" he said sullenly. "But I seen it. I never had nothing to do with that." He shuffled his feet. "I never moved it."

"Bert . . ." said Meredith firmly. "Where did you put the dead cat? The police want to examine it."

"Whaffor?" he retaliated, glaring at her. "Lot of nonsense. What do them bobbies want with a dead cat? I put it on me bonfire, if you wants to know . . . bonfire what I got going in the corner of the churchyard. And I'll tell you why, and all—it's because I'd get the blame if anyone saw it. They'd say I'd gone and put down poison for it . . . but I never did. I saw it dead there under that branch. You wants to do something double-quick about that, Bert, I says to meself. And I gets it out and burns it, so there!"

Meredith sighed. It might be wise to leave Markby in ignorance of this fact. "Where are your best vegetables, Bert?"

"Wrong time of the year to see my prize veg," he said. "Carrits was good. I got a first for me carrits. I got the spring greens coming along now." He pointed at the shallow tray he had set down. "Cabbidges. I grows 'em for folk to plant out. Walter, I promised him a dozen and he's supposed to come by for them."

Meredith looked about her. The garden was a miracle of neatness. She wandered towards the door of the shed and peeped in. There could have been no greater contrast. Tins, some of them rusted completely and without any labels, were stacked in corners. Ancient and broken implements hung from nails on the walls. Earthenware plant pots rose stacked in unsteady towers. Mysterious cobwebby bottles lined the shelves. Bits of string, odds and ends of sticks, foil milk bottle tops strung on black cotton, old seed packets, mouldy boots and paraffin lamps jostled together, hung from hooks or trailed across like Christmas decorations from one wall to another.

"Honestly, Bert," Meredith said in some awe. "How do you ever find anything?"

"I knows where everything is!" he said crossly. "Don't go touching nothing. Them p'lice was in there poking and prying already. That there bloke in charge, he come jawing at me about it. Get it cleared out, he says, it's a danger. We'll take it away for you if you can't get rid of it. I told him, don't want to get rid of it. It's all good stuff. And it's not dangerous to anyone but me and that's my business!"

Meredith poked at a pile of yellowed dirt-strewn news-papers and picked up the top ones. The headline on the one facing up at her read, "President Tito dies." She re-placed the top ones and read the faded ticket stuck on a bottle of the nearest shelf. It said four shillings and six-pence. An aged wooden carpet-sweeper was embellished with a seated lion over crossed Union Jacks and declared itself "Empire Made." A handleless mug containing some sort of oil showed a picture of George V and Queen Mary.

"All good stuff," repeated Bert obstinately. "And better than what you buys nowadays."

"Bert," Meredith said, seating herself on an upturned bucket. "How long did Mr. Lorrimer live next door to you?"

He rubbed his nose and fixed his rheumy, malicious lit-tle eyes on her. "Best part of four year. And he never done a day's honest work in all that time. Making them little pots all the time, that's all."

"Did he ever have visitors from outside the village? Family?"

"I never seen 'em. He had a little van . . . used to de-liver the pots in it to shops and that. But clutch went and last few months he never had no car nor nothing. Couldn't afford one, he told me. I told him he wanted to save his money and not go giving it to the pubs!"

Enough money for the Dun Cow, then, but not enough to buy a badly-needed new van.

She took the plunge. "You said he had girlfriends there."

He looked shifty. "Women, ah . . . them. Ought to know better. I hears 'em. I knows!" He put his finger to the side of his gnarled nose in the age-old gesture of cunning. He looked completely evil. "I could tell a thing or two, I could."

Meredith tried to control the sudden rapid pounding of her heart. "Have you told the police whatever it is?"

"No!" said Bert stubbornly. "Messing in my shed and telling me to throw away good gardening tools and fertil-izers and slug pellets and all . . . Why should I go and tell 'em anything? Let 'em find out. They's paid for that. Let 'em do a day's work. I'll tell what I know in my own good time, ah!" He moved away. "I got work to do. I can't stand about gossiping. Walter's coming for them spring cabbidges. I said I'd have 'em ready."

He was not going to talk to her any more. If she lingered she would outstay what little welcome she had had. Meredith asked, "If you do see the cat, Bert, try and catch him and come and tell me. I'll take him to the RSPCA."

He muttered at her.

Slowly Meredith walked back to the rectory. Eve was in the drawing room dealing briskly with her day's mail. She looked fresh and bright and wore white trousers and a shocking pink satin blouse with ballooning sleeves and a sash. The sort of outfit, thought Meredith, in which I couldn't stay looking clean and tidy for ten minutes. Eve was smiling indulgently at a sheet of vivid mauve notepaper.

"How sweet . . . This lady says she's been a fan of mine since I first started."

"She must be nearing fifty, then," said Meredith unkindly.

"Now, Merry . . ." Eve put down the mauve notepaper. "Age is immaterial. Look at Sophia, at Elizabeth, at Raquel. Look at me," she added serenely.

"I am looking at you and you look very nice, I'm the first to admit. It takes some doing and I admire you for it, truly. But, Eve—when if ever are you going to grow old gracefully? I mean are you going to look like that for years to come and then suddenly, overnight, turn into an old woman. Like that female in *She* who stepped twice into the fountain of youth?"

"If you look," said Eve confidentially, putting a scarlet-tipped hand to her hair, "I'm letting a few grey hairs show through, mingled with the blonde. My beautician advises it. But the secret is, watch what you eat. That's my advice. And it's what you feel inside, Merry, not just the outside. I feel young inside."

Meredith sat down in the nearest armchair and crossed her legs. "How young, Eve? As young as Lorrimer?"

The violet eyes snapped in a burst of real anger. "I'd like to say I don't know what you mean by that—but of course I do, and it's rubbish. I'm surprised at you, Merry! At least give me credit for good taste!"

For all the seriousness of the situation, Meredith had to smile. "Come clean, Eve. He was a very attractive young man. Were you tripping lightly down to Lorrimer's through the back gate and teaching him the things he didn't learn at mother's knee? Because if you were, Alan Markby will find out."

"I was married to Robert when I came here!" Eve said furiously. "I was very happy with dear Robert. He was the kindest of men!"

"And you miss him? Eve, it's not a crime! You can be lonely. But you've also got to be honest!"

"All right," Eve said calmly. "I'll be honest. No, I didn't have any kind of affair with Lorrimer. Do you really think I'd want to go to bed with some over-enthusiastic boy, pawing me around and talking a lot of romantic nonsense? You must be mad. Nor, incidentally, is Albie my lover."

"I didn't think he was."

"Is it that obvious?" asked Eve, mildly surprised.

"I saw the way he looked at you when I first arrived here. Very proud, kind and paternal. No lust in it. Which there should have been."

Eve was mollified by what she chose to interpret as a compliment. "I've a dear friend in London, as it happens. I don't see him often but it's often enough. He doesn't come here because of Sara. The poor child is hopelessly romantic and would want to marry me off, and marriage isn't in question. So there, are you satisfied?"

Meredith nodded. "Yes. Sorry, Eve, but I had to know. I'm certain Markby is more than efficient at rooting out these little scandals and while I'm more than prepared to fight for your corner, I have to know, when the bell goes, just what power my punches have. If I go out there protesting your virtue, I want to be sure I'm defending something which exists." She grinned. "Or exists as far as Lorrimer is concerned, anyway."

"I like men, and let's face it, any woman wants to be reassured she's still got what it takes," Eve said frankly. "But I'm not promiscuous. Above all, I don't go falling in love. Well, I did love Robert ... but in a friendly sort of way. The only man I ever really loved with passion was Mike."

There was a silence. Meredith looked away from her across the room and her gaze fell on the portrait. She wanted to shout, If you loved him, why did you lead him such a hell of a dance? Why did you drive him away and then, just when the poor bloke had got his life back together, snap your fingers and declare you wanted him back? He didn't know what to do. He was a decent man and you made his life a misery!

She said none of this but perhaps Eve sensed it. Slowly she said, "I did love him, Merry."

"Sure," Meredith said. In her own way, Eve probably had. Well, it was ancient history now, anyway. Dead is dead and gone for ever. Life goes on. She shook herself and got to her feet. "I'm driving into Bamford to do a bit of shopping. Do you want to come or can I bring back anything?"

"Um, no ... yes, some postage stamps, first class. And if you go by that little delicatessen, they sell a locally made cheddar and you could bring a pound of that. Lucia is very fond of it."

Meredith set off. At the outskirts of the village, she passed by Rose Cottage and saw Peter Russell standing in the drive. At her approach he looked up and signalled urgently to her to stop.

She wound down the window as he ran up and asked, panting, "Can you give me a lift? You are going into Bamford? My car won't start."

"Sure, where to?"

"The health centre. I'll show you where you drop me off."

They drove on until the junction with the main road and when they had turned into it and were heading straight for Bamford in a stream of other vehicles, he asked, "How is everyone at the rectory?"

"Bearing up well. You mean Sara, I suppose. She's holding out. She's still pretty nervous underneath it, but I think she'll come through."

There was a silence. Meredith overtook a pantechnicon. Russell asked quietly, "Is it that obvious?"

"I saw how you looked at her after the inquest."

"Making a fool of myself, aren't I?" he said soberly.

"I didn't say that. She's a pretty kid, full of life, why shouldn't you take a fancy to her? Only be warned, she thinks you're keen on her mum."

"People would be more forgiving if I was, wouldn't they?"

"I'm not criticizing you. I'd rather you than Lazenby, frankly. But at the moment I have to say she only has eyes for the unspeakable Jonathan."

She felt sorry for him. She liked him, but there was nothing she could do or say. You can't always have the person you love. I ought to know that, Meredith thought.

She put him down outside his surgery, drove on into the centre and parked. She carried out Eve's commissions first because if she forgot them Eve would be sadly reproachful like a spaniel whose owner has omitted to bring back the doggy chocs. She bought the cheese and some pâté, a postcard of old Bamford to send Toby and went along to the post office and bought the stamps for Eve and for her own postcard. Then she found a store in a side street which sold in bulk to the catering business and persuaded them to sell her a giant-sized bottle of Lea and Perrins sauce. She put the lot in her carrier bag and retired to the little restaurant she had previously visited with Eve.

It was nearly lunchtime now. The shop did light meals and a sprinkling of shoppers and local business people were beginning to arrive. Meredith asked for soup and home-made bread and whilst waiting for it, settled down to write her postcard. "Village soulless and inhabitants apt to be murdered," would be truthful but inappropriate on an open postcard. She wrote, "Had a good journey. Weather fine. Hope all goes well." That was about as uninteresting as a postcard could be. Meredith chewed the end of her biro. "Dramatic events but trust they won't interfere with wedding. Will tell all when I get back." That would give Toby something to mull over. The thought of his frustration as he speculated gave her a moment's pleasure.

It was at this point that Markby came upon her. He had

made a resolution not to skip lunch for once and good re-
solves are obviously rewarded after all, because when he
walked into the restaurant the first person his eye lit on
was Meredith, bent over a postcard, scribbling furiously
and smiling to herself. His first impulse of pleasure at seeing her was immediately tempered with an unreasoning
desire to know to whom she wrote with such concentra-
tion—and smiling away like that.

He walked over to her table, put his hand on the back
of the chair opposite hers and said "Hallo." She looked up
startled. "Mind if I join you?" he continued, adding apologetically, "It gets very crowded in here around lunchtime."

"What brings you in here?" she asked, putting away her
biro and postcard.

"My lunch." He smiled amiably at her and requested
chicken salad when the waitress came.

She tossed back her thick brown hair. "How are your in-
vestigations going?"

"Oh, coming along . . ." Markby's glance had fallen on
to her carrier bag on the floor. A peculiar thin-necked bottle of some dark liquid poked out of it. "What's that?"

She glanced down. "It's a bottle of Lea and Perrins
sauce. I'm taking it back for a friend. He's addicted to it."

Markby's heart, which seemed to be acting on a will of
its own which he could not control, now insisted on sinking. "Oh? He's, um, he's English, this friend, is he?"

"Yes, he's my vice." She must have seen the startled
look on his face because she added kindly, "My vice-
consul. Toby Smythe."

He knew he looked embarrassed. He ought not to have
sat here. It was with relief he saw that Meredith's soup had
arrived. She gave him a smile and asked, "You don't mind
if I start, do you?"

"No, go ahead."

Markby watched her pick up her spoon. It would be un-
realistic to assume she hadn't some man in the background. The slight feeling of gloom increased. Not that it
mattered to him, of course. She was just an important witness in a murder inquiry. But she was interesting, intelli-

gent and he didn't quite know why he had first thought her plain. Firmly he told himself to stick to business!

"I'm trying to find out who last saw or spoke to Lorrimer." Was he imagining it or did her hand shake slightly, spilling a little soup?

"It was very early in the morning when I found him. I don't suppose anyone saw him. The murderer didn't have to be there, did he? Not with poison." But someone had been there ransacking the cottage, someone who knew Lorrimer was dead . . .

"I still want to know his last movements. The old man saw him early the morning of the previous day and there was another argument about the cats. You saw him at mid-morning and helped him home since by then he was suffering cramp and vomiting. That's our last firm sighting. What did he do during that afternoon and evening? He wasn't in the Dun Cow. Was he at home, ill?"

Meredith put down her spoon. She looked flushed but his chicken salad had arrived and the conversation was broken. Markby picked up his knife and fork and peered closely at the offering. He was aware that she was staring at him in an antagonistic fashion. He was getting used to that but he wished it were otherwise. He would rather like to see more of her smile. He moved a piece of potato salad to the side of his plate after giving it a speculative glance. "How do you find England after so long abroad?" he asked curiously.

"I do come home fairly often!" The hazel eyes snapped at him, then she added honestly, "I find it odd, to tell you the truth. I feel a stranger. I don't have family except Eve. No brothers or sisters, no parents. If I did have any of those, I'd feel differently about home leaves, I dare say."

"What made you pick a job which takes you away so much?" He realized as he asked it that it was basically a foolish question and an impertinent one as well. The look he received from her told him so. "Sorry," he apologized. "I shouldn't have asked that. It doesn't have anything to do with present inquiries."

She was staring thoughtfully at his salad as if its composition puzzled her. Markby was beginning to have serious second thoughts about it himself.

She said quietly, "Why does anyone take up any kind of job? What made you a policeman?"

"A fascination with the practical application of the law and with what used fashionably to be called 'the criminal mind'. I have a sister who is a practising solicitor, and very good she is too, but that kind of paper-shuffling, small-print-reading law isn't for me."

"Between you," she said, "you seem to have the legal process tied up."

He grinned at her. "No, we lack a judge in the family."

She said soberly, "It takes a particular kind of person to be a judge. You have to be able to stand aloof, not let emotions prompt you, and be sure that the one thread you have picked out of the tangled skein is the right one."

"No," he said, "that is being a detective."

She studied him for a moment and it occurred to him ruefully that she had no idea how expressive her thickly lashed hazel eyes were. Suddenly she said briskly, "Well, I was good at languages, wanted to travel, don't mind a reasonable amount of paper-shuffling or getting called out at odd hours. It seemed a career which would suit me." She stooped and picked up her bag. "I'm sorry I can't stay until you finish your lunch. It's nice to see you. Enjoy your salad."

She had caught him on the hop. He had just taken a mouthful of food. He attempted to stand up, clutched at his napkin and knocked the menu in its plastic stand off the table.

"Please, don't bother!" said Meredith graciously and walked off before he could do much other than mumble through a mouthful of chicken at her. He saw her pause by the cash register to pay her bill. She didn't look his way again. Markby pushed away his uneaten salad.

Meredith went back to her car and sat in it, staring unseeingly through the windscreen. She was glad she had only ordered soup because she felt sick. It was stupid to let a short, fairly simple conversation upset her, but it had on two accounts.

There was Sara of course. Poor Sara was by no means the actress her mother was and Markby must have realized she was hiding something when they had talked in his office. Had he worked out that Sara had been to see Lorrimer that last afternoon, despite her claim that she had not seen him for months? That she was probably the last person to see and talk to him? The common assumption was that the last person to see a murder victim all too often turned out to be the killer. However, poison was different, especially in this case which involved slow poison over a period of time. She wished Sara had told Markby the truth. Her failure only worsened an already unsatisfactory situation. This is how complications come about, she thought. First you're less than frank about something trifling and you end up being downright shifty. Then you can't come clean.

The consequences of Lorrimer's death were not alone in upsetting her. Ever since her arrival, or perhaps ever since receiving Eve's invitation, the ghost of Mike had been resurrected from his uneasy grave to hover about her. Why did you join the consular service, Meredith? Because I'd fallen in love with my cousin's husband, that's why. Because I was desperate to get away to an entirely new life among people who were only ships that pass, who wouldn't ask questions about me and basically couldn't care less. People like Toby, who knew she was Eve's cousin, could be curious, but she had become adept at fending them off.

It had been a funny sort of love-affair to carry on her back through life. Like Sinbad with the Old Man of the Sea she was unable to set her burden down. It had begun when a leggy bridesmaid in an unsuitable dress had developed a crush on the bridegroom. Such things had happened before. But in her case, instead of growing out of it, she had grown into it. She'd become older but no wiser, gone to university, made a career and throughout had continued to carry that little passion in her heart. No boyfriend had ever come near to rivalling it.

As for Eve, in that time she had become more beautiful and capricious. She was repeatedly unfaithful but always contrite, promising never again. Mike, bewildered, had seen the girl he married turn into someone he could not understand or whose attention he could not keep. Meredith had been the one into whose sympathetic ear he had poured his troubles. Meredith, ever loyal, as she thought wryly now, providing tea and sympathy and eventually more than that . . .

No wonder, she thought as she took up the ignition keys, that she was out of sorts now. Markby had roused a veritable hornets' nest of memories. He was a nice man, Alan Markby. An attractive man, but her priority now was to get this whole leave over with. To get away back to her job and the world she knew and with which she could cope. To that end, this business of Lorrimer had to be cleared up pronto. Time to do a little sleuthing on your own account, Meredith. The engine sprang into life.

It took a little while to find the depot of the dairy. She looked up the address in a tattered telephone directory in a roadside kiosk and discovered it lay out of town. When she found it at last it was easily identifiable by a row of milk vans similar to that which delivered to the rectory parked in the forecourt. Meredith got out and sniffed. The place emitted an insidious, sour-cream smell. A notice pinned on the nearest van read, "Ask your milkman about potatoes." In a large building like a hangar crates rattled and bottles chinked.

In the office was a tallow-haired girl who said, "Gary Yewell? You'll have to go over to the loading bay for him. Hang on, though, he might be having his tea break. Round the back."

Gary wasn't round the back or in the loading bay. He was tracked down at last in the maintenance area for the vans, where he was talking to another youth in a greasy overall. Here the sickly smell of the milk was replaced by the acrid odour of exhaust fumes and fuel. Gary himself was pale and spotty and sullen.

"Who are you?" he asked sulkily. "I suppose none of you will be satisfied until I loses me job. The fuzz has been here I dunno how many times and old Cooper 'as had me up to the office twice. I dunno nothing about it. I just put the milk outside the door."

"I'm sorry to take up your time," said Meredith. "I just

want to know. . . . You come very early to the village. Is anyone about at that time? Do you see many people?"

He shrugged. "No. What, at that hour? The old bloke in the other one of them cottages, he's sometimes up and about in summer-time digging in his blooming garden round the back. That's me great-uncle Bert and he's a miserable old sod and I don't go near him. I hears him coughing but I don't see 'im because I puts the milk down in the front."

"By the front door?" Meredith frowned. "You never saw Mr. Lorrimer in the mornings?"

"Bloke what got done in? No. Never. Not outa bed. Place always quiet as the grave . . ." Gary paused and sniggered. "Anyway, I only ever saw 'im on a Friday evening when I went round the village and collected the money."

"You're related to Mrs. Yewell who cleans at the rectory, I understand?" she asked him.

"Yeah . . . Auntie Pearl. Married to me Uncle Walter. I goes round there on a Friday evening after I got in the money and 'as me tea."

"Does Mrs. Yewell ever talk about the rectory? Her job, her employer?"

"Naw . . ." Gary looked disgusted. "I used to ask her 'cos I thought she might let slip something I could sell to the newspapers. Well, they pays for that kind of thing, don't they? But she never says nothing. Nothing interesting . . . no sex nor nothing. What's your interest, anyway?" Gary's close-set eyes blinked at her.

"Personal!" said Meredith firmly. "Here, have a drink on me!" She gave him a fiver.

"Oh, thanks!" he said. "Sorry I can't help you, love."

Meredith returned to the office and asked, "Can I buy a pint of milk?"

"Yeah, suppose so," said the tallow-haired girl. "Thirty-one pence. Here, you can have this one. It's today's. I only just brought it in." She produced a bottle from a table behind her on which stood an electric kettle and a bag of sugar.

Meredith took her bottle back to the car and wedged it carefully in with Toby's Lea and Perrins. She drove half-

way back to the Old Rectory and pulled into the farm gate
where she had previously stopped on the way back from
the inquest. She recovered the milk bottle and sat studying
the top for a few moments. Then she ran her fingernail
carefully under the foil rim, turning her hand palm up-
wards. It was possible. The foil cap lifted off neatly in one
piece without so much as a bend in it. She replaced it. It
was possible, all right, but it suggested something . . .
something she didn't like at all. She wondered whether
Markby had tried the same experiment and whether the
same thought had struck him.

Nine

The weekend started badly but perhaps that was only to be expected. On Friday, just before lunchtime, a buzz heralded an arrival at the gate and a white Porsche swept up the drive and drew up with a flourish before the front door. Jonathan Lazenby got out. He was wearing a green quilted sleeveless body-warmer over a pullover and a checked cap. He adjusted the cap dashingly over his eyes and went to take his suitcase from the car.

Meredith, watching all this from the window, reflected that if driving in them had not been impractical, Lazenby would certainly have worn green wellies. He looked the complete townie down for a country weekend. His general turn-out and demeanour indicated point-to-point meetings and perhaps a spot of shooting. It was spoiled by being all brand-new. He should have thrown a bit of mud at that body-warmer, she thought. Just to give it that authentic stable yard touch.

Meredith went out into the hall and called upstairs to Sara who came running down and threw herself into his arms with a shriek of "Jon—darling!"

It struck Meredith that Lazenby's response was adequate but a little perfunctory. Perhaps it was just less uninhibited. He was a curiously passionless young man. It seemed to her that the brash aggressive manner was a substitute for genuine emotion and she wondered if he was aware of his own shallowness. She doubted it. Meredith shrugged and retired to the drawing room with some idea of doing the crossword but found Eve already there, staring helplessly at a caterers' invoice.

"I suppose this is right. You will take a look at it, won't
you, Merry? It's all beyond me . . ."

"Lazenby's here," said Meredith bleakly.

Eve brightened visibly. "I'm so glad he's come. It will
cheer poor Sara up. She's been moping. She misses him."

"How do you get on with his family?" asked Meredith
casually, sliding into a chair.

"Dreary people!" returned her cousin with energy. "No,
that's mean of me. The truth is, Merry, that Jonathan's
mother is a good woman and I'm a bad one . . . She makes
me feel humble and I hate it. Who wouldn't?"

"How are they likely to react to a murder on the doorstep just before the wedding?"

Eve sighed. "It will give them even more cause to look
down their noses at us. As if they had anything to be su-
perior about!" she added in a renewed burst of ferocity.
"Oh, I shall be so glad when this wedding is over!"

Jonathan and Sara joined them for a pre-luncheon
sherry. He was looking more than usually truculent and
Meredith wondered what the lovebirds had been talking
about. More tendentious matters than an exchange of
sweet nothings by the look of it. Sara looked subdued, her
earlier vivacity quite gone. Remembering her impulsive
greeting of Lazenby, Meredith felt a movement of anger
against him. His wedge-shaped, clever-handsome face was
flushed and his hair brushed flat across the top of his head
so that his features seemed set in a triangle. He stood before the fireplace with one hand in his pocket and his glass
in the other. He had taken off the green body-warmer and
wore a cashmere sweater and suede chukka boots with immaculate twill slacks.

"I don't like the way this has been handled. We're all in
a spotlight here."

"They'll go away," Eve said plaintively. "They do eventually—the press I mean. One just has to ignore them."

"This isn't showbiz!" he said sharply. "Any publicity
isn't better than no publicity!"

Albie Elliott, who had drifted in as he spoke and lurked
behind Eve, now put out a thin pale hand and briefly

touched Eve's shoulder. "You're just a little out of date, sonny. Bad publicity we can all do without."

Lazenby flushed. "We could certainly do without this! What have the police come up with?"

"They're doing their best," said Meredith, wondering how Alan Markby would take this tepid vote of confidence, were he able to hear it.

"I'll get in touch with the Chief Constable," Lazenby muttered. "This has got to be bloody well cleared up before we all get dragged into it. They'll mix reports of the murder hunt with reports of the wedding and the whole thing will be a complete shambles. The press have already had a field-day. There was a photograph of this house in one of the tabloids, obviously taken through the gates. I'll get on to the local nick about it and if they continue to do that sort of thing, I'll write to the Press Council."

"You're going to be busy," said Meredith. "Contacting all these people."

"Merry!" exclaimed Sara in shocked tones.

Lazenby's mouth tightened and a pulse jumped in his neck. "I came back from the States twelve hours early because I know how these things can get out of hand! Now then, the cook and the daily cleaner must be warned about the dangers of talking to anyone outside the house. They are the sort of people the yellow press pump for titbits of information."

"You're a trifle late," Meredith informed him. "We've already been through all that. I think you'll find the police haven't much sympathy with our press problem."

"What about that chap Markby? Isn't he a copper? He's supposed to be a family friend. What's he doing about it, apart from damn-all?"

"He's working very hard on what is a tricky and nasty case!" Meredith flared up, a little startled to hear the vehemence in her own voice. "And it is very nasty, in case you haven't thought about the practical physical side of it. I found him and he didn't present a very pretty sight!"

"Don't, Merry, please . . ." Sara whispered.

There was an awkward silence. "Sorry," Meredith said ruefully.

"What were you doing down there, anyway?" Lazenby

asked her. Suspicion leapt into his eyes. "Why were you messing about in that studio?"

"I wasn't messing about!" Meredith said angrily. "I went to see what was wrong with the cat."

"If you'd left it alone, we wouldn't be in this fix! Why couldn't you have just left him there and let someone else find him?"

"You'd better not let Alan Markby hear you talk that way!" she retaliated.

"Maybe," said Elliott mildly, "we should just leave it for now. It can wait."

"Yes," Eve said quickly. "I'm sure Lucia has lunch just about ready. Jonathan dear, do open the wine." Meredith noticed that her hand was gripping Elliott's on her shoulder.

Meredith went out for a walk after lunch, mainly to avoid Lazenby until dinner. She passed him on her way out through the hall, speaking on the telephone to someone he was at school with whose father played golf with the Chief Constable—or some such hazardous connection. She ran down the drive and out into the lane, walking quickly through the village, brow furrowed and hands thrust in pockets until she reached the old schoolhouse. Mrs. Locke was in the garden. Meredith slowed down.

"Good afternoon!" she called out over the wall.

"Ah, Miss Mitchell, just the person!" cried Mrs. Locke brandishing a pair of secateurs. She beckoned with these furiously.

Meredith moved up to the gate. Mrs. Locke opened it and was revealed to be wearing a plastic apron with an illustration of common British wild flowers on it and gardening gloves. She stood aside for Meredith to enter.

"What a pleasant garden," said Meredith and was not being merely polite. It was an old-fashioned country garden with flowers not so much seen now but formerly common, such as hollyhock and michaelmas daisies.

"It's my hobby," confided Mrs. Locke, obviously pleased. "I mean, my husband cuts the lawns and trims the hedges but all the flower-beds are mine. He doesn't have the patience for seeds. And he has his own hobby of course, military modelling."

"Ah ... I see," said Meredith.

Mrs. Locke heaved a sigh. "I've always wanted a proper garden. When we were in the army we were always moving. Sometimes I had a small plot of ground but quite often we were in flats or somewhere where I really had no time to do anything. We promised ourselves, Howard and I, that when we retired we would find somewhere in the country where I could have my garden and Howard do his models in peace. That's why I planted that rose over there—it's called Peace—when we first moved in."

Meredith smiled. It was really rather touching. Especially the way in which Mrs. Locke said "we" when referring to her husband's army career. She understood exactly what Mrs. Locke meant. The same speech could have been made by many a diplomatic wife.

"In fact," Mrs. Locke was saying sadly, "it hasn't really turned out as well as we had hoped. We thought country people would be friendly, but they aren't. Not towards us, anyway. We had terrible trouble over a right of way when we first came. They really just resented our turning the schoolhouse into a residential property. It was so silly. I mean, it was empty and there was never going to be a school in it again. Did they want it just to fall down?"

Meredith found herself scrutinizing the front of the Lockes' home for the first time. It was built in worn, warm red brick and there were poignant traces of its original use. Over the front door letters in haut-relief read "Boys" and further along, over a pair of french windows, an equivalent sign "Girls" balanced the other. The original asphalt-surfaced playground had been removed and replaced by topsoil but somehow there was still a feeling of absent occupiers about the place. The building and its surroundings still seemed to be waiting for the start of a new term and the return of those for whom they had been built. It would take very little imagination to fancy the click of glass marbles bouncing along the ground, the jangle of the school bell, treble voices upraised in a morning hymn.

"You're looking at the house." Mrs. Locke sounded pleased. "It wasn't easy to convert into a proper dwelling.

The right of way problem was only one of many, albeit a very important one. We had to get it cleared up but we had no help from the planning department of the council at all. Howard started a petition over it." She hesitated. "That's when we had a very nasty exchange with young Mr. Lorrimer. I know one ought not to speak ill of the dead, but that young man was a wolf in sheep's clothing, if ever there was one. He'd always seemed so pleasant and suddenly he turned quite—well, nasty and sarcastic. Not very nice at all. I mean, he was a newcomer too and we thought . . . well, I'll say no more about that. We got the right of way changed in the end. It was a very trying time. And then we found that we had blocked the access of the sewage emptier. I had to relocate a whole flower-bed of perennials."

Meredith had opened her mouth to make some suitable reply when a movement in a shrubbery caught her eye. "Good Lord!" she exclaimed. "There's Tom! I've been looking for him everywhere!"

Tom, seeing her, stopped and sat down under a weigela to fix her with a basilisk stare. He looked fit and trim.

"Yes," said Mrs. Locke hastily. "Lorrimer's cat. That's what I wanted to talk to you about. I found him hanging about the back door, obviously very hungry. I'm rather fond of cats. I fed him and he sort of adopted us. I didn't mean to take him in—but he seemed to assume he had a home here. Cats do, you know. The thing is, I dare say he's quite valuable. I don't want to be accused of enticing him. I know I fed him . . . but that was only because he asked so persistently. I suppose I should have rung the RSPCA or the police."

"I'm sure," Meredith said, "that if you want to keep him, no one will object. The RSPCA have more than enough unwanted animals to find homes for. Chief Inspector Markby told me they are having difficulty tracing next of kin for Lorrimer. I'm sure no one else will claim Tom. I'm glad you've taken him in, I was quite worried about him. Lorrimer was very fond of the cats."

Mrs. Locke looked relieved. "I'm so glad. That's all right, then. It does seem strange, taking in his cat when we had quarrelled with Lorrimer himself. He was such an odd young man. Would you like to come inside and see the house, Miss Mitchell?"

"Thank you," Meredith said. "I should."

They passed beneath the arch marked "Boys" and found themselves in a long narrow hall.

"We had to subdivide the existing classrooms," said Mrs. Locke. "There were only two main ones. The head-master's study is now our kitchen. We should have liked to keep the original windows but of course we had to put in a false ceiling and upper floor so that sadly the windows got chopped in half, as it were. But we kept the top of the biggest and turned it into the bedroom window. Come and see."

She led the way upstairs and threw open the door proudly. Meredith saw what she meant. The school, a Victorian foundation, had sported a huge window with mock-Gothic tracery rising to the roof in what must have been its assembly hall. Though curiously shortened now by the creation of an upper floor which, thought Meredith, cut the window off at its knees; the pointed arches of the original now gave the master bedroom a moated grange appearance from inside. In fact, there was something endearingly peculiar about the Lockes' whole home.

They went downstairs and Mrs. Locke ushered her into a drawing room. At last Meredith found herself in that England which exiles always dream of. Here were the chintz-covered chairs, the faded watercolour paintings, the Staffordshire pottery knick-knacks, the well-read books on oak shelves and a profusion of mementoes of the Lockes' time abroad. Mrs. Locke insisted she sit down and bustled away to bring them tea.

Meredith relaxed on the cushions of the flowery sofa and let her gaze drift round the room. A brand-new cat basket by the fireplace showed Tom had found a place to stay for good. There was a rubber mouse in it.

When Mrs. Locke returned with the tea, Meredith asked, "Tell me, does Tom—the cat—drink milk?"

Mrs. Locke shook her head. "He doesn't touch it. I tried him several times."

"That's why he's still alive and prowling around," Meredith said. "Unlike his unfortunate brother Jerry who obviously fancied the odd saucer of milk. Perhaps Tom tried the milk once and it made him sick and put him off it." Mrs. Locke was staring at her over the teapot. "The police think someone may have poisoned Lorrimer's milk. He drank a lot of milk, apparently."

"Oh dear," said Mrs. Locke. "How unpleasant. It is all very unpleasant, isn't it?" She stared mistrustfully at her own milk jug. "How is dear Eve bearing up?"

"Oh, pretty well. Especially now that the press seem to have taken themselves off."

"I'm so glad. And dear little Sara. It seemed so unfair. Especially after all the trouble they had. Poor child. Of course, in view of what we went through, I'm not surprised."

There was a sound of a door and a footstep. "Muriel!" cried a voice. "Where have you put my glue?"

"I haven't touched your glue, Howard dear. And Miss Mitchell is here."

The drawing room door opened and Major Locke's red face appeared. "Ah, didn't know you were here—nice to see you. Lost my glue. Are you sure, Muriel? Oh, tea . . ."

He came in and sat down expectantly. His wife sighed and went to fetch another cup.

"How's life?" asked Major Locke cheerily.

"Rather eventful at the moment."

"Oh, yes . . ." Major Locke chewed his lower lip. "No loss, that boy. Bad lot." He rubbed at his moustache. His fingers were smeared with red paint. He seemed to become aware of it and added apologetically,"Battle of Waterloo. I'm making a diorama."

"That's interesting. You do a lot of research, I imagine."

"My word, yes. The Bamford library is very helpful. I spend a lot of time there. I've my own books showing uniforms and so on as well. People get things wrong," said Major Locke ferociously. "No hussars deployed at Waterloo, you know. Yet every time you see a painting of the battle, there's a hussar, stuck slap-bang in the middle of it."

"I see."

Mrs. Locke had returned. "Here's the glue, Howard. You left it on the dresser."

Major Locke took the tube and peered at it suspiciously.
"So it is. You've squeezed the top end of this, Muriel."

"No, Howard, I haven't. Are you taking your tea back
to your workroom?"

Her husband took the hint and departed with teacup and
glue.

"Howard's hobby," said Mrs. Locke. She leaned forward. "Howard's deserved a peaceful retirement. His
health isn't very good. I try to protect him from all the
fuss and bother. I do my best."

Meredith smiled and drank up her tea. "I really must go
now. Thank you for showing me the house."

"Not at all, my dear. Thank you so much for putting my
mind at rest about the cat."

Meredith walked slowly back to the rectory. Mrs. Locke
had evidently got wind of Sara's former wild lifestyle. It
was as the gates opened with a buzz to admit her, that she
thought, I suppose that's what she meant . . .

"Look what Jon brought down!" cried Sara triumphantly after dinner, brandishing a small package. "It's a
video of one of your old films, Mummy! It's been re-
released and we can all watch it!"

"Goodness," said Eve, adding cautiously, "Which one?"

"Adventurers on Planet Ipsilon!" declared her daughter.

Eve said, "Oh . . ." faintly.

Meredith said, "Hey, that's the one I like, where the
monsters chase you."

"It is one of my earlier ones," said Eve. "I wish you'd
brought *Spying for Love*. That was a much more worthwhile part."

"Lucia's got to come in and see it too!" ordered Sara,
arranging them all in front of the television.

Lucia was brought from the kitchen and sat overflowing
a rather small chair and with a large handkerchief ready.
Sara herself, once the film started, sat down by Lazenby's
feet.

"Dramatic music," said Meredith.

"The colour's awfully bright, Mummy."

"It was the sort of film they used then, dear."

"Golly, look at the controls on that spaceship!" hooted

Sara after a while. "They look like the dials on a washing machine! Who could fly to Mars on that?"

"The starship *Enterprise* came after that, darling, and changed everyone's notion about space travel. You forget."

"That's Ralph Hetherbridge playing the villain, isn't it?" asked Lazenby suddenly. "I thought he was a Shakespearian actor?"

"He was," said Eve. "He didn't come to films until he reached the age people retire at in other professions. He never turned in a bad performance."

"Brought a touch of class," said Meredith. "If anyone else had had the villain's role, it would have been plain funny. But old Ralph really made people believe in him being evil . . . Ah, this is where the giant lizard nearly has you for lunch, Eve . . ."

"You are so beautiful!" sniffled Lucia from the handkerchief. "Ah, so beautiful, signora! That man, he is so wicked!"

"I was overweight, my goodness, quite a podge!"

"Bursting fetchingly out of that bikini, Evie!"

"What I can't work out, is why that reptile is chasing you in that funny way. I mean, was it just because it was clockwork or was it supposed to be a bit retarded?"

"Old Ralph, I mean the villainous overlord, was controlling it from his lair, darling."

"Oh yes, I forgot that bit."

"I'm surprised a distinguished actor like Hetherbridge descended to this sort of thing!" intoned Lazenby.

"Hey!" said his fiancée, twisting her head against his knee, "this is one of Mummy's finest moments!"

"I wouldn't say that, darling!"

"I saw him on film as Polonius. Wish I could have seen him when he was young and turned in the famous Hamlet in when was it? Before the war. Thirty-seven or eight?" Lazenby turned his head to stare at them.

"None of us know, we're not that old!" said Meredith drily.

"So beautiful," moaned Lucia gently. "That man he was so wicked. He should die."

"He did die, didn't he? Old Ralph, just after the end of filming?"

"Yes, he did, darling. He was eighty-four. You would never have thought it."

"So wicked," said Lucia, "to persecute you, signora!"

Ralph's villainous overlord fell victim to his own monsters, the rickety spaceship blasted off back to earth, music swelled and credits rolled.

"They don't make films like that any more ..." said Meredith with satisfaction.

"I would say, just as well!" Eve announced.

"It was beautiful!" said Lucia fervently "It strike me here!" She placed a hand on her ample bosom and smiled benevolently.

Sara got up from the floor and switched on the lights. "Didn't Daddy work on that script, Mummy?"

"Mike? Yes, he did ..." Eve said. "But he left in the middle of it. It would have been a far better script if he'd stayed. The other chap, I forget his name, whom they called in to replace him, wasn't half so good and always suffering from a hangover. We ran out of dialogue altogether at one point. We all sat round with the director and argued about what would happen next. Old Ralph sat by himself at the back and after we'd argued ourselves blue in the face, boomed out, 'Improvise, my dears! Improvise!' "

"Why did Daddy walk out in the middle?" Sara asked.

"Oh, I forget now," her mother said vaguely. "He didn't get on with the director. They kept changing things."

From the corner where they had forgotten him but whence he had been watching the video unroll with grim intensity, Elliott said, "I directed on that one, Evie honey."

At the sound of his mild voice, Eve turned a dusky red. "So you did, Albie darling, I quite forgot. How silly of me."

Meredith got up and went to pour herself a drink. Didn't get on with the director, my eye! You were carrying on with that plastic idiot playing the male lead and Mike had taken all he could stand from you, Evie. You were making a fool of him.

"I still think," Lazenby said obstinately, "that it was an inglorious way for Hetherbridge to finish a very fine career."

Meredith glanced at him. "Do you? I admire him for

tackling something completely new in a strange medium at his age."

"Absolutely!" Eve cried. "Old Ralph had such zest for everything!" She still looked flushed and added suddenly, "Do open the window, Jonathan dear. It's so dreadfully warm in here."

That night, as Meredith was preparing for bed, there was a knock at the bedroom door. She opened it, half expecting Sara again, but it was her cousin who stood on the threshold in a white satin garment, holding a gin bottle in one hand and two small Schweppes tonic waters by the necks in the other. She held them up.

"What are we going to drink out of?" asked Meredith, standing back to let Eve into the room.

"Oh, damn, forgot the glasses!" Eve pulled as exasperated face.

"Don't worry, I'll fetch a couple of tooth mugs."

They sat down with their tooth mug gins and toasted each other silently.

"What are these midnight student capers in aid of?" asked Meredith.

"Jonathan really can be unspeakable," said Eve. "Asking us if we remembered Ralph's 1938 Hamlet! I wasn't born until 1944." She swilled gin round the mug and stared into it. "I did look young on that film, didn't I? All plump and cuddly."

"Hey, is this going to be a maudlin session? How much gin have you put back already?"

"Our lives turn out so different to what we hope," Eve said mournfully. "I really wish Jon had brought some other video. You know why Mike really walked off that film set, don't you?"

"Yes," Meredith said soberly after a pause, "I do."

"It didn't mean anything!" The exasperated look returned to Eve's face and voice. "It was only a stupid film set flirtation. I did love Mike."

"Don't brood on it, Evie."

Eve tossed back her drink. "I want Sara to be happy, Merry, because I owe it to Mike and I messed up my own life. Things went wrong for me and Mike. Marriage to Hughie was hell. Robert died."

"Listen, Evie, go to bed and get a good night's sleep and don't knock back any more firewater. I'll take the bottle back downstairs out of temptation's way."

Eve obediently set off back to her own room. Meredith gathered up the bottle of gin and the two dead tonics and by clasping them to her bosom was able to grab the used mugs as well. She set off carefully downstairs. There was still a light on in the drawing room, shining under the door. Evie forgot it, she thought. She pushed the door open with her foot.

Lazenby, standing by a little writing desk, turned quickly. "Oh," he said, "it's you. I thought everyone was in bed."

"So they are. I'm just bringing the booze down. I was sharing a nightcap with Eve. What are you doing?" she added curiously.

He pushed an open drawer closed. "Working. I brought some papers down with me. I thought Eve might have some Liquid Paper."

"I've got some, but it's upstairs. I'll fetch it down if you need it urgently."

"No, not urgently!" he said hurriedly. He moved away from the desk. "Look here," he said, "I think Eve is putting away too much of that stuff. I wish you wouldn't encourage her to drink."

"For your information!" Meredith retorted angrily, "it wasn't my idea and I haven't encouraged any such thing. She is my cousin, you know. I do care about her too."

He flushed. "Yes, I know you're her cousin and that's why I think it's up to you to say something to her about the booze."

"She holds it pretty well as far as I can see. I haven't noticed her weaving from side to side!"

They glowered at one another. Meredith walked over to the drinks cabinet and replaced the gin bottle. Lazenby, watching her, said unexpectedly, "I am quite keen on the stage, you know. I used to do a bit at Cambridge— Footlights Revue and all that. I actually think Eve isn't a bad actress—she just made a lot of bad films. I think she ought to go for a stage role."

"Let her know what she does best," Meredith said. "Or do you think a stage role would be more respectable than this soap opera one she's after?"

He stuck out his jaw obstinately. "I admit I am against that."

Meredith eyed him thoughtfully. She walked back towards him and stood before him with folded arms. "If you're an actor, the choice is between working and not working. I think Eve has a pretty fair idea of the extent of her own talent. Tell me, are you really in love with Sara?"

"That's a damn insulting question!" he snapped, reddening.

"It's a perfectly fair one. Are you or not?"

"Yes!"

"In sickness or in health? If things go wrong?"

"Yes, dammit!"

"Bad publicity or good? Mother-in-law a soap queen or in legit theatre? Racy stories in Sunday papers?"

"I don't know what you're getting at—" he began, but she interrupted him.

"Like hell you don't!" she said crisply.

In a low, hard voice, he said, "Of course, I can't have scandal! I'm in the financial world. I handle people's money. I have to be seen to be above reproach—it's like being a judge."

Meredith thought about Markby. "We don't have any judges in this family," she said. "Look, I think that when you go back to London on Sunday night, you should take Sara with you. It's not good for her down here. She's had a bad shock and I think she ought to get back to that job of hers, take her mind off things."

"All right," he said after a pause.

Meredith drove into Bamford on Monday and parked outside the public library. Lazenby had taken Sara back to London the previous evening. Both Eve and Meredith had watched Lazenby go with some relief. Eve had been less enthusiastic about Sara's departure.

"It's that job of hers, at the refuge. I'm always afraid

she'll have some trouble there. Even get attacked. But she's so keen on it."

"Let her get on with it, Eve. It sounds worthwhile and better than hanging out with a lot of Hooray Henrys as she was before."

The library was bright and pleasant. There were two women at the desk, one young and one older. The younger one, in a pink cardigan, asked Meredith if she could be of assistance.

"Yes. I'm staying with Miss Owens who has tickets for this library and she's lent me one. Is that all right?"

The older woman looked up quickly from what she was doing and seemed about to speak but then looked down again.

"Oh, yes," said the girl in the pink cardigan. "Quite all right."

Meredith moved away and circled the library shelves until she came across general medical books. As she was perusing them, the older librarian came round the corner and asked, "Is it something specific you wanted?"

"Yes." Meredith hesitated. "Something on herbal medicines."

The woman stared at her intently through steel-rimmed spectacles. "We've *Culpeper's Herbal* ... but I think it might be out at the moment. If you don't mind me asking ..." She paused.

"Yes?" Meredith prompted.

"You said you were staying with Miss Owens. I wondered—" She paused again, looking confused and put-out. "That dreadful murder ... You've no idea, I suppose, how the police are getting along with their inquiries?"

Meredith eyed her carefully. It could just be idle curiosity, but the woman looked agitated. "Making the usual progress, I suppose." She threw out a line. "I only met the young man a couple of times. Very sad."

"Yes!" The woman seized on it. "He was such a nice young man."

A prickle ran up Meredith's spine. "Did you know him, Mrs—?"

"Mrs. Hartman. No, not *know* exactly. But I remember

him. He was in the library just a few weeks before the murder."

Meredith tried to keep her voice casual. "Did he want anything in particular? Did he take out any books?"

"No, no books at all. He wanted to use the photo-copier."

Another library customer drew near and glared. Obviously they were in the way. "Is there somewhere we can talk?" Meredith asked quickly and quietly.

Mrs. Hartman led the way to a cubby-hole housing a gas-ring and a selection of cups and coffee necessities. She closed the door carefully. "I've been worrying about it, whether I ought to tell the police. But it was such an in-nocent sort of thing and what could I tell them, after all? I first noticed the young man over by the copying ma-chine. It's just inside the door next to the microfiche cat-alogue. He had his back to me. He was wearing one of those leather jackets and jeans and I thought he might have been a student from the college down the road. They come in sometimes to use the machine, copying each other's notes."

"Did you see what he was copying?" Meredith asked.

Mrs. Hartman shook her head. "No, you can't. But he ran out of change and he came over to the desk to ask if I could change a twenty-pence piece into two tens, be-cause the machine uses tens. We don't like doing it be-cause we have to use the fines box, then when people want change to pay a fine, there isn't any, if you see what I mean. Only, he was such a nice boy . . ."

A nice boy. At least I wasn't alone, thought Meredith wryly.

"Well," said Mrs. Hartman, blushing. "Not a boy, ex-actly. He looked a bit older when he came close to and I decided he couldn't be a college student after all, because they are all about nineteen."

"And what happened?" Meredith prompted impatiently.

"Nothing . . ." said Mrs. Hartman. "That's why I don't feel I can go to the police. I just gave him two tens for his twenty because he was so polite, really quite charming. I mean, you should see some of those students! The boys are yobs and the girls—well, I wouldn't like to say! And they are supposed to be the bright ones, benefiting from higher education! It seems to have all gone wrong to me."

Meredith dragged her back to Philip Lorrimer. "You gave him his change and presumably he went back to the photo-copier."

"Yes, that's right. Then someone came to the desk and I was distracted." Mrs. Hartman frowned. "When I looked up again, he was leaving. I called after him to ask if he'd taken his originals. Because sometimes, you know, people leave them in the machine. He said, yes, he had them safe."

"Those were his words?" Meredith pressed her.

"Yes, I think so. He called back, "Don't worry, I've got those safe!" "

Them. He had copied several items. But what and why? Why did he want to keep the originals "safe"? Because they were valuable, to him at least. To anyone else? Were these originals what the murderer had sought when ransacking Philip's cottage so hurriedly?

Meredith left the library deep in thought. There seemed no point in moving the car so she left it and walked the short distance into the main shopping area. A well-known chain of booksellers did not have any books on herbal medicines. only on growing herbs in your garden. They were, they said apologetically and without irony, only a small branch. A small independent bookshop in the market square did have a book but it covered a limited range of preparations aimed at relieving aches and pains. She stepped out of the shop and as she stood uncertainly on the pavement a car drew up and Alan Markby put his head out and hailed her. "Where are you going?"

"Home," she told him, going up the car and stooping. "I left my car by the library."

"I wanted a word with you," he said. "If you've got a moment. Got time for a cup of tea? Let me park and I'll meet you in the tea-rooms where I saw you before."

The tea-room was fairly empty. Meredith took a window seat and when the waitress came up said, "I'm waiting for—for a friend."

"Righto, I'll come back in a minute, then," she said cheerfully.

Markby arrived five minutes later. Meredith saw him come in and exchange a word with the waitress who obviously knew him. The girl pointed towards Meredith's table. Markby came over and joined her.

"They have very good cream cakes." He raised an inquiring eyebrow.

She shook her head. "Just a cup of tea. I've eaten substantially over the weekend and put on pounds. Lucia created all kinds of fantastic Neapolitan dishes."

"Special celebrations?"

"No. Well, Sara's boyfriend was down for the weekend."

Something in her voice made him smile. The waitress came back and he ordered the teas. "Press giving any more trouble?" he asked affably, when the girl had gone.

"Found something more interesting for the time being, I think. I haven't noticed them around. Why was it you wanted me?"

He wished he could say, I just wanted to sit and talk to you. But that wasn't why he was here. He heaved a mental sigh. Who'd be a policeman? "You went calling on Gary Yewell at his workplace, I understand?" he said. "After we last parted."

"Yes. Is that it? What you wanted to see me about?"

"Yes, it is. Why did you go?"

Her fine eyes met his and that mulish expression he both dreaded and was beginning to get rather fond of returned to her face. "I wondered what time in the morning Philip Lorrimer was up and about."

"Look, Meredith," he said. "You don't mind, do you, if I speak bluntly? I do understand how frustrating it is for you. You're on holiday. You came to what you thought was a nice quiet English village and when you go out for an early morning stroll you fall over a dead body. Next thing the place is swarming with reporters and photographers and policemen. You'd like to take a broom and sweep us all out. You're not the sort of person who sits around and does nothing. So you've decided to hurry our departure along a little by doing a little private investigating. It may have worked for Hercule Poirot but it doesn't work in real life. Leave it to the professionals."

"You?" The hazel eyes snapped at him.

"Very rude," he said.

"All right, very rude and I didn't intend it to be so. But I can't see my asking a few routine questions of Gary Yewell can make any difference to you. If it keeps me harmlessly occupied and out from under your feet, I'd have thought you'd be happy to let me get on with it."

"It doesn't keep you from under my feet!" he said firmly. "It puts you there. It also might be called tampering with a witness, you know."

"Oh, rubbish!" she exploded crossly.

The waitress brought the tea and provided a timely break in the conversation.

"We've spoken to Yewell on three separate occasions," Markby said. "An unlovely youth, defensively monosyllabic. He doesn't like policemen."

"You see?" Meredith said triumphantly. "He might tell me things he wouldn't tell you!"

"And did he?" Markby's gaze held hers.

"I don't know. I don't know what he told you and I don't suppose you'd tell me. He didn't tell me anything much. In the mornings he never saw Philip, who was always in bed when Gary called. He saw him on Friday evenings when he went round the village collecting the money."

"Can you imagine Gary tampering with the milk bottles?" Markby asked, sipping at his tea.

"No, frankly. He's not subtle enough. Why should he, anyway? He saw Philip once a week and took the milk money off him."

"You bought a bottle of milk at the dairy."

Drat the man! Meredith fumed. Had he missed nothing? She wanted to burst out, How dare you check up on me? But that was his job, checking up on people.

"Yes," she said coldly. "Is that illegal?"

"No, it's curious. What did you do with it?"

"Drank it," Meredith said promptly.

"Meredith," Markby said gently. "Leave the detective work to me."

She picked up her shoulder-bag and stood up, hazel eyes blazing. "This is a free country, isn't it? I can go where I like and talk to whom I like. I'm not in your way and certainly not tampering with witnesses! Good luck with your inquiries, Chief Inspector!"

As she stormed out, Meredith reflected that she ought to have told him to go and see Mrs. Hartman. But then she thought, I should only be accused of trespassing on his territory! If he wants to do it all himself, let him get on with it!

By the time she reached the corner of the street, she had calmed down a little. The lights were against pedestrians and she stood waiting for them to change, squashed between a young woman with a pushchair and an old woman with a shopping trolley. Both manoeuvred their wheeled appendages with careless abandon. Meredith wondered if the young woman was trying to get rid of the baby, because she had pushed it out into the oncoming traffic well before the green man appeared to signal them to cross and heavy goods vehicles roared past within inches of the child's toes, enveloping the unfortunate infant in exhaust fumes. Then, as she stood there, she saw it. Right opposite her on the corner facing.

A. J. PERRY.
ARTIST AND CRAFT SUPPLIES.
PICTURE FRAMING.
GALLERY.

The lights changed. The young woman with the pushchair charged forward, the elderly one hauled the trolley in brisk pursuit. Meredith followed after and stopped on the pavement, peering through the window of the shop.

It was dingy and untidy. The contents of the window were faded, dusty and fly-spotted and did not appear to have been changed for years. One or two old hand-coloured prints of Bamford were so brown and faded as to be almost unrecognizable. Meredith pushed open the door, its frame painted a sun-dulled brown, and a bell jangled noisily overhead.

There was no one in the shop but from the rear premises came the sound of energetic hammering. Perhaps A. J. Perry was doing his picture framing. She supposed he had heard the bell. Meredith glanced round. From dusty pigeon-holes tubes of paint and different sized brushes peered out. Samples of frame were tacked up the wall in a line of superimposed upside-down V's, all kinds from strictly plain and modern to ornate gilt such as cradled Victorian oils. The prices of picture glass were hand-written on a piece of curling card. An African violet in a pot looked suspiciously dead, dark furry leaves hanging limply over the edge. Meredith probed the compost with an experimental finger. Dry as a bone. Meredith opened and shut the door again, causing the bell to jangle anew.

This time there was a reaction. The hammering stopped and a small, bald-headed man with a Tolstoyan beard appeared abruptly through a bead curtain and glared at her.

"Oh, it's someone," he said grudgingly. "I thought it was those damn kids skylarking again."

Meredith apologized for disturbing him and explained what brought her.

"Philip Lorrimer? Oh, yes, I remember him all right." Mr. Perry, supposing this was he, moved round to stand behind his counter and leaned his hands palm downwards on its cluttered top. From the looks of his blackened fingernails his aim with the hammer was erratic. "He used to buy bits and pieces here. He said he was a potter and I read it in the local rag when he was bumped off. Never saw any of his work—the pottery that is. Saw one or two paintings."

"Paintings?" This was the first time anyone had mentioned that Lorrimer had done any painting. "I didn't know he did any. I thought he was strictly a potter."

"Ah," said Mr. Perry. "Got to keep body and soul together. That was what he kept the pottery going for, or so he told me. Really would have liked to turn his hand to portraiture. I've got a little gallery here . . ." He nodded towards the bead curtain. "He brought in a couple of pictures to see if they'd sell."

Meredith tried to quench the excitement in her voice. "And did they? Are they still here?"

"Now that's a funny thing," said Mr. Perry, his stubby fingers searching in his beard as if he thought a few odd picture nails or tacks might have got lost in there as he worked. "One was a picture of a cat and an old lady bought it. Don't care for cats myself, but I suppose as a picture of a cat it was OK. Animal pictures usually sell so I didn't mind giving it house-room. Because between you and me, he wasn't really that good a pictorial artist. Clumsy brushwork. But he was good at capturing a sort of likeness, if you know what I mean."

"The other picture. . .?" Meredith said in a tight voice.

"Oh, yes, that was of a girl. Young girl with long fair hair, pretty sort of girl. Quite a pretty picture but I had doubts about it selling. But *that* was the funny thing." Mr. Perry leaned forward. "Young fellow bought it. Came marching in here one day, very stroppy. Belligerent sort of bloke. Bit of a smart-aleck. City type, not a local chap. You know the type?"

"Yes," Meredith said, "I know."

"He said he understood I had a painting here by Lorrimer. Didn't ask to see the gallery, mind you! Just asked about that painting. I showed him the picture and he said yes, that's the one! And he took out a cheque book and says, 'How much?' in a very brusque way. I nearly told him he couldn't have it, just to put him in his place! But there, I thought young Lorrimer would be pleased and a sale is a sale. But I stuck another tenner on the price. He paid up too, without a blink. Stuck the picture under his arm and marched out. Never asked about framing . . ." added Mr. Perry resentfully.

"I see . . ."

"No, you don't," said Mr. Perry, waggling his beard. "I haven't finished. That wasn't the end of it. Couple of days later, Lorrimer himself came storming in here, white as a sheet, nearly busting a gut with rage. He went dashing straight through into the gallery and came out twice as quick as he went in. 'Where's the bloody picture?' he yells. I told him, sold it. 'What did you something-well do that for?' Well, I was in the Navy meself so I give him a bit of that sort of language back. He calmed down a bit, turned sort of sulky. 'I wanted it back!' he said. I told him I didn't know that. I tried to give him the money for it, less my percentage. He wouldn't take it. '*You* keep his bloody money!' he said. 'Little bitch!' and he went storming out again. I never saw him after that. He must have bought his materials somewhere else."

Meredith thanked him. She drove back to the rectory muttering, "Idiot, idiot, idiot!" to herself. She went straight through to the drawing room and up to the portrait of Eve on the wall. Yes, the brushwork was clumsy. Of course, the artist's name hadn't meant anything to her when she first arrived. But she should have remembered it even so, especially when she met him . . .

She peered into the corner of the picture. Yes, there was the signature, just above a sizeable chip in the frame which had been disguised with gold paint.

"I was hoping you wouldn't notice that."

Meredith spun round. Eve stood by the door, elegant in pale green silk crêpe. She came slowly across the room and stared at the painting with dislike.

"Why didn't you mention Lorrimer did this, Evie?"

Eve shrugged. "Is it important? Surely it would be tactless to remind people now? Especially Sara. I didn't sit for that portrait. It was done from a photograph. Robert used to come out this way on business—before we bought this house. That's what gave him the idea to move down here and how he came to know of the house standing empty. I don't know how he met young Lorrimer but Robert was interested in young people. He liked to encourage young talent. He had the young man do the portrait from the photo, to surprise me. We'd only just got married and he did that sort of thing. It turned out well, considering. Robert liked it. He insisted it hang there. Mind you, I think that looking at it made him think he'd done a good turn, helping out Lorrimer with a commission. It made him feel good and was one reason he liked it so much. But I never met Lorrimer until we came here to live. Frankly, I found it embarrassing—the painting on the wall here and the artist such a scruffy young man living a stone's throw away. But after Robert died, I couldn't take it down . . . You know . . ." Eve finished obscurely.

There was a lot she didn't know, Meredith thought, or hadn't known but was beginning to learn. She went upstairs and sat looking out of her bedroom window, down the main drive. Then she opened a notebook and balancing it on her knee, wrote:

"Robert visits on business and meets Lorrimer who paints Eve from a photo.

"Robert buys the house and moves Eve and Sara down here.

"Robert dies and Sara meets Lazenby at his funeral and gets engaged.

"Lorrimer has at some point painted Sara and put the picture for sale in Perry's shop but Lazenby learns of it and buys it. Lorrimer subsequently tries in vain to get it back.

"Lorrimer uses the photo-copier in the library."

Meredith closed the notebook. Time to talk to Sara and this time, no nonsense! she thought grimly.

Ten

"For heaven's sake, Alan!" said Laura crossly. She leaned against the door jamb with folded arms and surveyed the patio and the stooped figure of her only brother who appeared to be haranguing a pot of geraniums. "You're not another one who's started talking to plants? I know the best people do it, but I don't think I can take it."

"No!" he said indignantly. "I was thinking aloud."

"Pottering round those flower tubs, talking to yourself. One thing about you, Alan, there's never a problem what to buy you for birthdays or Christmas. A bag of bio-fertilizer and you're happy."

"Better than getting ties and socks I don't want!"

They both returned to his kitchen. "I came to ask you over to lunch on Sunday," Laura informed him. "The kids haven't seen you for ages."

"That's not true," he defended himself. "I had you all over to lunch—we had a barbecue outside. I've only just managed to get the grease marks out of the patio."

"Once in a blue moon. Anyway, it was at least two months ago. More. It was when Eve Owens first asked you to give away the bride." He mumbled and moved away but Laura followed him accusingly. "Uncle Alan is turning into a mythical figure like Santa Claus. It's a wonder they don't think you are Santa because you appear once a year at Christmas bearing gifts and then vanish for a twelvemonth. What's the matter, don't you like my kids?"

"I love 'em, but that little 'un is always in bed when I come round. It's like a perishing Victorian invalid."

"She, Alan, she! Not It. Children are not sexless. Shall

we be seeing you on Sunday? Paul says there's football on the TV and you can watch West Ham with him."

"Thanks." Markby prowled round a cyclamen on the Welsh dresser. "I'm rather busy, Laura. Kind of you to ask and so on."

"You can't work on Sundays. Well, you can but you needn't and you shouldn't. You're getting to be a workaholic!" she told him severely.

"No, I'm not!" he defended himself. "But I've a peculiar case on my hands at the moment."

"Look, *I* have work on my hands but I take time to eat!" She sounded exasperated. After a pause she asked, "Is it this chap who got himself poisoned next door to Eve Owens?"

"That one. He had it coming to him, I imagine, but it's a nasty sort of death." Markby scratched his chin. "I prefer the bullet and blunt instrument cases to poisonings. Furtive thing, poison."

"Compared with blunt instruments, you might say it was almost sophisticated," she argued.

Her brother looked up, his gaze sharp and Laura reflected not for the first time that her brother's amiable manner was an effective cover for an exceptionally alert mind.

"Yes, a woman's weapon, they say. But perhaps that's an old-fashioned idea from the days when women were weak and feeble and every house had a tin of arsenic in it to keep down rats."

"What worries you, Alan?" Laura asked quietly.

"I'm worried that there's no apparent motive. He was an unpleasant oick but if everyone of that description was murdered tomorrow the population would be decimated. It's not enough. He lived alone. He was self-employed and self-sufficient in his way. He owned that cottage. He bought it outright and told the estate agent it was money left to him by an elderly relative. So far we've failed to come up with any other family. Why should anyone worry about him enough to want him dead? Incidentally, his unpleasantness wasn't immediately apparent. Outwardly he could be a charmer. That's always the nastiest type."

"But he didn't use it to prey on simple-minded women of fortune," Laura pointed out.

"How do we know that? Perhaps we just haven't found out yet who his victims were. That boyish charm was damn effective. Even Miss Mitchell thought he was a nice chap and she's nobody's fool."

"Oh?" Laura said.

He hunched his shoulders. "Laura, if you were a woman—"

"Thanks a lot! What am I, then? Some kind of android?"

"Listen. If you were not my sister but another woman, okay? What would you think of me?"

"Untidy," she said promptly. "Sadly in need of a female hand to guide, iron that shirt, remind you to get a haircut, stop you talking to yourself or plants."

"She's not that kind of woman, the shirt-ironing kind."

Laura pounced. "Whom are we talking about? You haven't fallen for the *femme fatale,* the goddess of the silver screen, ageless Eve, have you?"

"No, and don't be bitchy. Eve Owens, I can tell you, is a remarkably well-preserved woman."

"I have a remarkably well-preserved Georgian card table. For Pete's sake, Alan! If you are going to make that kind of remark, you had better carry on talking to plants. If Eve Owens heard you describe her like that, she'd sue— and I'd represent her!"

"I'm talking about Meredith Mitchell," he confessed.

"What does she look like?" asked practical Laura.

"Oh, tallish, thirty something-ish, nice hair, good skin, intelligent. She's in the consular service."

"Pity you can't bring her to lunch," Laura said with real regret. "But you can't, I suppose, until this case is over. Not since she's a material witness. She did find the body, didn't she? Influence and all that. Defence would seize on it."

"I doubt she'd accept any invitation of mine, in any case. She looks at me as if I'd turned up in her consulate with a rucksack and worry beads, claiming to have lost my passport. It's not much fun being a copper, sometimes. You find yourself barging in and asking all manner of tom-

fool and highly personal questions and people resent it."
He paused. "She doesn't know anything about plants or
flowers."

"Bonus, in my book," said Laura with feeling.

"No, you miss the point," her brother said seriously.
"She doesn't, but whoever killed Philip Lorrimer does."

Meredith locked the car carefully and checked that nothing remotely of interest could be seen lying on the back
seat or shelf. This was not the spot she would have chosen
to park the car but it was the nearest she could get to her
goal. She looked around her. Blocks of red-brick flats
stretched uniformly on either side, many of the lower windows boarded up. Graffiti were scrawled on the walls,
most of them meaningless, some aspiring to art. She put
her keys in her pocket into which she had already trans-
ferred essential items normally carried in a shoulder-bag.
To walk about here carrying a snatchable bag seemed asking for trouble.

The car looked sad and abandoned as she set out briskly
along the street, past the flats and a block of shop premises
comprising a launderette, a seedy newsagents with a window festooned with hand-printed personal advertisements
on cards and a building apparently empty but with open
door and frequented by a group of aimlessly lurking
youths. She was aware of their appraising, hostile glances
as she walked past.

Around the corner was marginally better, rows of pre-
war terraced houses with bay windows which had escaped
the blitz. Some seemed to be residential, some turned into
flats, one—almost surprisingly—was a doctor's surgery.
Double yellow lines precluded moving the car here, however. A side street. She crossed it. Another bay window,
this time obscured by thick lace curtains but displaying a
comic postcard sellotaped to the glass and bearing the leg-
end, "If you're in the mood, wink." It was impossible to
guess who waited behind the lace curtains for customers
so discreetly hailed. Better than a red lamp or girls in the
window pinging their suspenders Meredith thought,
amused.

She stopped before one of the bay-fronted houses. It had

steps rising to a front door and another set running down
to a basement with a grilled window from which seeped a
cooking smell, onions and boiling water containing rice,
potatoes or pasta. Meredith glanced up to check the
number, climbed the steps to a battle-scarred front door
and pressed the bell beneath the label reading, "St.
Agatha's Women's Refuge."

After a few moments footsteps approached and the door
opened a few inches with an accompanying rattle of a
chain. A face peered out and summed Meredith up.

"I'd like to see Sara Emerson," Meredith said.

"What's your name?" asked the face's voice suspiciously.

Meredith gave it, adding, "I'm a relative."

"Just a second," said the voice. The door closed, the
chain was disengaged and the door reopened, this time
wide enough for Meredith just to squeeze through.

A plump girl in a tee-shirt and jeans refastened the door
and chain. Meredith glanced about her during his proce-
dure. This hall was bare with aged, broken linoleum on the
floor though the pale blue paintwork looked recent, if
amateurly applied. Somewhere a child cried and a Radio
One disc jockey was relentlessly cheerful. A clatter of feet
on the uncarpeted stair preceded the arrival of another
young woman, cigarette in hand, who came half-way
down, saw Meredith, turned and bolted, but not before
Meredith observed she had an horrific black eye.

"We have to check," said the plump girl, scowling at
Meredith. "You can tell if it's someone wanting shelter.
You don't look as if you do. You're sure you're not the
council or the social services?"

"Absolute. Ask Sara herself."

"Not a journalist or anything?"

"No," Meredith repeated patiently.

"They come round to count how many we got in," said
the plump girl. "The council. They keep saying, keep
down the numbers. Fire hazards and health and all the rest.
But we can't turn them away, can we? And the social
come about the kids. What with them and the husbands
and boyfriends trying to kick the door in and the press
hanging about for stories, it really gets to you sometimes."

"I'm none of those," Meredith assured her.

"We don't have many in at the moment, as it happens." The plump girl seemed possessed of a mind which ran on rails and, having taken one set of tracks, carried on until it reached the equivalent of a set of points.

"Sara?" prompted Meredith firmly.

"Oh, yes, in the crèche—down the hall."

The crèche was a large sunny room at the back of the house. It was spartanly furnished but brightly painted with the same blue paint which extended to the surround and smoke-hood of the grate. On the walls were pinned cray-oned children's pictures. A geranium stood on the win-dowsill. Sara sat on the floor cradling a snuffling baby, the child Meredith had heard crying. Two little girls squabbled over a toy xylophone and in the corner on his own sat a small boy, slowly and with desperate intensity placing plastic bricks end to end.

Meredith sat on a shabby armchair. One of the little girls looked up and smiled and then hit the other one with the hammer of the xylophone.

Sara, rocking the baby with one arm and reaching out with the other to settle the xylophone dispute, said defi-antly, "Go on, you might as well say it. The area is awful, the hostel is shabby and we're barricaded in. I ought not to be here."

"I won't say it, because I don't think it. You've every right to be here doing this if it's what you want. The hos-tel's not so bad, or what I've seen. Nice new paint."

Sara relaxed and tossed her head to shake back a lock of hair. "Yes, Joanne and I painted nearly all of it. It took us ages because we had to do it at night when everyone was in bed out of the way and the children wouldn't touch the wet paint." She paused. "This is the first thing I've ever done in my life which is even partly worthwhile." The baby squawked and she joggled it about. "Joanne's here full-time with Mark and Jen. Lucy, Mark's girlfriend, takes care of the cooking. It's all vegetarian because that's what she is. Joanne organizes things. I just help wherever needed, mostly here in the crèche."

"What does Mark do?" asked Meredith curiously.

"He drives the transit van. Would you like coffee?"

"I just want a talk. A serious one, Sara. Don't mess me about. I want to know what hold Philip had over you and what he threatened to do and why."

The set look returned to Sara's face. She stood up, still clasping the baby and went to the door and called, "Joanne!" into the hall. Turning back, she said in a small, tense voice, "I don't want to discuss it here. I'll tell you but not here. We're not so busy this morning and Joanne can take over."

The plump girl appeared and arrangements were made. "We can go to my flat," Sara said. "It's not all that far from here."

"Fine. I'd like to move the car, I left it round the corner and there were some youngsters hanging about."

The car was still there but the windscreen wipers had gone. "Could have been worse, I suppose," said Meredith resignedly.

"It will be okay outside the flat." Sara was staring fixedly into the distance as she spoke.

Sara's flat was on the ground floor of another bay-fronted house of terraced look-alikes. But these were better kept up and some showed signs of recent improvements. There had been a rash of double-glazing and wooden doors more suited to moated granges than nineteen-thirties houses. Macramé pot holders hung in a few windows and the nearest thing to lace curtaining were screens of wooden beads on threads such as mask doorways in the casbah.

Sara showed Meredith into a cheerfully chaotic folksy room, splashed with bright patches of colour from patchwork cushions and crocheted blankets.

"My," Meredith said. "You're quite green-fingered."

The plant pots were everywhere. They lined windowsills and shelves and jostled for space on tables. A yucca in a tub stood in the bay window opposite a rubber plant which reached up to the ceiling. A spider plant dangled tentacles from a basketwork holder above Meredith's head.

"Oh, Jon gives them to me," Sara said vaguely. "Sit down, Merry, and I'll fetch the coffee."

Meredith sat down not sure whether it felt like sitting in a log hut on the Russian steppes or in a greenhouse at

Kew Gardens. She could hear Sara making coffee in the kitchen. On the book shelf nearby, lodged in a narrow spot between two hefty tomes on sociology, was a framed photo of Jonathan Lazenby. It gazed out severely at the crowded little room as if in rehearsal for the day when Lazenby made it to chairman of the CBI.

Sara came back with the coffee on a tray and Meredith moved books and papers aside on the table so that it could be set down.

"Whence the sociology books?" Meredith asked.

"I was thinking of trying for some sort of qualification. I can't do a degree course. I haven't the basic A levels. I might be able to get on a tech college course." Sara pushed back her hair nervously and handed Meredith a cup. Then she sat back and clasped her hands, fiddling with the ruby cluster again in a way which Meredith was beginning to find increasingly significant. "I'm glad you saw the refuge. Until I began to work there I had no idea that anything like that existed—that women could lead lives like it. I honestly thought that sort of thing went out with Dickens."

"Who introduced you to St. Agatha's?"

"A friend of a friend. It was all a bit of a chance. Some of the women who come there have had dreadful experiences. Some are just frightened and some actually injured, lots of bruises and so on. Often the children, if they bring their children, have behavioural problems and are deeply disturbed. The women are hurt on the outside, as it were, but the children are scarred inwardly. Several of the women have told me that they themselves were battered when they were children. You'd think, wouldn't you, that a child like that, when she grew up, wouldn't have anything to do with a man who knocked her about? But they do. It's hard to understand, but that kind of thing has always been a part of the pattern of life for them. Often they leave us to go back to the men. They don't have anywhere else to go. They don't have families who'll help, or they are ashamed to go to their families. They don't have any money or a place to live. So back they go. Sometimes they go back saying it might be all right this time, but really knowing that it won't. But sometimes they feel they just must go back. As if they were gluttons for punishment."

"What about the men?" Meredith asked. "Do they make much trouble?"

"Occasionally, but not always in the way you'd expect. Some of the husbands, when they arrive on the doorstep, look very respectable. They don't look like monsters. Some are plainly hard cases, of course. But I remember one chap who assured us that everything his wife had said was lies. He was well-spoken and dressed and very plausible. If we hadn't seen the bruises, we might have been tempted to believe him. Afterwards, his wife told us it was a sex thing . . . I mean, he couldn't get going unless he beat her up first. It wasn't drink or anything and he'd got a responsible job and he was scared his employers would find out his wife was in our refuge. Another one said we were holding his wife against her will and threatened to take us to court. People behave in the most amazing ways." She stopped abruptly.

"Yes," Meredith said and waited, sensing that Sara would go on with her story when she was ready. After a long pause, Sara recommenced.

"The men who look all right but are monsters underneath it always remind me of Phil Lorrimer. He didn't look like a monster either, but he was." She sighed. "If you'd seen me three years ago, Merry, you would never have imagined I'd be doing anything like the refuge. But I was lucky, you see. When I began to mess my life up I did have someone who could and would help. I had Mummy and Robert and they really got hold of me and sorted me out. I didn't appreciate it at the time, of course. When we moved out of London down to the rectory, I hated it. I shut myself in my bedroom and cried buckets just out of temper and self-pity, quite frankly. I was desperately lonely and missed all the people I still thought of as my friends, although they weren't really friends at all, and I missed the parties and all the rest . . . I used to get back to London whenever I could. Most of all I wanted to talk to someone about what was happening. Robert made me feel so ashamed, so I couldn't talk to him, and he was quite old. Mummy and I just squabbled when we tried to talk which made us both miserable, so I couldn't talk to her. I wanted to talk to a young person, someone outside the family, who wasn't committed to either side. Someone I thought would give me a fair hearing and an unbiased opinion."

"So that's when you started to make a confidant out of Philip?" Meredith asked.

Sara nodded. "We got talking over the cats. Then I started going down to his place every day. I used to go through the garden gate across the little lane they call Love Lane—it's a funny name, isn't it? Anyhow, Phil seemed so *nice*—then. He was unconventional, being an artist, and funny. He made me laugh. He used to mimic old Bert going on about his 'cabbidges and carrits'. He described Bert going round his garden putting out saucers of beer for the slugs to fall in—only Tom and Jerry went and drank it and were both sick. Bert was cross because they spoiled his slug traps and Phil was cross because the cats were sick. But afterwards Phil laughed and made me laugh. He'd scurry round the studio just like Bert, shaking his fists and cursing 'them foreign varmints!' And Phil let me watch him work and I painted some of the vases for him when he had a rush order. I even tried throwing the clay but I wasn't any good at it. It was all so different from the life I'd been leading. Phil didn't worry about the things my other friends worried about. He didn't want a flash car or to go ski-ing at St. Moritz. He had a couple of pairs of jeans, two or three sweatshirts and a leather jacket and I honestly think that was all. I never saw him wearing anything else. He used to spend money on proper food for the cats but he never bothered much for himself. He drank a lot of milk and that kept him going. Anyhow, in between painting vases and clearing up the studio after him, I told Phil everything. All about the parties I'd gone to and who was there and what they did. Some of them were well-known names. I mean, not the people I'd known themselves, but some of them had famous parents, in the government and all sorts, not just theatre or TV people like Mummy."

"So Phil got a lot of potentially very damaging information about you and others?"

"Yes," Sara said in a small, dejected voice. "But it

didn't seem to matter because he was a friend. He got hold of other things, too, photos and a letter."

"How did he do that?"

Sara shifted awkwardly in her chair and looked both shame-faced and angry. "It was my fault. A friend sent me the letter—a nice long gossipy one about the parties I'd missed and what pranks my friends had been getting up to. She really told me everything. I realize now it was the sort of stuff that if the wrong people got to hear about it—But she only meant it for me to read. I suppose,"—Sara's face reddened—"it wasn't really a 'nice' letter at all."

"Probably not. It was a foolish one too."

"She only meant me to see it! She thought it would make me laugh and cheer me up!" Sara said defensively.

"So you promptly showed it to Phil, is that it?"

She thought for a moment that Sara was going to jump up and run out of the room. But then her god-daughter shook back her long hair and met Meredith's eye firmly. "Yes, I did. I was wrong to do that because it betrayed a confidence—she really hadn't thought I'd show it to, well, to an outsider, not one of our crowd. And it was wrong because the gossip in it was malicious, even if it wasn't true."

"All the more reason for her not to pass it on."

"You needn't sound so prim about it!" Sara said resentfully. "It seemed amusing and fairly harmless at the time. It was about people having fun. There were photos too, taken at a party when everyone was well and truly drunk and things had got out of hand, as they do at parties. Haven't you ever been to a party like that?"

"Yes," Meredith admitted ruefully. "Not recently, but in my time. I never let anyone take any incriminating snapshots though."

"Well, these people had. And there were a few earlier photos off the same reel which had me in them. They were taken at one of the last parties I went to." Sara paused to take a deep breath. Her fists clenched and unclenched and she wiped damp palms on her knees. "The letter and photos arrived while Mummy was away filming a TV advert. I was lonely and reading the letter made me desperate to talk to a friend. It seemed I was missing everything! I took the letter and the photos down to Phil's cottage and read him parts of the letter to make him laugh and perhaps to let him know what fun I was used to having in London. I was sort of boasting, I suppose. I know it was stupid. I was stupid then. I don't pretend I wasn't. But I read bits out and he did laugh. I showed him some of the photos, too. Not all of them. Some I left the envelope—it was one of those big brown manila ones. Then I put the letter and the rest of the photos back in the envelope and Phil and I talked about other things and drank coffee and quite a bit later I went home, back to the rectory. I'd forgotten the envelope completely and didn't remember it until next day— and then I couldn't find it. I realized I'd left it over at Phil's. I admit I was a bit annoyed about it, but not seriously because after all, I thought Phil was a friend. I didn't worry. There seemed no need for that."

"But he refused to give the envelope back?"

"It wasn't quite like that. I went back to ask for it and he was working in the studio. He said he was busy and I could go up to the cottage and search for it myself. So I did but I couldn't find it. I asked Phil again and he said, was I sure I'd left it there? Perhaps I'd dropped it on the way home, somewhere in Love Lane or in the rectory garden. So I searched all over both those places with no luck. Phil said he'd have another look around his place some time and if he found it, he'd give it back. I was a bit worried I might have dropped it in Love Lane and a villager had picked it up. But I didn't worry about the possibility it might be at Phil's because Phil was a friend. I didn't think it mattered because I trusted him!" The last words came out as a desperate wail. "He lied to me! He had them all the time. He was my friend and he did that, kept them and lied!"

Silly little bitch, thought Meredith sadly. "And when did he stop being your friend?" she asked aloud. But she knew the answer to that already.

Sara drew another deep, shuddering breath. "When I got engaged to Jon. Phil changed completely. I couldn't believe what I saw and heard. It was eerie! He was so jealous. Why? I mean, our relationship wasn't like that! We weren't lovers, we were friends! Phil never even kissed me. Now he started acting as though I'd betrayed him. I couldn't understand it!" She fixed uncomprehending blue eyes on Meredith. "He said I'd been playing games with him but he could play games, too. He wanted me to break off my engagement to Jon. He said he'd make me do it. I thought he'd gone mad. Then he told me he had the letter and the photos, he'd had them all the time, and I began to be frightened. I couldn't understand how anyone could change like that."

"Phil thought you'd used him," Meredith said cruelly. "And you had really, hadn't you? He was a young man, Sara, not an old granny to whom you could just pour out your heart. He was a young man, however flawed, living in a community which disliked and despised him. He lived on his own with a couple of cats and suddenly there you were, a pretty socialite, haunting his studio, helping with his work, sobbing on his shoulder and making him feel needed and strong and clever, none of which things he really was. He was weak and had trouble making friends and carried a chip on his shoulder. Who knows, he may even have been impotent. But you made him feel like the most successful young stud around until you pulled the carpet from under him. You did that when you produced that whizz-kid with his Porsche and his Savile Row tailoring and his jetting here and there on business!"

"Stop it!" Sara shouted. "That's not how it was! Phil was horrible! Don't defend him! You wouldn't defend the men who attack and bully the women in our refuge, so don't make excuses for him!" She clenched her fists tightly and the ruby cluster glowed on the pale skin. "He wouldn't have dared behave like that if Robert had still been alive. He said such awful things and played revolting tricks. He sent me a dead bird in a parcel. It must have been one the cats killed. But it was lying in a little gift box, packed in with tissue and all wrapped up with pretty paper. When I opened it, there was the bird, dead and maggotty. There were other things, too."

So Albie Elliott was right, Meredith thought wryly.

Sara shivered and hugged her bare arms. "He made such embarrassing scenes, too. It wasn't just the abuse he came out with. He was violent. He slapped my face once but I didn't tell Mummy that. He did go to the rectory and shout at me in front of Mummy. She told him to get out and he grabbed a table lamp and threw it across the room at her and only just missed her. It knocked a piece out of the picture frame. It was after that Mummy had the security gates installed."

"Did either of you tell the police about this?"

"No!" Sara bounced in her chair with frustration. "We didn't want Jon to know of it! Jon doesn't like adverse publicity because of his job, and as for his so-nice family ...! Mummy couldn't risk it either, being so well known. Besides, if Jon had found out, he might have got the wrong idea about me and Phil. My going down every day to the studio and so on. . . . He might have misunderstood my motives."

"Yes, he might. Lorrimer certainly did. And don't kid yourself Jonathan knows nothing about it. You let Lorrimer paint your portrait, didn't you? When you first dropped him, he took it to a little gallery in Bamford and asked them to sell it."

Sara swallowed. "I know. I begged him to get it back. Eventually he said he would. But he didn't. He lied and said it had already been sold."

"He wasn't lying, Sara. Jonathan bought it."

For a moment, Meredith thought Sara was going to faint. She swayed and her eyes glazed. Then they filled with panic. "No—that's impossible! He didn't know about the picture."

"He knew all right. Somewhere Jonathan has a source of information we don't know about. Lorrimer went back to the gallery but he was too late. Lazenby had got there first. Lorrimer realized who had bought it. It was the worst thing which could have happened from his point of view."

"Oh no," Sara said with desperate obstinacy. Then she looked up with a spark of anger in her eyes. "You still sound sorry for him! He was such a horrible man! Why do you blame *me?*" Her voice rose to a new wail of anguish.

Meredith sighed. "I don't blame you, Sara, not altogether. You were feeling sorry for yourself and your thoughts were entirely self-centred or you might have spared one to consider what kind of effect you were having on Lorrimer. But you weren't the only one in your family to let him down. The whole damn show did. Robert took him up briefly and gave him a commission painting your mother from a photo. You can bet Lorrimer sweated over that. He probably saw a whole new career opening up. But it came to nothing. Robert never recommended him to anyone else and then he died. Eve never liked the picture. It hung on the wall because Robert had bought it. She could have put a word in for the artist, but she didn't. When he threw the lamp, did that happen in the drawing room? Was she standing by the portrait?"

Sara nodded and Meredith added, "Then think about it. There she stood in front of the picture he had painted of her, telling him to get out and that he was a scruffy little nobody with nothing to offer anyone. He didn't throw the lamp at her and miss, Sara. He threw it at the portrait and hit the frame! I'm not excusing him! But he wanted to be a serious artist. Yet the only pottery he could get regular sales for was junk stuff and the only picture he ever really sold on the open market was one of a cat! Failure makes people bitter and it's only too easy to make an enemy of someone like that."

This time the silence was longer. It was interrupted by a thump on the ceiling as if someone upstairs had dropped something. Sara made no comment on it. Instead she pushed back her long hair with both hands and said quietly, "So I got it wrong. It still didn't give him the right to behave that way. I still didn't deserve all that. It hurt me, Merry!"

Pity mingled with Meredith's exasperation. "You should have told the police, Sara."

"They can't do anything in cases like that! Mummy knew that because she went through all that sort of thing when she was trying to divorce Hughie. The police don't interfere in domestic squabbles."

Meredith stared thoughtfully at a Swiss cheese plant in front of her and thought about Gary Yewell. "Tell me," she said, "did Phil threaten to sell all he knew to the tabloid press?"

"Yes!" Sara stared at her in astonishment. "How did you know? He said one of the tabloids would pay for a nice scandal involving Eve Owens's daughter and the children of the idle rich. All those society names, all that drugs and booze and sex. He had the photos and letter too, to back it up. That's why I told you it wasn't ordinary blackmail, you see. Selling a story to a newspaper, that's legal, isn't it?"

"It's a fine point!" Meredith said ruefully. "It's a modern sort of blackmail, I suppose. The perpetrator can spend his ill-gotten gains quite openly. It's still dirty. Is that what Phil wanted, money?"

"No, I told you it wasn't ordinary blackmail!" Sara said passionately. "Not for money, anyway. He wanted me to break off my engagement. He said if I did, he'd keep quiet. If I didn't, he'd send it all to the gutter press and Jon would be so furious and embarrassed that he'd break the engagement, which is true."

"Doesn't say much for Jonathan!" Meredith said grimly.

"Don't blame Jon!" Sara defended him. "He hasn't got any choice. He has to consider his job and his family. But it would have hurt Mummy, too. Robert had only just died and she was very low. Because she was mourning Robert I didn't tell her about Phil's threat to sell the story. It was bad enough that she knew he was jealous and making scenes. Don't tell her, Merry! It just gets worse and worse!"

"And Phil sent you photo-copies of the letter and photographs he had, to put on extra pressure, I take it?" Meredith asked briskly.

Sara shook her head. "No. He didn't need to. I knew he had them. He said they were hidden away safely and it would be no use my searching the cottage or studio. He'd got them stored somewhere else."

But he did make copies, Meredith thought. He made them on the library copier and Mrs. Hartman saw him. She frowned. Sara was undoubtedly telling all she knew, however subjectively. But possibly she didn't know all. Possibly Philip had played a much more devious game. . . . He might have started out only seeking revenge and trying in a crazy wrong-headed way to keep the girl he thought he had a right to, but then something else happened. Something else. . . . Yes! thought Meredith suddenly. And I know what it was!

"I should have told you before," Sara said despondently. "I've been so scared. That last time I saw Phil, when you and Mummy were in Bamford, we had yet another row and he said it was my last chance. I'm not sorry he's dead. When I heard about it, it was like a great weight lifted from me. I was glad!" She looked up through a fringe of long hair and fixed wretched blue eyes on Meredith's face. "Merry, don't despise me."

"I don't," Meredith told her. "Let me tell you two things. One—your father would have been proud of you. Two—you don't need Jonathan Lazenby to help you sort out your life. I think you're quite capable of doing that all on your own!"

Sara's face burned crimson and then she said quietly, "Thanks . . . for the first anyway. I'm not sure about the second."

Markby was sitting in Mrs. Hartman's little cubicle, drinking Nescafé from a pottery mug. It was quite an attractive little mug, long and slightly fluted and coloured with a blue wash which graduated from light to dark. Mrs. Hartman was telling her story again. It was the first time she had told it to a policeman and her thin face was unusually tinged with pink. Her spectacle lenses seemed to gleam with their owner's excitement and, because the police inspector really was a very handsome man, or so Mrs. Hartman thought, and had such nice manners, from time to time she patted at her permed grey curls with a nervous hand.

"I mean, as I said to the young lady, I would have come to the police but it seemed such a little thing . . . I really didn't have anything to tell you at all."

"Quite the reverse," said Markby gravely. "You've been very helpful, Mrs. Hartman." Which was more than Miss Mitchell had been! he thought grimly.

"I am sorry . . ." said Mrs. Hartman unhappily. "I mean, I should have come to see you straight away. I realize that now. What a good job you came to see me, Chief Inspector."

"Yes, isn't it?" said Markby blandly. He drained his mug. "Well, thank you for the coffee and your time. I won't take up any more of it."

"Not at all, not at all," fluted Mrs. Hartman.

They both stood up. Markby, in the act of replacing the blue mug on the shelf, impulsively turned it upside-down. On the bottom was an almost illegible label. "Hand-made pottery by Philip Lorrimer," Markby murmured aloud. "Church cottage . . ." The rest of the address had rubbed off. But there was a circular stamp impressed in the clay which read "Philip Lorrimer Pottery" in a round robin, the words all joined into one.

Markby showed it to Mrs. Hartman. "See that? One of his . . ."

"Fancy that!" said Mrs. Hartman. She took it from him and studied it thoughtfully. "You know," she said suddenly, "now that you've told me I shan't be able to drink out of it again. Neither will Holly Loomis. I really wish you hadn't pointed it out."

Funny little coincidence, thought Markby as he got back into his car. Perhaps it was a good omen. Or a bad one. "At least," he said aloud as he switched on the ignition, "now we have a motive."

Eleven

Sara offered to make lunch, but Meredith refused, explaining she had one or two shopping errands and offering to take Sara with her to the West End and buy them both lunch instead. But Sara wanted to go back to the Refuge.

"I've left Joanne doing my job. It's not fair. She held the fort for me while I was down at the rectory. I'd better get back."

She accompanied Meredith out into the hall. As they reached the front door, the clatter of high heels on the stairs caused them both to look up. A slender ash-blonde with beautifully made-up features and a long white imitation but nonetheless expensive fur coat appeared and stopped to stare at them both with sharp grey eyes.

"This is Fiona," Sara said. "She lives upstairs. My cousin, Meredith Mitchell, Fi."

Meredith nodded politely at the woman who, she thought, must surely be some sort of a model.

The ash-blonde tossed back a tumbling mane. "Hi! Are you just leaving? Is that your car outside? You aren't going up West by any chance? I'm late for a photographic session."

Meredith opened her mouth to suggest telephoning for a taxi, but some instinct made her stop. Instead she offered, "I'll give you a lift if you like."

They set off. The sun was not very strong, but Fiona donned smoky-lensed glasses and leaned back against the head-rest. "I can drop you in Orchard Street," Meredith asked meekly, "down the side of Selfridges—okay?"

"Yah—great."

The car slid along, Meredith driving slowly and waiting.

Without turning her head, Fiona said abruptly, "Sara's in some kind of trouble, isn't she?"

"Is she?" Meredith turned a corner smoothly and drew up at red lights.

Now the car was temporarily stationary, the ash-blonde mane moved on the head-rest and the sunglasses faced Meredith. She could feel but not see the intentness of the sharp grey stare. "It's to do with that Lorrimer, isn't it?"

Meredith was pleased to think her instinct had not let her down and that this bimbo had indeed cadged a lift in order to find out what she had been talking about with Sara, but her surprise at hearing Philip mentioned openly was such that she almost stalled the car when the lights changed. For a second or two she was at a disadvantage and could not reply at once. When she did, she asked in startled tones, "Did you know Philip?"

"Oh, come on," said Fiona dismissively. "Do I look as if I'd have anything to do with someone like that?"

"No," said Meredith honestly.

Fiona took this as a compliment. Her tone mellowed slightly. She grew confidential. "Sara told me about him. I've known Sara quite a while, before her mother and stepfather moved down to that place in the country. Sara hated it when she first went there. It was the back of beyond. She used to write to me about it. She told me about this guy next door who made ash-trays and jugs, for crying out loud. I told her to stay clear. He was such an obvious nohoper. That type always ends up causing trouble. You can never get rid of them. Then the other day, when Sara got back to town, she told me Lorrimer was dead. It was murder, or so the police thought. I wasn't surprised."

"Why not?"

"I told you," said Fiona impatiently. "You never get rid of that type. They're like leeches. I bet you poor Sara wasn't the only one he'd battened on. No wonder someone did him in. If it had been me, I would have done. Only I wouldn't have let him latch on to me in the first place."

Meredith's eye caught a space between cars at the kerbside. She pulled into it and switched off the engine.

"Right," she said briskly, turning to the woman, "what

is it you want to know—and take those ridiculous glasses off!"

Fiona removed the sunglasses unperturbed. "I want to know if Sara's in trouble. She's a friend. And she's engaged to an old boyfriend of mine, Jonathan Lazenby."

A pattern was beginning to emerge. "Tell me," Meredith said. "Before Sara went to live in the country—did you and she go to the same parties? Share the same friends?"

Fiona shrugged. "Some. Doesn't everyone? I mean, go to the same parties and see the same people there?"

It depended what social circle you moved in, Meredith thought and avoided an answer. "How do you come to be living in the same house?"

"Easy," said Fiona confidently as if she had expected a trickier question. "Sara wanted a flat. I saw Jon Lazenby in a night-club one evening and he told me about it and I said no problem, the people below me are moving out. I was pleased to think Sara might be moving in because I already knew her. Jon was pleased, too."

You bet he was, thought Meredith, because now he had a spy to keep an eye on Sara for him.

"Convenient!" she said drily.

"Yah—wasn't it?" The woman consulted what appeared to be a Cartier wristwatch. "I'm going to be late."

Meredith drove her to Orchard Street and let her out. She drove round for another ten minutes looking for somewhere to park and when she had locked up the car she went into Selfridges. The restaurant was already busy so she avoided it. She bought the one or two items she needed and went back to put them in the boot and feed the meter. Then she walked to Portman Square behind the store and entered the museum housing the Wallace collection.

There were few people in here and no one thought it odd if anyone just sat. Meredith sat and stared at Fragonard's girl on a swing. Lazenby was a brash, shallow yuppie, but that kind is ruthless. City-smart. He knew a great deal more about what went on than she had supposed. Than any of them had supposed. He knew more of Sara's past than Sara thought and almost certainly his informant had been the willowy Fiona who would not have spared him any details. With friends like that, as the old saying went, Sara certainly did not need any enemies.

However, it explained Lazenby's jumpiness. No wonder he was worried. He already knew what Philip had threatened to tell and as Sara rightly said was above all desperate that it did not reach the press. What he did not have was the decency or moral courage to go to Sara, lay his cards on the table and tell her he knew.

He had not done it because it would reveal what an unedifying hand he had been playing to date. Instead he preferred to snoop around his prospective mother-in-law's home and receive reports from his spy-in-residence in London, Fiona. By keeping quiet, if and when the storm broke, he could look shocked and innocent and exclaim, "I never suspected!" and then take off in a cloud of offended dignity, never to be seen again. Meredith wondered whether, in such an eventuality, he would ask for his ring back.

"You bet!" she muttered, "and the next thing we'd know, Fiona would be sporting a similar ruby cluster on her finger! That's certainly her intention, anyway . . ."

An elderly gentleman with a shock of white hair standing out in a halo, bearing a resemblance to Einstein in his last years, and who had been staring besottedly at the courtesan on the swing, turned mildly puzzled eyes on Meredith.

"I'm sorry!" she apologized. "I was just looking at the painting and got thinking . . ."

"I understand," said the elderly gentleman in Central European tones. "I come often to see her and she always enchants. I believe I have been in love with her all my life since when I was a young man and bought a picture postcard of her from a bookseller in Vienna. Such fidelity, eh?" He chuckled.

Meredith looked up at the girl on the swing and smiled. But as she walked away she thought, Fidelity . . . that's the most difficult thing. It's the most painful. How do you go on loving when the object of your love is faithless? Does love always die? Does it turn like Philip's for Sara into a stupid and vindictive destruction? He did love her, surely. And she threw him over, even though she can't see it her-

self. Just like her mother in so many ways. Oh, Mike. . . .
Did you really always go on loving Eve despite all her be-
trayals? Or did you mean all the things you said to me?
Could you really have ever walked away from her? Had
she only to crook her little finger to bring you running
back?

Meredith set out to drive back. The weather had clouded
over and the air was oppressive. She felt low-spirited. I'm
just hungry! she admonished herself, realizing that it was
almost four and she had had no lunch. She drove on into
increasingly open country until she saw a reasonable-
looking pub which advertised bar snacks all day. She
pulled into the car park and got out with a sigh of relief.
She needed time to think. The sun was just starting to go
down. A slight breeze bowled along dry leaves and scraps
of paper but otherwise it was very still. The car park was
nearly empty and the pub, a large red-brick mock Tudor
affair, looked quiet, solid and respectable. It was the sort
of place businessmen driving about the country made for.
Its lunch menu probably had steak and kidney pie and it
kept a wine cellar of sorts.

She made her way into the lounge bar. It was a little
gloomy but in a good state of decoration with Dralon covered seats and plenty of fake dark Jacobean oak. Meredith
asked for the Ploughman's Lunch.

"Cheese or home-made pâté?" asked the young man sta-
tioned behind the bar. He wore the kind of golfing sweater
beloved of Albie Elliott and managed to convey the impression that even if they were quiet at the moment, the
rush was about to begin.

"Pâté," said Meredith, thinking that the ploughmen
hereabouts had a lifestyle all their own. Her eye fell on a
notice pinned up behind the young man saying that bed-
and-breakfast was available.

"Can I have a room for tonight?" she asked.

It seemed she could. She concluded the necessary arrangements and went to find the public telephone and ring
through to the rectory and explain she would not be back
until the morning. Lucia answered the phone and took the
message.

Meredith went back into the bar and found the pâté had arrived. It was accompanied by French bread, foil-wrapped butter, a small lettuce leaf and half a tomato. She was not doing any more driving that day so she ordered a glass of the house red. Nothing in the English countryside was as it had been.

"Pubs sell wine, ploughmen eat pâté and baguettes, film stars live in vicarages and milkmen deliver potatoes . . ." she murmured. It was an uneasy mix. False as a film set. And as heartless.

The bedroom was plain but reasonably comfortable. The wardrobe door didn't shut properly and there was a fair amount of noise from an adjacent bathroom, but it faced away from the main road so the traffic noise was muted. It would not have disturbed her in any case. Meredith switched on an elderly television set in one corner and watched for a while before turning in early and sleeping like a log.

Bert Yewell turned over in the big old double bed he had once shared with Ada and woke up. He lay there thinking about the past, as he often did at times like this. It was a rum thing, but somehow the past seemed more real than the present. He could remember the past so well and yet, dang it, he couldn't remember where he'd put them seeds last week or what it was he had meant to fetch back from Bamford the last time he'd gone in there on the bus. Couldn't have been that important, Bert consoled himself, or I'd have found I didn't have it by now.

People, now. He remembered people who were dead and gone fifty years or more better than those around him now. His niece Pearl, she said that young fellow who delivered the milk was young Andy's son, but blowed if Bert could remember him. Come to that, how could young Andy have a son? He was only a kid himself. Although, come to think of it, Andy was born during the last war, so he must be a bit older by now than Bert reckoned. There you are, thought Bert with gloomy satisfaction. Time flies by and you lose whole lumps of it altogether, years at a time.

People, now . . . Bert liked cutting the churchyard grass because it was like visiting old friends. There were men buried there he'd been at school with, when the school house had been a proper school. He remembered which ones were good at football and which ones never had a clean shirt . . . and he remembered old Mr. Lewis who had been schoolmaster and took snuff on the sly—ah, bad-tempered old bird he had been. But Reverend Markby, he'd been worse. Holy terror, right enough.

"And that," muttered Bert, "is how it should be. Teach a bit of discipline. What's right and wrong. No one ever let me put a foot wrong. Got me ear clipped. I had to work hard from age twelve on. Not like that young layabout as lived next door. Making pots. Every evening in the Dun Cow. Fast women. Dead, poisoned, and that was a judge-ment that was. Struck down for his sins. And I never done it!" added Bert pugnaciously to the bolster.

He sat up with an effort and swung his legs out of bed. Puffing with the exertion, he managed to get out com-pletely and felt his way across the darkened room and out into his kitchen. Make a cup of tea. Helped when you couldn't sleep. He didn't put the light on because he didn't need it. Knew his own kitchen like the back of his hand. Born in this cottage. There was enough moonlight falling through the uncurtained window and its silver sheen made it like day, almost. Bert took the battered tin kettle to the sink and reached for the tap. He found himself staring straight out of the window and down his garden towards a faint, intermittent stab of light.

"Dang me!" he exclaimed and set down the kettle with a clang. "There's some bugger in me shed!"

Excitedly, he puffed over to the back door and dragged on his raincoat and struggled into his boots. Gipsies, most like. Well, they were due a fright! Bert took the heavy old torch left over from his ARP duties and let himself out of the back door. He made his way cautiously down the gar-den path and before the half-open shed door came to a quivering halt. Someone was in there right enough and turning the place upside-down.

"You come on out of there!" he ordered.

From inside the shed came a gasp. Something fell down with a clatter. Bert pushed the button on the torch and swung up the beam of light, directing it through the door. "Well, dang me . . ." he said.

It was noon the following day when Mrs. Yewell, finished at the rectory, pushed her bicycle squeakily down the front path of Bert's cottage and propped it against the wall. She heaved a deep sigh and wiped her forehead as she set off round the back. Uncle Bert never used his front door. She wouldn't be surprised if it didn't even open after all this time, swollen shut most like. Uncle Bert was something of a problem. He couldn't go on living on his own much longer but, as she had said to Walter only last night, you'd never get the old boy away from his garden.

The back door into the kitchen stood open. Mrs. Yewell bustled in. "Uncle Bert!" There was no reply. She looked about her in disgust and made distressed clucking noises. "Uncle Bert? Are you there? This place is a real pigsty. If Auntie Ada could see it, she'd turn in her grave! I'll come over this weekend and give it a real going over."

He wasn't here. He was probably down his garden somewhere. Mrs. Yewell put her head through the bedroom door. Look at that. Got up and walked out and not even made the bed. The old chap was all right messing about outdoors in that garden but he couldn't look after himself, it was a fact. She went back through the kitchen and set off down the long, narrow plot past the immaculate, regimented rows of vegetables and carefully tended soft fruit bushes, past the patch from which the onions had been lifted and which was as fresh dug over and geometrically oblong as a new grave, calling as she went, "Uncle Bert? I come for Walter's cabbage plants! You said as they'd be ready."

Not in his garden. That was odd. Over at the churchyard, maybe? The shed door was open. Mrs. Yewell, who had started to experience a prickle of unease, heaved a sigh of relief. Pottering in that messy old shed. Getting deaf, too. Here she was, shouting her head off and he couldn't hear a thing.

She walked round the pile of garden rubbish waiting to be burnt which stood between her and the shed and then she saw him. Saw, too, why he hadn't heard nor ever would hear her again. Mrs. Yewell began to scream.

Twelve

Alan Markby was getting steadily more irritated. It was pointless being irritable with a dead man, but Philip Lorrimer must have been the most incompetent book-keeper in the world, and it was not surprising that amongst the jumble of papers brought away from the cottage and now spread out on Markby's desk were several letters from the Inland Revenue. The tone ranged from the plaintive to the abrupt and all demanded details of Lorrimer's income. He had kept no kind of regular accounts at all. Odd bills and receipts were mixed together. Some were obscured with streaks of paint or clay fingerprints. The fingerprints could at least be checked but would prove to be Lorrimer's. There was some correspondence with gift shops regarding the pottery. A couple of complaints about late or non-delivery, too. In one case the order was cancelled in a curt note pointing out that if Lorrimer could not produce the goods when promised, he must expect customers to look elsewhere. Not a good businessman at all, Mr. Lorrimer. Pearce could check those. Markby's fingers closed on a different piece of paper. What was this?

It was an estimate for repairs to a Bedford van. Markby whistled softly between his teeth. Strewth, it would be cheaper to buy a good second-hand replacement. He frowned. There had been no van on the property. He looked at the address on the estimate, folded the bill and stuck it in his pocket and told Pearce he was going out. "Contact this lot," he said, handing Pearce the miscellany of letters and receipts regarding pottery ordered or supplied. Pearce looked gloomy.

The repair garage was a small one in a back street but the front was painted and the forecourt tidy and it gave every appearance of a reputable establishment. A young man in orange overalls came out, wiping his hands on a bundle of cotton waste as Markby got out of the car. When he identified himself, the young man looked distinctly nervous. There was probably good reason, but it was unlikely it had anything to do with the matter in hand. The youth said Markby ought to see Fred. As he set off to do this, he saw from the corner of his eye the young man scuttling towards a telephone. Counterfeit videos, dog-fighting, who knows? he thought resignedly. It was amazing what fell out when you tapped the woodwork.

Fred was also in orange overalls but proved to be an older man with horn-rimmed spectacles and hands so engrained with grease and dirt that Markby wondered if they ever came clean. He produced the estimate and explained his purpose.

"I remember that van all right," said Fred dourly. "But it ain't here. Heap of scrap, that's what it was. I told the young feller so. No point in fixing that! to get it up to scratch to pass the MOT you'd need to spend a small fortune on it and it wasn't worth it. I advised him to take it to Crocker's yard. I mean, we could've done the work but it didn't seem fair on the lad."

Markby made his way to Crocker's yard. It was out of town, a glorious jungle of rusty old cars and scrap surrounded by high wire fencing. On all sides of it, in complete contrast, lay fields bounded by tangled blackberry bushes. The late afternoon sun shone in Markby's face, as he turned into the sprawling yard, and glinted off piled metal as if the abandoned hulks signalled to one another. Two dark, gipsy-looking young men working at the end of an alley between twisted metal skeletons glanced up at his car and returned to their work. But they would be on hand if needed. This kind of place always conducted a fair number of discreet cash transactions and was a sitting target for casual violent robbery.

In the middle of the twinkling metal forest stood a Portakabin office guarded by a bad-tempered looking alsa-

tian dog which growled at Markby when he got out of his
car. Behind it, pop music issued from the Portakabin
through a half-open door.

"Mr. Crocker!" called Markby, finding himself backed
up against his car door by the intimidating canine. "Chief
Inspector Markby from the Bamford station. Can I have a
word?"

The music was switched off, the Portakabin door
opened and a thin man with jet-black hair and a moustache
appeared. "Better come in then, chief! Don't take no notice of the dog."

"He's taking notice of me," said Markby.

"Naw, he's a soft old thing. *Siddown!*" roared Mr.
Crocker suddenly in stentorian tones. The dog sank on its
haunches and put its nose on its paws. It watched Markby
climb the steps into the office with mistrustful tawny eyes.

"What can I do for you, then, squire?" asked Mr.
Crocker genially, shaking Markby by the hand. He wore
several gold rings, a heavy gold identity bracelet and an
expensive-looking wristwatch. "All the books are in order.
I don't deal in no hot cars nor nuffin'."

Markby explained about the van. Mr. Crocker frowned
and produced a grimy ledger with something of a flourish.

"We get a lot of old tin cans like that. The kids buy 'em
cheap, run 'em into the ground and then bring 'em here.
They ain't worth nuffin'. I gives 'em thirty or forty quid
for 'em. Just to be helpful, you know what I mean? Take
'em off their hands."

"Very good of you," said Markby blandly.

"Yus. I mean, you'd appreciate that, wouldn't you? I
mean, if it wasn't for me, they'd only abandon 'em somewhere and then your boys would have a lot of work,
wouldn't they? End up passing it on to the council and then
they gets on to me to go and fetch 'em away. . . . Here we
are . . ." He spread the open book before Markby's eyes,
pushing aside a transistor radio, an ash-tray full of stubs, an
empty lager can and a copy of a tabloid newspaper folded
open at a list of today's runners. There was also, Markby noticed, a cordless telephone on the table.

"Yes, you do keep detailed books!" he said a little sarcastically.

"Like I say, squire. All above board. I don't get rid of no cars what have been in funny business nor nuffin' like that. Everythin' what comes in this yard goes down in this book!" Mr. Crocker could afford to let the sarcasm roll over his head. He sat back, smoothed his jet-black hair with a beringed hand and lit a small cigar.

Markby ran a finger down the page. Mr. Crocker had parted with the princely sum of ten pounds for the van—scrap. "Good money," said Mr Crocker, reading the entry upside-down. "Considering it wasn't worth nuffin' really."

Markby closed the book. "Well, thank you, Mr. Crocker." His eye lit on a coloured postcard affixed to the wall. "Oh, Spain, is that?"

"That's right," said Mr. Crocker cheerfully. "I bought a villa there last year—just about here." He pointed to a white mass of concrete in the corner of the picture. "Well, not fer me, you know. The missus wanted it and you know how it is, got to keep the enemy happy!"

He conducted Markby back to his car, past the softly growling alsatian, and shook hands with him again. "Anything to help the boys in blue, Inspector!"

Markby glanced at the surrounding chaos. Somewhere in this elephants' graveyard Lorrimer's van rusted away. Unglamorous surroundings, but you could buy a villa in Spain on the proceeds.

"It's not what you'd call beautiful," said Mr. Crocker complacently, puffing blue smoke into Markby's face. "But it's an honest living, innit?"

Markby drove back to Bamford, wondering if he had spent his entire life in the wrong business.

"Oh, Mr. Markby, sir!" called the lad on the desk as he stomped crossly into the station.

"Yes?" he said sharply.

"Report just come in, sir. A woman found a body . . ."

The shape on the ground hardly looked like a real body at all. It was crumpled up, seeming very small and shrunken inside the baggy old raincoat, and the smashed skull might have been a Hallowe'en pumpkin head, it was so distorted and grotesque. The washed-out blue-striped pyjamas and the mud-caked wellington boots seemed tossed down like discarded contributions to a jumble sale, past selling.

"A Mrs. Yewell found him," said Sergeant Pearce. "She's a niece by marriage, as I understand. She lives in the village and works as daily in the mornings at the rectory—the Owens's place."

Markby looked up sharply. "Does she, indeed?" He looked back at the body. "Poor old devil," he said. "Didn't take much force to do that. Skull like an eggshell, probably. But why? What was he doing down here in the middle of the night in his pyjamas?"

"Heard a noise?" Pearce shrugged. "The weapon, sir— probably." He held up a transparent plastic bag containing an old heavy rubber-handled torch.

"These are the ones that really get to me," Markby said slowly. "The attacks on the very young and the very old. Stupid old blighter. . . . Why didn't he tell us what he knew? He'd be alive today and digging up his damned carrots."

"Think he knew something, sir?"

"Why the hell kill him, otherwise?" Markby scowled at the shed. "And why here?" He remember talking to Laura about poison and saying he preferred the blunt instrument cases. He wondered now what on earth had possessed him to say such a thing.

He stood by the roadside and watched them load Bert's body into the ambulance and take it away. The sheer wickedness of it all left him feeling impotent and furious, temporarily numbed. A small crowd of local people hung about on the triangular patch of green around the bus stop, watching and whispering together. Their faces were shocked but sullen too. This time the violence had come to one of their own. He could sense the smouldering rage. He felt like walking across to them and shouting, "Me, too! I feel that way about it, too!" But he didn't feel about it the way they did. Their resentment ran deeper, directed not only towards one murderer, but towards all those distant faceless forces which had conspired over the years to destroy their way of life.

A car approached from the direction of the main road,

drew up and a door slammed. "Chief Inspector Markby!" called a woman's voice.

He looked up. Meredith Mitchell was coming towards him. She walked quickly over the gravel, her face tense and anxious. "What's happened?" she asked in a low rapid voice.

"Where have you been?" he retorted.

"I went to London yesterday. I stayed overnight on the road back at a pub place that did bed and breakfast. I've just driven from there this morning. What on earth is going on?"

"I want a word with you, anyway," he said abruptly. "Lock your car up and come with me into the Dun Cow. The old man is dead, by the way."

He wanted to shock her and he succeeded. She drew a sharp breath. "How?"

"Blunt instrument. Probably a torch. During the night and in his garden, by the shed door. The niece, Pearl Yewell, found him at lunchtime when she called by to collect some plants."

They were walking towards the Dun Cow as he spoke. The door of the pub was open and Harry Linnet, the publican, stood framed in it, a glowering figure in an old pullover and grubby body-warmer.

"I know these aren't your opening hours," Markby said to him, "but I'd appreciate it if you could make a room available to me for an hour."

"You can have the snug," Harry growled promptly, leading them into a claustrophobic cavern with low timber beams and a sour odour of stale tobacco. "You just ask for what you wants, Inspector. We all of us wants you to get the blighter who done that to old Bert! And if you wants Pearl Yewell again, she's in our back parlour with my wife. Took very bad, she is."

"Local people are angry," Markby said, seating himself in a shadowy recess in the thick stone wall. There were horse brasses all over the place, tacked up along the dark ceiling beams, strung down the wall on strips of leather. Markby wondered who polished them all.

He watched Meredith sit down opposite him where a shaft of light from a small, dusty window fell on her face.

She put her clasped hands briefly to her mouth then said in a low voice, "They weren't angry when Philip died." She did not look at him, but fixed her eyes on the dull gold gleam of the horse brasses behind his head.

"He wasn't one of them. He was an outsider. A foreigner, as they'd see it." He paused. "Why didn't you come back to the rectory last night?"

"I was tired . . . I didn't want to drive any more. And I wanted to get away from this village for a night. It—it really is quite the most horrible village I was ever in."

"What makes it horrible?" Markby asked her. "The place, the people?"

"The soullessness of it."

He was silent for a while. She had rested her elbows on the little round table between them and her chin on her clasped hands. The curtain of glossy dark brown hair caressed her cheek.

"The last time we met," he said, and it seemed to his ear that his own voice sounded peculiar, as if it stuck in his throat, "I told you to leave the detective work to me, Meredith. You told me you'd parked your car outside the library, so I went along there yesterday to see what you'd been doing. You'd been talking to one of the librarians, a Mrs. Hartman, and she actually had something quite interesting to relate. But you didn't tell me about it. Why?"

She looked up, those wonderful thickly lashed hazel eyes defiant. "Sometimes, you know, you're not the easiest man to talk to!"

"I'm sorry about that . . ." He gave a little hiss of impatience. "But you should have told me. You didn't go chatting to old Bert, too, did you?"

"Yes. He kept dropping hints, but he wouldn't tell me anything, except that he found Lorrimer's cat dead in the churchyard and burned it on his bonfire because he was afraid he'd get the blame." She paused. "He made obscure accusations about Philip. Women and so on. Said he was always propping up the bar in here." She hesitated again. "Bert told Phil, he says, to save his money and buy a new van."

"Oh yes," Markby said. "I've found out about the van.

It's currently rusting in a scrapyard belonging to a Mr. Crocker."

A closed, frozen look had crossed her face.

He said gently, "Bert was not the nicest old man in the world, just as this isn't the nicest village. This isn't the best pub I was ever in. But they're all valid in their way. He was eighty years old and had lived here all his life. He deserved to die in his bed or drop dead in his potato patch . . . but not to have his skull caved in."

"Was it a very brutal attack?" she asked almost inaudibly.

"No, not really—not a berserk one, if that's what you mean. Just a couple of good strong blows . . . but one would have done the trick. Like knocking in a papier-mâché mask."

She twitched. He said, "Think about it." But he had no need to say that. She would think about it. He watched her stand up and walk out of the snug. She was tall enough to need to duck her head under the low beams. Markby sighed and went to see if Mrs. Yewell was well enough to talk to him.

Thirteen

A stony-faced Lucia let Meredith into the house and took her coat. In answer to Meredith's query, she said grudgingly, "The signora is resting in her room. She is not well. She has the very bad head. I make for her now camomile tea." She gave Meredith a defiant look from her black eyes. The cook had obviously omitted some matinal routine to her toilet which involved plucking out the dark hairs which sprouted on her upper lip and this afternoon she sported a distinct moustache.

"I'll take it up to her," Meredith said with calm authority. Lucia moved unwillingly to one side and muttered resentfully but did not argue.

Meredith climbed the stairs slowly with the pale yellowish tea splashing a little in the cup. As she reached the top there was a click and a door further down the upper landing opened. A shaft of light fell into the shadows and in it Albie Elliott appeared.

"Why don't you leave it?" he asked gently.

"She's expecting tea."

"Come on now," he said reproachfully. "You know I'm not talking about the goddamn tea."

It was quiet on the landing. Meredith put the cup down on a little table and moved towards him. He turned away and she followed him into the room. He pushed the door shut and they faced each other. He looked very much as he had done the first time she had met him, small, tidy, sleek. His undertaker's paleness and smooth skin seemed like an advertisement for his own embalming technique.

She said, "You were right about Lorrimer leaving those things about the place."

"Sure I was right, Meredith. Right about a lot of things. You go on back downstairs and let me take the tea in to Evie."

She shook her head. "No, I want to talk to her."

"No, you don't," he said patiently.

"I must."

He gave a little sigh. "Listen, it's never a good idea to ask questions, to go looking for information. Good news gets to you sooner or later and who the hell wants to hear bad news? If you start asking questions, Meredith, you get answers. The trouble is, they aren't always the answers you expect or want. You might learn a whole lot more than you counted on. Have you thought of that? Let it alone, sweetheart."

"I can't."

His patience snapped. His pale face flushed and grew animated, the muscles about his thin mouth twitching. "Then for God's sake, think of me! I need her! The show needs her! I've put together a real good package for her and me! Without her, it all goes down the tubes, baby!" In his agitation, his accent was slipping away along with his laid-back calm. A new kind of lifestyle was emerging from it. High-rise tenement buildings and iron fire-escapes, kids running wild and young loafers on street corners. Packages exchanged in public lavatories. Mothers who were hookers and fathers, if there were any, who never worked. Welfare stamps and petty crime. He must have fought hard to get away from that and he was fighting now, fighting to stop sliding back down into the morass.

But he was losing this round of the battle and he knew it. The anger in his face was mixed with desperation and with fear.

"Sooner or later I have to see her, Albie. It might as well be now!"

"You'll be sorry," he said vindictively. "Don't come crying to me! You'll be sorry—and you damn well deserve it!" He looked as though he was going to cry himself. "Why can't you damn well leave it alone?"

Meredith went back to the landing and retrieved the cooling tea. "Evie?" She tapped on the door and turned the handle without waiting for an answer. She sensed that

Elliott had come to the door of his room and watched but he made no move to interfere. His hatred was like an arrow between her shoulderblades. But it was hatred that sprang from impotence. The sort of hatred that had inspired Philip Lorrimer.

Eve was sitting with her feet up on a little sofa in the window embrasure, staring out at the back garden with blank violet eyes. The mellow late afternoon sun fell across the legs of her immaculate white pants. She was wearing the shocking pink blouse again and looked as she always did, bandbox fresh except for dark shadows beneath the eyes. Meredith put down the camomile tea.

"Sorry you're not feeling well, Eve. Here's Lucia's brew . . ." She fell silent, the words trailing away unhappily.

Eve turned her head and gave her a sad little smile. "Yes," she said.

"You haven't been at the gin, have you?"

"No—my head aches. I couldn't drink alcohol."

Damn this, Meredith thought. What a wretched business. Aloud she said, "I'm sorry I didn't come home last night."

"It doesn't matter," her cousin said in the same soft sad voice. "It didn't make any difference."

"It might have done." Meredith stood up and wandered over to the Victorian mantelpiece. It had been painted with white gloss and functioned solely as a decorative feature yet despite the fact that no fire was ever lit in it, feathery scraps of paper burned almost to ash quivered in the hearth and floated into the air in the draught caused by her approach.

"You found them, then," Meredith said slowly. "After all. This is all that remains of Phil's originals, isn't it? The letter and the photographs?"

Eve stirred slightly and picked up the tea. "Yes. He really was so tiresome, hiding them in that silly old man's shed. I searched all over the cottage and in the studio and I really couldn't think where he'd put them. Then I remembered Sara telling me about the shed. Phil had been in there and told Sara what a dreadful mess it was in. So I thought Phil would have kept the letter and those photos near at hand. The shed would be ideal. No one else went in it except the old man and he hadn't moved the contents for years. Phil could get in there virtually any time when the old man was out. All he had to do was tuck the envelope up into the roof. And that's what he had done."

Meredith said, "That was quite clever of you, Evie. But you shouldn't have hurt the old man."

"I didn't mean to!" Evie sounded aggrieved. She put down the teacup. "It wasn't my fault. It was two o'clock in the morning for goodness' sake! Why wasn't the silly old fool asleep in his bed? He suddenly appeared, looking just like a great big goblin and waving a torch and shining it in my face. Even then I wouldn't have hurt him. I would have explained that Phil had hidden something of mine and showed him the envelope . . . but he began shouting at me. Such stupid things!" Eve's tone became scornful. "He called me Jezebel and a scarlet woman! I ask you! He kept on about Sodom and Gomorrah. He said a woman my age ought to know better! I said he was a silly old fool and didn't know what he was talking about. Then he said he'd seen me leaving Phil's cottage very early in the morning, creeping about at first light . . . so he knew I'd been up to no good! He said I was old enough to be Phil's mother and I must know Phil had been carrying on with my daughter, which made it worse . . . and he started on about Sodom and Gomorrah again. Oh, it really was so tiresome!"

Eve broke off in exasperation and clapped her hands together. Meredith came back and sat down beside her on a little stool. "But he'd got it wrong, hadn't he, Eve?"

"Yes, of course he had! I wasn't having an affair with Phil! As if I would! And neither would Sara have been so silly. That's why it was all such a nonsense when Phil made such a fuss over her engagement. But you see, I couldn't let the old man go round telling people he'd seen me early in the morning at Phil's back door—because Alan Markby might have heard and he would have guessed the real reason . . ."

"Tell me what Phil wanted from you, Eve."

Eve shrugged elegantly. "Oh, money, what do you think? Common little blackmailer! He'd got hold of a letter and photos and gave me copies. He was going to ruin

Sara first and then he intended to blackmail other people too. So you see, I did the right thing in killing him. He would have been a dreadful nuisance. I got the idea of poison from the dreary Locke female. We get vermin in the gardens, foxes and so forth, and she found a poisoned one. Such a fuss she made, too. I began to think about poison and I remembered how years ago Lucia told me about making poisons from herbs. I didn't involve her this time. I experimented on my own. I bought some gerbils, funny little things, in a pet shop in Bamford and kept them in those derelict stables. No one uses them for anything or goes in there, not even Mr. Yewell when he comes to garden. The gerbils were quite easy to kill so I tried it on a rabbit. I realized I'd have to step up the doses considerably to kill a man. I knew Phil drank a lot of milk, so I thought of tampering with the milk bottles very early just after they were delivered. That way I would be sure he'd take a dose every day and it would build up. I knew that even if Lucia guessed what I'd done, she wouldn't say anything. She's totally loyal."

"But Bert saw you—and thought mistakenly you were creeping out of Phil's back door after nights of illicit passion."

"Yes . . . I told you, he was such a silly old man, getting up so early and quite obsessed with sin and sex. At his age! Disgusting! All that Sodom and Gomorrah business . . . I think he was mad." Eve turned reproachful eyes on her. "You nearly saw me, Merry. The morning Philip died I found him before you did. He wasn't quite dead. He was lying on the studio floor dribbling foam and gasping. It was very unpleasant. But I could see he was dying. I hadn't thought"—Eve frowned—"that he would have taken so long about it. But I saw I could search the cottage before anyone else found him. At least, I thought so!" A cross note entered her voice. "So I started going through the cottage and then, would you believe it?, that silly old man came out of his home and started swearing and shouting at one of the cats. It was behaving very oddly, dodging about in the bushes and making a queer noise. I was scared he'd see me. So I ran out of Philip's kitchen door while the old man was chasing down his garden after the

SAY IT WITH POISON 197

cat, ran back across the lane into the rectory garden, bolted the garden door and started to come back to the house. Then I saw you!" Eve's violet eyes opened wide. "You were coming down the garden. I had to hide in the shrubbery. You walked right by me. You opened the gate and went into the lane. I knew you'd find Philip. I just ran up to the house here and came upstairs. I heard you come back and phone Peter Russell. And then Mrs. Yewell came wailing up the stairs at me. 'Oh lor, Miss Owens, I don't know what's happened over at the studio ... !' " Eve mimicked the daily woman.

Meredith sighed.

"That silly old man," Eve said resentfully. "Do you know, he had seen me! Last night, after he'd called me Jezebel and all the rest of it and talked about seeing me in the mornings, he shouted, 'And I seen you on the morning he died, an' all! You was in his cottage, you was!" I had to kill him, Merry."

Eve leaned forward urgently. "You do understand, don't you? I had to shut the old man up and I had to get rid of Phil. I didn't want to do it, either time. They made me, both of them. I had to stop Philip's mouth for good. Jon Lazenby's family is so proper and Jon himself is the sort that cuts and runs when there's trouble and I knew there wasn't a chance he'd stand by Sara if there was a scandal. Nor could I pay Phil a lot of money. I don't have any. Oh, I know it looks as if I do, but I don't. All I have is what Robert left me. That's why I do need Albie's soap opera role so desperately and nothing must stop me getting it! Phil was just like Hughie and I know that type. They're spiteful, especially if they don't get what they want, and when Phil realized I wasn't going to pay him—couldn't pay him—there was no knowing what he might have done to get revenge. I was afraid he'd disrupt the marriage service. He might have slipped in at the back and jumped up when the vicar asks if anyone knows 'just cause or impediment' and started ranting on about everything. Or he might have let the marriage go ahead so he could get his money from Sara. He would have preyed on my poor baby for the whole of her marriage like a leech. He would have bled her white. That sort does. Do you think I don't know?

If they have a hold on you, they play it for all it's worth. I had to pay Hughie every cent I had to get him to agree to a divorce and go away. That's why I have nothing but Robert's money. Hughie took the rest, everything, and all the time laughing, laughing at me because I was power- less. Do you think I'd let Sara go through what I went through then?"

"But why had you to pay Hughie for a divorce?" asked Meredith curiously, remembering the tales she had heard and Eve, had told her of her second's husband's despicable behaviour. "You had grounds. He was no good. He drank, he beat you up, he cheated you, he wouldn't work—"

"Oh yes, all that," Eve said earnestly. "But I couldn't say so in court because, you see, Hughie knew what I'd done."

A cloud passed over the sun outside and the room be- came suddenly duller and colder. Elliott's voice echoed spitefully in her ear. "You'll be sorry!" Meredith shivered. It was as if a ghost had entered and stood at her elbow. She knew, deep in her heart, that to ask the next question was to invite a dreadful knowledge she did not want to have—but must. "What did Hughie know, Evie?"

"That I shot Mike. Hughie guessed it somehow and he always said if I wanted to dish the dirt, so could he. In the end, when he was tired of me anyway and tired of tor- menting me, he just took my money and went. It left me without a cent. But I was so glad to see him go . . ."

"But I thought," Meredith whispered, "the junkie . . ."

"Oh no!" Eve sat up, swinging her legs to the floor and sounding quite bright. "No, not at all. You see, I wanted Mike to come back to us—to Sara and me. I thought he would. He kept saying he had to think it out and so on, but I was so sure—" Eve sounded petulant. "I was so sure he would see it was right to come back to us in the end! That evening we went to his apartment and we had a couple of drinks and he said—he said . . ." Eve's voice grew incred- ulous. "He said he'd made up his mind and he wasn't coming back. Not ever. He'd found someone else, Merry! He wanted someone else more than he wanted Sara and me!"

Meredith shut her eyes tightly. Her head was throbbing.

The words of Mike's last letter whirled round and round in her brain like newspaper headlines. "I don't know what to do, Merry, except that I want to do what's right. You know I don't love Eve any longer, but there's the child. I feel I ought to give it another try for Sara's sake. Yet I don't think I can bear to stand by and watch Eve play around again, and she will, I know, once she thinks she's got me safely back in the corral. I honestly haven't made up my mind and feel a prize heel writing to you like this after all the plans we've made. Please be patient, darling, and try and understand. I'll settle it soon, one way or the other . . ."

He had done so. He had made up his mind and chosen her, Meredith. And it had been the death of him.

"I carried a little gun in my purse," Eve was saying in a curious sing-song voice like a child reciting a poem. "There had been a number of attacks on women when we first arrived and Mike bought me the gun, a silly little thing, like a toy really. We were still together then. I suppose he'd forgotten I still had it. I was so angry, I took it out and pointed it at Mike and he told me I was stupid and he said, 'You know you won't fire it, Eve'—so I did, just to show him! Just to show him he couldn't just leave me!" Eve's voice grew higher and more indignant. Her outrage showed in her lovely face, her mouth and chin quivering and her eyes blazing. "Anyhow, there he lay, dead. It was very odd. I mean, I'm not a good shot or anything. It wasn't my fault. It was bad luck. I knew no one had seen me come in because I came with Mike using his keys. So I washed up the glasses and put away the bottle and cleaned off the gun. Then I slipped out and dropped the gun in a dustbin."

She sighed. "Really, people are so tiresome. How was I to know that fool kid was visiting the janitor, his uncle, and asking for money and would go hunting about in the dustbins for something to sell? If people would only just mind their own business! But after all, that boy was better off in prison because he was only taking drugs and stealing and so on. So it didn't matter that he got the blame."

Meredith said in an expressionless voice, "You didn't drink your tea, Eve."

"Oh, so I haven't," Eve said calmly, picking up the cup.

Meredith swallowed. "You've had a very—very stressful time, Evie. I think I ought to call Peter Russell and have him come over and give you something for your nerves."

Eve considered this. "Yes, you're right. Dear Peter will know what to prescribe. I really don't sleep very well. I'm very tired now. I'd like a really good night's sleep."

Meredith closed the door gently. Elliott was standing by his own door, hands folded, waiting. "I told you!" he said pettishly. "You wouldn't leave it alone. I warned you."

"You knew . . ." Meredith swallowed and forced out the words. "You knew about Mike, that she killed—"

He hunched his thin shoulders up under his ears. "Of course. I was directing on that film at the time. I reminded you all the other evening. She came to see me after she'd done it. She was babbling away but after I got her to calm down I realized that if she just kept her cool no one would be any the wiser. She'd already kept her head enough to clean off the tumblers and the gun. We didn't have to worry about any other odd prints around Mike's apartment because she was still his wife and her prints might be expected there." He frowned. "She really couldn't understand that he was going to file for divorce. It was hard on her."

"Hard on everyone," Meredith said bleakly.

"If you'd just keep your head this time," he said wistfully, "if you would just keep quiet. We can get away with it again. But you won't, will you?" Without waiting for her reply, he added sadly, "It's a real pity. Worse, it's dumb. Real dumb." He turned and walked back into his bedroom and closed the door.

Peter Russell was just leaving his Bamford surgery. He promised to hurry and arrived twenty minutes after she telephoned him. To Meredith it seemed an interminable time during which she sat in the drawing room and stared at Eve's portrait. Yet it was not Eve she saw, but someone else. He was there as an invisible yet real presence. When she moved about the room, trying to force the feeling away, he followed her, so in the end she sat huddled on the sofa, eyes fixed on the painting, imagining Lorrimer hurling the lamp at it in his rage, bitterness and grief.

She knew that these feeling did wear off, intolerable as they were, there was worse to follow. The guilt would come. Again.

The sound of the gate's buzz signalled relief. She jumped up and managed to reach the door before Lucia. "It's all right," she told the cook. "It's only Dr. Russell. I called him to see if Miss Owens needed anything."

"She not need anything from doctor," said Lucia sulkily. "I make for her." She waddled back towards her kitchen, outrage in every plump line.

"What's wrong?" Russell demanded abruptly, pushing past Meredith into the hall.

Meredith indicated silently that he should go into the drawing room and when they were there she made a determined effort to pull herself together and face him squarely. "I would like you to go up and see Eve. You'll find her in a—in a rather nervous state. And I—I would like you to stay here for a while . . . until . . ." She fell silent and then tossed back her hair and met his curious and antagonistic gaze unflinchingly. "Until the police come."

Russell twitched. "Lorrimer?" he asked in a jagged voice and she knew he was thinking of Sara.

"Yes, Lorrimer. He tried to blackmail her. He threatened Sara. She desperately wanted Sara to marry Lazenby. She couldn't bear anything to hold up her going to the States and taking on that wretched soap part . . . and I think she felt guilty about Sara—and she does love her. She is a mother." The explanations tailed away. What, after all, was there to say? No one can excuse murder. Cold-blooded, carefully plotted murder. Much less the casual viciousness that had struck down a feeble old man.

Russell's long pale face gained an even more lugubrious expression. "You're sure about this?" he asked doubtfully.

"Quite sure, Peter. She's been telling me all about it. I—I haven't rung the police yet. I wanted to be sure you would be here. She'll need you. She's—she's not normal, you know. A jury will take account of that, won't it?"

"A good lawyer will make sure they do." Russell was

still watching her closely. "Would you prefer it if I rang the police?"

"No, no, it's my responsibility," Meredith said. "She doesn't think she's done anything wrong, you know. She doesn't think she's to blame. It's all the fault of others."

Perhaps some of it is mine, she was thinking. If I had come back last night Bert might still be alive—and if I hadn't told Mike I loved him he might be alive, too. But "if" and "might," as Markby had said, were the great imponderables.

Aloud she said, "It's Sara—I'm worried about Sara. Lazenby will ditch her. She might go to pieces."

Peter Russell said obstinately, "I'll take care of Sara."

If she'll let you, thought Meredith. She might, for the time being. She watched Russell go out and heard his footsteps on the stair. As she picked up the telephone and rang through to the Bamford police station, she found herself asking, Would I be doing this if it weren't for Mike? Lorrimer was really only a nasty little blackmailer just as Eve said and Alan Markby agreed. Bert wasn't the nicest old man in the world. No one is grieving for either of them—not even Pearl and Walter in the long term. They're shocked, that's all. The knowledge and the trial and the scandal will tear Sara's life apart again. Lazenby will take off in a cloud of dust. If she accepts Russell's comfort, it won't be for ever. He's going to get hurt, too. And of course, there's Albie. . . . He'd take Eve away to the States and watch over her. No one need know a thing. . . . Why don't I just put down this phone and forget about it? I could tell Russell I thought Eve was rambling and hadn't meant a word of it. Eve would go to the States and star in her soap opera and everyone would be happier and no one hurt any more.

A voice was speaking in her ear and automatically she asked if Chief Inspector Markby was available. As she waited the impulse to put the telephone down became stronger and stronger. In the end, she pressed it against her chest and said aloud to the empty room, "No, this is for you, Mike. . . . This so that you'll have justice . . ."

Then Alan Markby's voice came on the line, asking, "Meredith?"

She opened her mouth but before she could speak there was a commotion outside the room. Footsteps clattered down the stairs. The door burst open and Peter Russell appeared wild-eyed and crossed the room to where she stood holding the telephone in two long strides.

"Call a bloody ambulance!" he ordered.

Meredith stood staring at him. Markby's voice, tiny and distorted, came from the receiver shouting, "Meredith? Meredith, what the hell is going on?"

"Give me that!" Russell snapped, reaching out a hand.

The paralysis left her. "No—I'm talking to Alan Markby already . . ." She put the receiver to her mouth. "We need an ambulance, Alan. . . . And we need you." Her hand shook and composure deserted her again. "Oh God, Alan, do come quickly. I need you . . ."

Fourteen

"The tea! Oh, dear God, she put something in the tea . . ." Meredith whispered.

Eve lay on the little sofa as she had left her but now her head was thrown back, her violet eyes were open wide in astonishment, her lips parted and her whole attitude frozen. One slender beringed hand gripped at the pink satin bosom of the blouse as if she would have torn it open to aid a desperate last search for breath. The cup which had contained the camomile tea stood empty on the table. Automatically, Meredith stretched out her hand towards it. Peter Russell struck her aside and said sharply, "No! Don't touch it!" She drew back in horror and he went on urgently, "Do you know what it was? Pills? Had she pills or powders? It still might not be too late . . . there's a faint pulse. If the ambulance gets here in time and we know what she took—!"

Meredith interrupted him, shaking her head. "No, you don't understand. I don't mean she took it intentionally! I'm sure she didn't mix it herself. I don't think it's the sort of drugs you're thinking of, sleeping pills or anything like that. I meant Lucia—Lucia put something in the tea, something she made up herself."

"The cook?" He glared at her. "Make sense, Meredith! Why should the cook want to harm Eve?"

"The signorina is right," said a heavy, flat voice behind them. They both jumped around to see Lucia standing in the doorway, massive, black-clad, triumphant. "But I not harm her. I keep her safe. I know what she do," the cook nodded. "I know when I hear that boy sick that someone give him something. And when he die, I know she do it.

204

But I say nothing. He was bad, that one. He threaten her and the little one. He come here, shout, make trouble. My ladies, they both very frightened. I think maybe I make something to make him go away. But then he start to get sick and I know I not need to. She"—Lucia lifted a hand and pointed at the sprawled figure of Eve—"she did it already. So I do nothing, only wait. I not think you find it out what she did. And I not let you take her away, put her in prison with bad women. She is like a bird, so beautiful, you must not put her in a cage. You cannot shame her. He was so wicked that young man to persecute her so. He should die!"

"Oh no," Meredith whispered, "I thought you were talking about Ralph Hetherbridge. I should have realized . . ."

"She not suffer," Lucia said proudly. "I make it right." She turned and plodded out of the room.

"What was it, you old witch?" Russell yelled, diving after her.

"She won't tell you," Meredith said in a flat voice. "You're wasting your time, Peter." She looked down at her cousin's beautiful, surprised face. "Goodbye, Eve. It did all go wrong and I was part of it. I'm sorry."

It seemed to her that for a brief moment the violet eyes widened even more as if acknowledging her words. But perhaps that was imagination on her part—or a muscular spasm on death.

Markby and the ambulance arrived together. They carried Eve out on a stretcher, past Lucia who sat in the hall, her broad features impassive.

"You'd better take care of the cook," said Markby in a low voice to Pearce who had come with him. "Take her back and charge her with administering a substance with intent . . . you know the sort of thing."

Pearce, looking rather green about the gills, although this was not his first murder case, moved towards Lucia who glanced up at him scornfully. At that moment Albie Elliott, whom they had all quite forgotten, appeared at the top of the stairs, his eyes bulging and his whole face the twisted mask of a man possessed. He uttered a blood-curdling inarticulate cry, leapt down the staircase, paused to stare wild-eyed at the retreating backs of the ambulance men and then launched himself at the maid, screaming abuse. His outstretched hands caught at the woman's hair, braided in thick plaits round her head, tearing it loose from the pins. Then he struck, clawing at her eyes as she threw up a brawny arm to fend him off. Markby, Russell and Pearce all rushed to intervene.

"All right, sir, all right," panted Pearce as soothingly as he could while grappling with the writhing Elliott. He grasped the struggling man's arms expertly and pinned them to his sides.

"He's out of his wits with grief," Markby muttered. "Seen it before. Can you give him some kind of sedative?" he asked Peter Russell.

"Only if he asks for one."

But Elliott had abruptly fallen silent, limp and unresisting in Pearce's grip. "Goddam it," he was muttering tearfully. "Goddam it. Goddam the lot of you."

After their fine Indian summer, the day of Eve's funeral was drizzly and cold. They gathered in the open cemetery on the northern outskirts of Oxford, unprotected from the driving mist of rain and the chill wind. During the spoken graveside service the words were half-drowned by the roar of traffic passing by on the Banbury road.

They buried Eve alongside Robert Freeman. To Meredith, it all seemed unreal. It was difficult to believe that Eve lay in that coffin. Difficult to imagine that she would not suddenly appear among them, elegant and bright, and charmingly thank them for the beautiful flowers. There were a lot of flowers. Eve would have liked that. There had been quite a number of well-known faces amongst the mourners too, despite the circumstances, and Eve would also have appreciated that. But these attendants had now all drifted away and only a handful of people remained.

Sara, her fair hair plaited into a long pigtail which hung down her back and made her look even more like a schoolgirl, was red-eyed and silent, her pale face wooden in grief. Peter Russell, looking equally grief-stricken but for a different reason, hovered protectingly at her shoulder. Jonathan Lazenby had predictably gone on a sudden unforeseen business trip. Officially the wedding had been delayed because of the funeral, but everyone knew it was off altogether. The only person still crying—in fact the only person actually to shed tears at the graveside—was Albie Elliott who stood by himself, bare-headed in the rain, grasping a bunch of red roses, tears and raindrops mingled on his white face. Meredith has tried to speak to him earlier but he had only stared at her as if she spoke some foreign language.

Meredith walked forward awkwardly, teetering down the plank laid on the mud alongside the open grave. The hole was draped with green baize to shield the freshly turned earth from the gaze of the mourners. She stooped and scooped up a handful of mud, soiling her hastily bought black gloves, and threw it in. It struck the coffin lid with a dull hollow thud just above the brass plaque.

That was that. In the distance, the undertaker's men hovered, waiting, damp but decorous, like crows on a fence. Russell had taken Sara by the elbow and she had turned towards him. Meredith was not needed there. Elliott uttered a choking sound, lurched forward suddenly in a disjointed fashion and dropped his bouquet in the grave. The effect was neither dramatic nor romantic, only grotesque. He was lost in his private world of despair and Meredith was not needed there either. The cars on the Banbury road sounded their horns uncaringly as they tried to overtake one another.

She turned away and walked through the neat rows of graves towards the car park. This was an urban council burial place and it had none of the chaotic neighbourliness of the village churchyard. Alan Markby, in a black tie and the dark raincoat he wore at funerals, moved out from behind a headstone and followed her. He caught up with her by the parked cars. She was pulling off her soiled damp black gloves. She rolled them into a ball and threw them into a rubbish basket. Then she looked up at him.

He said, "I've got a thermos of coffee in the car."

"That was prudent of you."

"Not me. Laura, my sister, stopped by the house and gave it to me. She said I'd need it. She's a bit inclined to fuss."

They sat in the front of his car, damp and uncomfortable, and drank the coffee out of plastic mugs also supplied by Laura, who for reasons of her own had thoughtfully put in two. It tasted stewed but it was hot and got the blood flowing.

Meredith, gripping her mug in both hands to let the warmth seep into her chilled fingers, wondered if Markby remembered her cry of appeal down the phone that last fateful afternoon. She had no idea why she'd said it. Stupid. She supposed it had been the stress of the moment. She hoped he hadn't noticed or had forgotten. If he had done neither, then she trusted that at least he wouldn't mention it. That would be too excruciatingly embarrassing.

Aloud she said, "I gave the doll to Sergeant Pearce . . . the one Lorrimer left for Sara to find. You can put it in your black museum if you've got one."

Markby grunted. "You know you should have handed it over immediately. It would have brought us in sooner and that might have kept him alive and in turn left her—Oh, for God's sake we've been through this already. You know." He broke off, cursing his clumsiness silently.

She stared straight ahead through the rain-spotted windscreen. "You once told me that 'if' and 'might' were the great imponderables. If I'd told you about the doll and the heart and the other things which Albie found and poor Sara received, you might have tracked them to Lorrimer, and then what? A court case, Lorrimer making all kinds of wild accusations to justify what he'd done and Lazenby, the creep, running for cover and ditching Sara."

"What you describe would have been preferable to murder, a double murder as it turned out. I don't see Lazenby here today. I suppose that means he's taken himself off anyway."

Meredith opened the car door to tip out the dregs of her coffee. She put the empty mug down by her feet. Her shoes were muddy and had left black smears on the floor of the car. "Sorry about the mess . . ." she mumbled and let him interpret that any way he wished.

He put out a hand awkwardly and touched her elbow. "I'm sorry about it all. I know she was your cousin and I really can't discuss any aspect of this case objectively with you. I would like to say something comforting. But it's not possible, is it?"

"No, but it's like any other pain. One learns to live with it."

He stirred uneasily in his seat. She glanced at him. He was scowling at the figure of Elliott, stumbling between graves towards the far corner of the car park and a hire-car.

"You know Albie guessed it was Lorrimer leaving those things to be found. And Lucia knew what Eve was doing as soon as Lorrimer fell sick. I'm not saying I wasn't the only one to keep quiet when I might have spoken up, but I wasn't."

"Leave it!" he said suddenly in a sharper voice than she had heard him use to her before.

"What will happen to Lucia?"

He shrugged. "The defence will almost certainly enter a plea of diminished responsibility. She's a simple woman, isolated in a foreign culture and she was abnormally devoted to her employer. She certainly intended to kill, but not out of malice. She'll be charged with manslaughter and as to whether the plea regarding her mental state will be accepted that's not for me to say. She may well finish in a psychiatric hospital rather than in a prison. What worries me is the thought of someone with so much knowledge of poisons and so little grip on normal definitions of right and wrong being released into the community within the foreseeable future—particularly if there were any question of her working as a cook again! But policemen only catch the criminals, they don't have any control over what society chooses to do about them."

"She might start scattering the wrong herbs on the pizzas in that Pasadena restaurant if she disliked the customer, I suppose," Meredith said and added by way of explanation, Eve told me Lucia has a relative who runs a pizza parlour and wanted her to go and help him out."

"There you have it then! Oh damn," he added softly, "there's a press photographer still hanging about the cemetery gates. I can see him from here."

"Who cares?" she returned wearily. Then she added, "Eve would—care, I mean. She'd be disappointed if there weren't any pressmen here. It was a good turnout, especially on such a dismal day. She had a lot of friends in the business."

"Russell seems to be taking care of young Sara. I suppose I shan't now be giving her away to Lazenby. Do you think Eve picked on me because she wanted a tame copper who would be a smokescreen if there were inquiries about Lorrimer?"

"I think she picked you because you'd look good and your name is carved all over that churchyard. I'm not being rude, just objective."

"Fair enough. I know she didn't pick me because I was Bob Freeman's nearest crony because I wasn't."

"Freeman shouldn't have asked Lorrimer to paint that portrait," Meredith said thoughtfully. "That may have started it all off. Even before he met Sara, Philip had had his hopes raised and dashed by one member of the family. Now Russell's in love with Sara. I hope it turns out better."

Markby said, surprisingly unkindly she thought, "Someone always will be. She'll never lack a shoulder to cry on. Don't worry about her, Meredith."

"I can't do anything, anyway. She's almost twenty. She has what's left of Bob Freeman's money." Meredith busied herself putting Laura's thermos and picnic mugs back in the bag they'd come in. Her mug had Bugs Bunny on it. "I tried it myself, you know, opening a milk bottle so that the top could be replaced unmarked. It isn't such a very difficult thing to do especially if you've got long nails. I thought it likely then, that Lorrimer's killer was a woman." She gave a little exclamation of exasperation and added aggressively, "I was so wrong about Phil Lorrimer! It makes me feel a bit of a fool, to say the least. I frequently deal with people I've never seen before and have to make a judgement about their reliability, whether they are telling me the simple truth or spinning me a line. How could I be so dumb as to be taken in by a boyish smile and a lot of fake charm?"

Markby smiled at her. "You didn't have the chance to know him well enough to change your mind. And he wasn't just any casual small-time liar. He had the makings of a first-class con-man and speaking as a policeman I for one am glad he set out to be a potter and only came to crime late, by chance, and, as it turned out, unluckily."

She nodded but observed, "Funnily enough, despite it all, when I think of him, I still think of him as—likeable. It was as if he'd once been a nice person and been spoiled. A tragedy really, how such a person can become twisted and vicious."

"Necessity drives people to unexpected extremes," Markby observed. "And the opportunity to do evil is curiously tempting. Lorrimer is a good example. First of all the only thing he wanted to do was break up Sara's engagement with Lazenby. He was abusive, he played macabre practical jokes such as the ones with the heart and that doll. He threatened to send the letter to the press, but in the end he might not have carried out that particular threat. If his motive had remained solely to get Sara back, he must have realized that actually to publish the letter and photos would alienate the girl for ever."

"He did have a vicious streak," Meredith said slowly. "He might have done it out of sheer spite. And he was sick in his mind. He must have been to play those repulsive jokes. Who knows how logically he was thinking."

"The point is," Markby said patiently, "that at that early stage all he wanted was to get Sara back, all to himself. Money didn't come into it."

"But then the van broke down and he couldn't afford to replace it," Meredith said, "Such a—a small thing."

"Not to him. He needed a transport desperately. The shops wanted the goods in time for the onset of the Christmas rush and he was losing orders because he couldn't deliver. Sending the goods by post was out of the question. Large quantities of pottery are heavy, besides being breakable. And we mustn't forget the personalized mugs. That was a new line he was anxious to launch and the shops were interested, but he had to be able to ensure he got the goods to them on time. He needed to buy a new van urgently and he wasn't going to get one with the ten quid Crocker gave him for the old one."

"So he thought he'd go to Eve and ask for money."

"Yes—and then he realized for the first time just how

much money the letter and photos might represent. The
prospect of so much easy money changed Lorrimer's ideas
and he stopped being a bohemian young fellow who just
wanted enough beer money to spend in the Dun Cow or
even just to replace a clapped-out van. There was not just
Eve, there were the other parents. Couple of 'em MPs, one
or two with titles, several prominent in the City—and all
anxious to pay to keep their kids' misdemeanours out of
the press. Even if we'd got their names, we could have interviewed them until we were blue in the face and it would
be unlikely any one of them would have owned up to being blackmailed. It would be interesting to know if he had
contacted any of the others."

"He should have gone to those others first, not to Eve,"
Meredith said bluntly. "Eve hadn't the money to keep
shelling out to a blackmailer. She could have made him a
small one-off payment for a new van, but she knew it
never stops at that with a blackmailer. She knew that from
her dealings with Hughie."

Markby nodded. "Yes, it isn't just the money which
brings them back to their victim again and again, it's the
power. The knowledge that they have someone outwardly
so successful, so completely under their thumb. For the
first time in his life probably Lorrimer found himself in
the position of calling the shots. Heady stuff. Envy played
its part, too, no doubt. Envy in this case of someone who
was frustrated in his artistic career towards someone who
seemed to have it made. He probably blamed Eve for
Sara's engagement to Lazenby and there was a revenge
motive as well. A dangerous young man."

"And there was poor old Bert," said Meredith with a
sigh, "who really had nothing whatsoever to do with it. He
just happened to see Eve prowling around Lorrimer's back
door. He thought it was lust!"

"Naturally," said Markby with a faint smile. "He belonged to a generation which never discussed sex openly
but thought about it all the time and saw it everywhere!"

And so am I thinking about it, one way or another, he
thought to himself ruefully. Even in this unlikely spot and
on this inauspicious occasion. But then, whatever we in-

tend, sex and death make the real decisions for us in the end. You can't argue with either of them.

The car windows were beginning to steam up. He wound his side down a couple of inches to let the glass clear. "You know," he said awkwardly, "I was rather hoping, when this is all over, that we might stay friends . . . keep in touch." He paused and added even more unhappily, "But I suppose you'd really rather forget it all."

Meredith avoided his eye. She had sensed he was working himself up to saying something along these lines. At one time it would have been out of the question because of Mike. But Mike's ghost had been thoroughly exorcized now. She said quietly, "I can't forget it. As for—us, it's too early, Alan."

"I know that. Just—send me a postcard when you get back, will you?"

She smiled. "Yes, I will."

He returned the smile. "Perhaps one day we'll make that trip down to Greece together."

"Perhaps."

"Then we'll leave it at that for the time being. All right?"

"Yes," she said. "That's all right. We'll leave it for the time being."

Epilogue

Bert Yewell was buried in the churchyard where he had tended the grass, joining the company of the friends of his youth. It was the first burial there for some years. Ada's grave was reopened and he was laid to rest with her, but no one got around to adding his name to the tombstone because, as Pearl said, there didn't seem much point in it. They knew Uncle Bert was there and no one else cared.

As it turned out, it was lucky they didn't put out good money on updating the headstone. No one else was found who was prepared to take care of the grass in the graveyard as Bert had done. No one else knew how to use the scythe or was prepared to do the job for so little financial return. So the decision was taken to level all the graves and the headstones were all uprooted and stacked in a corner round the back of the church.

After that the council sent a couple of men out from time to time with a petrol-driven motor mower on a lorry. One of them leaned on the wall and watched as the other drove round and round on his miniature tractor over the flattened ground, slicing up the long grass untidily and leaving it where it fell. Beneath it Bert Yewell's remains mouldered away, slowly becoming part of the soil he had spent a lifetime tending.